Advance praise for *A Tomb on the Periphery*

"Few novels can stand up to the promise of tour de force, but here, John Domini is at the top of his form, writing beautifully, humming along like Fabbrizio on his Suzuki. This is a delightful crime novel, with a setting to die for, and at the same time a moving story that should interest a wide range of readers. *A Tomb on the Periphery* is a wonderful read."

 —Jay Parini, author of *One Matchless Time* and *The Last Station*

"Archeology is a kind of destruction even as it discovers. John Domini's new novel, *A Tomb on the Periphery*, deconstructs the conventions of detection and pieces it back together in startling fashion. The writing fragments, splinters, shatters, and each shard one finds a clue, a cure, a sacred relic. The book reveals as it conceals, and it adheres as it tears you apart."

 —Michael Martone, author of *The Blue Guide to Indiana*

"In *A Tomb on the Periphery*, John Domini gives us a suspenseful story of the underworld and the netherworld, the ancient world and the modern. A simple tale about a stolen necklace turns into an insightful commentary on the collision of cultures in contemporary Italy."

 —Rita Ciresi, author of *Pink Slip* and *Sometimes I Dream in Italian*

"*A Tomb on the Periphery* takes the reader on a fascinating tour of a part of Naples most visitors never see: a labyrinthine world of antiquities and thefts and fabrications. John Domini is a master of suspense and of psychological complexity. The result is an edgy, richly peopled and thoroughly absorbing novel."

 —Margot Livesey, author of *Eva Moves the Furniture* and *Banishing Verona*

Other Books by John Domini

Talking Heads: 77 — novel
Earthquake I.D. — novel
Bedlam — short stories
Highway Trade — short stories

A Tomb on the Periphery

a novel

by John Domini

Arlington, Virginia

Published by Gival Press, an imprint of Gival Press, LLC.

For information please write:
Gival Press, LLC, P. O. Box 3812, Arlington, VA 22203.

Website: *www.givalpress.com*
Email: *givalpress@yahoo.com*

First edition ISBN 13: 978-1-928589-40-2
Library of Congress Control Number: 2007935328

Book cover artwork: "Antique Figure" © Galdzen / *Dreamswork.com* Used by permission
Photo of John Domini by Lettie Prell
Format and design by Ken Schellenberg

Acknowledgments

to Robert Giron and Gival Press, for splendid work;
to Ken Schellenberg, for the cover design;
to Lettie Prell and Faye Bender for essential readings;
to Allison Mackin for the copyedit;
to Ognissanti and my Neapolitan friends and relations.

Financial support came from Northwestern University Center for the Writing Arts and elsewhere.

A writer finds nothing so galvanizing as other writers, and Naples and the other elements in play in this novel open onto a whole library of catalytic figures, working in a wide array of languages. I could begin with Diodorus Siculus and the earlier commentators on whom he relied… I could end with the latest article in *La Repubblica* about the manufacture and sale of fake antiquities… and then there would be the novelists, from Sciascia to Herling to Hazzard to Parini and beyond. *Mille grazie, tutti.*

Lettie: *sempre meglio.*

ANTONIO: ...Will you grant with me
That Ferdinand is drowned?
SEBASTIAN: He's gone.
ANTONIO: Then, tell me,
Who's the next heir of Naples?

— *The Tempest*

First Evening

It wasn't midnight yet, to judge from the moonlight, the clarity it gave to the exposed skeleton. The bones of the lone uncovered arm glistened. Anyone could see, though the limb was folded tight at the elbow, mummy-style, that the interred hadn't yet reached full size. The skull and shoulder looked to be adolescent. Most of the corpse remained under the dirt, since for a discovery like this the dig crew worked with teaspoons, with watercolor brushes. But the visible bits might've been some subterranean neon, more tawny than white, its electricity uncovered while still abuzz. Also you could make out just a wink of tomb jewelry.

Or you could so long as the moon hung postcard-full. Already however Fabbrizio understood he'd made a terrible mistake. Terrible, *sicuro*.

Didn't he know better? Fabbrizio wasn't the kind of crook who put himself in harm's way. He didn't think of himself as a crook at all, never mind the sardonic jabs he heard from his older brother. A crook was one of those nuts out of Quentin Tarantino, a guy who spent half the movie with a gun to his head. Hadn't he proved himself smarter than that, Fabbro? He'd confined himself to the technical end, an artisan rather than a thug, and the intricacy and heart he put into his "black work" surely mitigated the venality of the black marketplace (though he couldn't say just how, and he knew better than to try that argument on his brother). Nonetheless here he stood, down in the illegal dirt, with plenty of light in his face. If he were caught now, he'd be in another sort of movie, one of those Hollywood teen-sex comedies, and his role would be the doofus virgin surprised with his pants around his ankles. He'd gotten himself into this mess because of a woman—an American.

"What is it, Fabbrizio?" she asked now. She knew her interrogative Italian, the accent on the verb.

Shanti was still squatting at his feet. She didn't wait for an answer, turning away to block his view of the bones, picking at something to do with the neck and shoulders. Shanti or whoever she was, occasionally wiping off her hands with unfussy swipes at her butt. For breaking and entering, she'd pulled on a summer rain-jacket, material so light the gravedirt slid off the sleeves. Beneath that however his accomplice wore a tank top that appeared better suited for a lipstick ad, clingy, gleaming. Her cleavage made the moon seem like bedroom lighting. Fabbrizio could only go on staring, flabbergasted, sinking deeper into the sorry certainty that he'd never have taken such a risk for an Italian girl. If all he'd wanted was to get into some woman's pants, he could've done that at any number of unpoliced nooks and crannies around the Neapolitan periphery. *L'Americana* however had got him to take her into a necropolis from the Greek era, still under excavation. For a place like this, security was arranged in Rome.

And it'd taken so little for her to make him crazy, hardly more than her looks and the fact of her traveling alone. She'd sunk the hook with nothing but some hippie-girl mumbo-jumbo about summoning the Goddess. For what could this "Shanti" be except a hippie girl? What else, when she'd first tracked him down in Salerno, in a mob front of a coffee bar? An *Americana* traveling alone, and strolling into a place like this, in a port town on the far south of the Naples periphery—certainly it fit the profile, Fabbrizio's overheated fantasy profile, that she'd come here with some New-Age hoodoo in mind.

Shanti had claimed she knew a ritual that would put them in touch with the Original Mother Herself. She believed she could pull off a pagan resurrection, hauling the distant past into the present density. The Goddess, that's Who she was after: the Queen Who cradled a pomegranate. Fabbrizio hadn't gotten the whole wild story at their first meeting, of course (and had it been only three days ago, just this past Tuesday, that she'd first walked into that Salerno bar?). Even *l'Americana* had seemed to understand the danger, there in the Café Sempre, a bar illegally zoned in a suburb filled with dockworkers; she'd sensed enough of a threat to rein in what she'd had to say (and wouldn't that alone, her pouting savvy about whoever might be listening, have made him suspicious if he'd had his usual wits about him?). Rather she'd saved the more psychedelic details of her plan for her second meeting with Fabbrizio, later that same Tuesday night. They'd hooked up again across a wicker table, in Naples itself, in a rendezvous piazza she said reminded her of Greenwich Village.

Up in the old downtown Shanti had rattled on about her intended ritual freely, breathlessly. Her "sisters" everywhere, she'd declared, needed to re-encounter the Great Hag. They needed to know again the power of the Crone, a vitalizing comfort in an era when a woman's only worth lay in her skin, her face. And Shanti had taught Fabbrizio a new piece of American slang, "fuckable."

Myself, she'd asked, cocking her sharp, almost Arab chin to look him straight in the eye, *what am I, if I'm not… 'fuckable?'*

Fabbrizio had no answer for that. As he eyed the woman he might've spotted a fraction of something that required no translation, a tic of angry neediness. But the insight flickered shut, he believed in what he'd glimpsed but it was over just that fast, and after that the one way out of his hesitation was to pick up a line of thought from his abandoned schoolwork. His schoolwork, plus the reading he used to do for fun. Fabbro pointed out that the First Feminine, call her Hera, call her Dione or whatever, had held onto believers well into the Christian era. Early converts to the faith out of Galilee had known better than to reject the Goddess outright, here in Campania Felix. Rather the new sect had made the old one over, transforming the womanly Demiurge and her fruit scepter into Madonna and child.

Shanti had kept nodding, the tips of her hair spider-walking along her shoulders. She'd had no reason to tie it back, that night: rich hair, full, black as the baked corpses of Pompeii. Fabbrizio wondered whether this somewhat older *turista* (she might've been 30, even) had American Indian blood (that would've been a first for him), or merely an ancestor from the Middle East. In fact they were talking in an open-air restaurant run by Palestinians. He'd suggested this piazza, Bellini, because here a man didn't call attention to himself by talking to foreigners. He saw too that when excitement flushed her face, she darkened to a shade not far from red ochre, whereas Italian girls tended towards lavender. It didn't escape his notice, either, that while this Shanti carried on about "ceremony," about "making the unseen manifest," she'd underscored her university Italian with prolonged touches of his knee.

His trouble-antenna, otherwise so finely tuned, wasn't equipped for such interference. *By the end of the night,* she'd said, *imagine the power we might unleash!* Now here they stood, a long way before the end of Friday night, and it was another she-god they'd called back to life. It was the Siren, mistress of destruction.

Simply to get out of this busted tomb would require a dirty climb hand over hand. Throughout the surrounding dig, a graveyard nearly three thousand years old, ground-level itself remained unstable and sunken. Just to get back to the driveway cleared for the work crew, let alone the nearest paved road, would be like climbing a stairway in which several steps had gone missing. But Fabbrizio's companion was moving in the opposite direction, digging lightly at his feet. From her shoulder bag—the bag that was supposed to hold incense and such for the ritual—she'd pulled a pair of needle-nosed pliers. He tore his eyes from the moon-glimmers in her ponytail, in the pseudo-silk of her windbreaker, and tried instead to read this lower site. He hadn't lost his head entirely; he retained enough of his own university training to see that the deceased had been a girl. He recognized the tomb furniture, the styles of the half-exposed vases. Nor could he miss what Shanti had uncovered, in picking over the upper skeleton. The youngster had been laid out wearing some sort of ornamental necklace. The moon lit up alternating stripes of shadow-green and mineral-yellow: Baltic amber and, perhaps even, gold.

Beh, listen, little *Greca*: you aren't the only one overdressed for your own funeral. Fabbro was wearing suede pants, dance-club threads, too warm and tight for this. Before he'd rung for Shanti at her hotel he'd sprinkled on Caprifoglio, the honeysuckle cologne out of Florence.

"What *is* it, Fabbrizio?" the American repeated, drawing herself to her feet.

The necklace lay draped over her open hand, its brightest bits glittering as if it had waited twenty-six or -seven centuries for just this opportunity to shine. Fabbro had heard what Shanti had asked—he'd heard her the first time, when she'd just gotten the necklace uncovered and unhooked—but he couldn't respond.

"But what *is* it? Why, why show me this, this face of surprise?" A moment's trouble with the Italian. "I know you didn't come here to talk with the dead."

Stung, he worked up a smile, something cynical.

"You didn't come out here with the cute tourist for, for something mystic."

Such idiocy. Even now his mental theater briefly screened an earlier fantasy, L.A. bikini-stuff.

"*Beh.*" As if she read his mind. "Fabbro, now think of something else. Think of your business, your work. I know well what is your work."

The way she smiled. "Listen, not even a week after I arrived in Italy, while I'm asking some question in Pompeii, in Paestum—not even a single week, I heard of this young man Fabbrizio. He's got a real head for this, Fabbrizio. And the copies Fabbrizio makes, they're the best."

"Enough." This reminded him of her rap about the Goddess. "I understand perfectly well. You have a *buyer.*"

This last was English, the same throaty *y-r* sound she'd made a moment ago, when she'd first finagled the tomb-goods from around the buried upper vertebra. He'd used the word before, it came up often in his line of work, but just now it left him nervously plucking at the suede over his thighs.

"But truly, a *buyer.*" Finally she lost her smile. "From New York, understand? He has money."

Had Fabbrizio been a child, earlier this same week? Had he honestly failed to see how dubious their original meeting had looked? Throughout the quick-and-dirty neighborhoods nearby, in the slapdash *palazzi* that scabbed over so much of the southern Neapolitan periphery, Café Sempre was well-known as a front for the local branch of the bad guys, the Camorra. Fabbrizio had been called into the Sempre for a couple of consultations, over the eighteen months since he'd dropped out of the university. Once too, he'd provided its owners a better service than merely looking over long-ago jewel-smithing and telling them what he thought. Once he'd done some smithing of his own, down in the shop the *Camorristi* had set up in the café cellar. Beneath the coffee-flavored floors, beneath a hatch itself hidden under rollaway kitchen shelving, he'd put in several hours over his picks and solders, beside a small charcoal fire. But to hear Shanti talk, that day she'd strolled into the Sempre, you would think she'd known all about his lone visit to the work-space under its floors, the most crooked thing he'd ever done. The woman had even mentioned the illegal dealing in antiquities.

Her magic, she'd claimed, would never work in some ruin open to the public. "I require," she'd said, "a place of purity, some location where the hegemony of the ancient Queen hasn't yet suffered desecration."

Fabbrizio had shared a glance with the man behind the bar, but in fact he'd rather enjoyed the woman's idea, in all its nuttiiness: some uncorrupted situation which could revitalize the surrounding world.

"A place," the sweet-faced crank had gone on to say, "where there have never been grave-robbers."

She'd known the slang for grave-robber, *tombaroli*. This hardly fifteen minutes after she'd come in and ordered a drink that at once underscored her American-ness: a latte, too heavy on the milk for this late in the day, if you were Italian. She'd been surprised at how the drink was served, too, in what she called a "Coke glass," tall and clear with a pinched middle. But then before she'd emptied that glass, the pretty foreigner had all but asked how a person might break into a restricted archeological site. Again Fabbrizio had eyed the barista, a more toughnecked type than you usually found slinging coffee. The man's cell phone no doubt had the café's invisible partners on one-touch dial. But Fabbrizio had an idea, as of Tuesday afternoon he'd still had his brains, and he'd coughed up a sardonic laugh. Loudly, he'd told the woman she should try this kind of crazy talk up in Piazza Bellini.

"Go up there tonight," he'd told her, wondering if she could connect the dots of his glance as it swung from her to the barman. "They love this hippie nonsense."

She'd got the message, oh sure. Up in Bellini, just three hours after she'd gone sulking out of the Café Sempre, Fabbrizio had found Shanti waiting for him over a plate of hummus. She'd praised his "good judgment." He was a sharp one, wasn't he; he wasn't just some *settebello*, coasting on his looks. And when they were into their second beer, and she'd begun to touch his thigh, she'd told him their "best opportunity" would be a site only recently discovered. A fresh grave.

Beh, since then he'd dug his own.

Before he'd picked her up at the hotel tonight, Friday night, he'd managed not to lose that judgment entirely. He'd understood it wouldn't be difficult to bribe one of the security officers on the Paestum graveyard site. The very evening after he'd promised *l'Americana* that he would try, Fabbrizio in fact had spotted his pigeon. Not that a mere sometime consultant like himself, a youngster whose primary assets were his eye and his fingertip, had ever arranged a bribe before. Or not exactly; of course he'd paid in the way that a million other southern Italians did, and especially the families who shared the quick-and-dirty apartment blocks, shelling out a few bills to protect a parking spot or to get the garbage hauled away. But among the watchmen on the Paestum site, there was one that even a rookie couldn't miss, an officer who made no effort to hide his requests for night shifts and weekend duty. These days you found men like him all over greater Naples. Fathers with one kid too many and a taste for good American cigarettes, or perhaps a car with two more cylinders than necessary, these guys sought to squeeze every paycheck they could out of the Cultural Ministry. Rome had insisted on round-the-clock surveillance of any significant sites. The safety of Italy's "artistic patrimony" was defined as a top-level concern, following the recent earthquake.

That quake had hit some serious numbers on the Richter scale, at least as bad as the *terramoto* of 1980. In the six weeks since, security had become the most common Neapolitan boondoggle—either security, or all the scams having to do with the new temporary identification papers, the so-called "Earthquake I.D." The rent-a-cop business was the less dangerous of the two enterprises, the work more often legitimate. It was magic: you button on one of those uniforms and, abracadabra, your monthly bills disappear. Or at least the pile dwindled, especially if a man were willing to spend an entire night, even a whole weekend, sitting around in uncomfortable gray polyester and keeping an eye on nothing in particular. Nonetheless, even officers on the midnight shift had to make do with an hourly rate and a full month between checks. This guy on the Paestum dig was plainly one of those for whom a month was too long to wait.

The guard wore his uniform to breakfast, and he took his cappuccino and brioche at one of the spendiest places around. You found him along the pedestrian walkway out front of the tourist site, the ruins of the three temples and marketplace. This wasn't far, as the crow flies, from the half-undug necropolis the man had been hired to protect. Greeks tended to bury their dead outside the city walls, in this case no more than three hundred yards inland. But the guard took his breakfast among the Germans and Swedes, the lucky ones not yet sixty and already on their pensions, or among the Milanese on a day-trip off this summer's cruise. And he would complain about his paycheck. He didn't much care for the view across the walkway either, the roofless holy sites and the lichen-riddled amphitheaters, Paestum c. 600 B.C.E. Rather the guard's thoughts were with the racks of postcards, the chatter of tour groups. There had to be, in all this, some way to turn a buck. Fabbrizio learned the man's name—- though he then took care to forget it, as soon as he'd arranged for someone else to make the contact.

He'd have to be one dumb pretty boy indeed, if he himself were the one to pay his way onto the protected inland site. No more than seventeen, eighteen months, now, had Fabbrizio been piecing together contracts that never made the accounting ledger, but already his face had grown too familiar, among his colleagues south of the city, for him to simply stroll in among the pastel-clad tourists and pull out his billfold. Any major transgression like tonight's, a break-in that held out the possibility of a sizeable score, was reserved for the men who ran things. If a freelancer tried to sneak a piece of their action, he was in for a short career. In the movies their game would end with a blast from a shotgun, a snubnosed *lupara*, but more often the local Camorristi used a knife. The two hoods who worked out of Café Sempre came across as a classic pairing of brains and muscle, but word was, even the smaller of these two preferred the knife. The little Scarface preferred a face-to-face comeuppance, when some dilettante got foolish.

Happily Fabbrizio, given his particular niche in the *malavita*, had other friends too. His work had taken him around the entire periphery, Salerno in fact was a long way from his home suburb of Secondigliano, and he'd also made connections downtown. One of those was a hashish dealer Fabbrizio had first gotten to know in the dance clubs. This dealer's primary clientele wasn't rave kids (who were usually looking for Ecstasy anyway), but rather the African community by the central train station. In that way the hash man minimized his dependence on the mainstream mafia, and at the same time got away with flamboyant affectations like his street name: Monte Zu. Fabbrizio had learned he could trust that flamboyance, enough for this transaction anyway, and he figured Monte Zu could boost his profits with a short trip south. Around Salerno you had colonies of African laborers, immigrants who worked the tomato fields. Better still, by calling in a couple of favors,

Fabbrizio could see to it that his friend showed up in a flashy German convertible and a knockoff Armani suit.

~~~

So the Euros had changed hands, and Monte Zu had filled him in on the arrangements the guard would make as he began his shift on the last night of the working week. Wasn't that the best night for breaking and entering? The most quiet? Then as Friday's heat began finally to cool, over the highway asphalt, he'd gunned his Suzuki down to Shanti's hotel. The bike would be easier to park out of sight, but that wasn't why Fabbrizio had chosen it. He could just as easily have taken the family Fiat, an early-'80s 600 that no one would have looked at twice. On weekends his brother was always home with his sociology texts, the drawbridge up and the gate closed on his academic's castle in the clouds. Poor Uldirico was nobody's idea of professor-track these days; since their father had died the *primogenito* hadn't gotten downtown for a single exam, and Fridays and Saturdays too he let the Fiat sit.

But for the younger brother, his ride had to be the bike. Only the motorcycle offered the close clutching, the American breasts pressed into his back.

As she emerged from the Positano hotel—so trendy a town and expensive a place, that too should've made him suspicious—he believed he saw America in the combination of pulled-flat hair, second-skin tank top, and the easy-breathing jacket and exercise pants. She'd told him something of her highway-stretched life: born in Iowa (he'd shaken his head at the name, and she'd lost her smile a moment), educated in San Francisco (*ah*, he'd said, in brainless English, *San Francisco is beautiful*). For a few years now she'd been based in New York. The woman claimed no Native American blood, nor any touch of Arab, but rather a couple of Jewish uncles; she speculated that some lingering throb of Jehovah had drawn her to the older Mediterranean religions. And tonight she crossed him up further, her hair sending new signals; this afternoon she'd taken time to dab in vermilion highlights. Very I ♥ NY, post-9/11.

Fabbrizio drew more upright on his banana seat as he watched her approach. The bike also leant him bulk, even his delicate wrists, the legacy of a family that used to work in shell-carving—his mother's family. These wrists took on extra heft when he gripped the accelerator and gearshift. And at the same time the bike made it obvious he carried no gut. Sitting in a model's twist, he made of his waist a neat slant v: Italic. Not that he did anything like exercise, unless you counted the runaround required by his contracts. One day he'd buzz north to Cuma and the next, like today, way down south. Still, whenever Fabbrizio struck a pose on his bike, he entertained half a notion that someone might think of a demi-god out of Hollywood, sleek as the machine he rode on and impervious to bullets. Half a notion, this was, a movie-moment that Fabbrizio could sustain for at most a few ticks of his copycat Rolex. In fact, he knew better. He wasn't that kind of crook. The only weapon he carried was the *telefonino* at his hip, and the only trick he could rely on was fast talk.

Nevertheless tonight everything seemed to be working for him as he and Shanti roared off. She snugged her breasts and crotch against him, both, leaving the pack she'd brought for the ritual strapped to the rack over his rear wheel. The Paestum temples were less than an hour down the road, even with the wiggly and spine-tweaking coastal stretch out of Positano, even with the Friday traffic in summertime. Only Fabbrizio's helmet interfered with the joy of the ride. The fiberglass that oval'd their heads turned any connection between him and the girl into a tuneless clonk. But up in Rome, not long before the earthquake, they'd passed strict laws against riding unprotected. The last thing Fabbrizio needed tonight was to have the highway patrol pull him over. He went with the headgear, trying to find the sublimity in it. He did enjoy the shifting prismatics in the visor. Lines of color radiated like a comic book *Boom!*, erupting across the tinted glass whenever it caught either the lowering sun or its burning reflection off the sea.

At the exit for the ruins, Fabbro throttled down but remained on the bike, getting as close as the pedestrian walkway would allow. Behind the uncovered agora, the farther scraps of home-foundations, the horizon was beginning to change color. The columns that ringed the temples lost their wear and tear, like chipped teeth growing whole again. All east-facing, Greece-facing, their doors forever open to the

Queen in her mountain home: one, two, three Erector-Set behemoths of sandstone, amid a low, fluttering mélange of wild roses.

All had survived this latest quake, even the oldest, a dowdy Heraion to the far south. The stone was good Cilento stock, the work a stacking-block method like they'd used for the Pyramids, and there'd been retrofitting at the turn of the most recent century. Fabbrizio knew these things. He hadn't lost the fascination that had driven him through nearly three years at the university. Granted, the stinginess of his father's former bureaucracy, the smallness of their widow's comp, had wound up sweeping away his pretty imaginings of life as a conservator. Granted, he'd learned enough about the ornaments of a body and a downtown (or perhaps he'd always known enough) to grasp how the artifacts which remained from the ancients, whether temple-grand or earring-tiny, lay at the far end of the affective scale from the ugly suburb in which he'd grown up. A Secondigliano like himself, one with some calling as an *artigiano*, would be drawn naturally to the polar opposite of the bleak and shoddy block-and-tackle work he saw in the housing all over the city's periphery. A good two-thirds of the palazzi he'd lived in or visited had been thrown up illegally in the 1960s and '70s. They called to mind embedded lice, vermin who'd first burrowed in seeking some bloody taste of *la dolce vita*. What remained these days were cracked and naked exoskeletons, concrete riddled with exposed wiring, pus-yellow, infection-green. The only place for him and Uldirico to kick a ball, back when the brother would still get out and kick a ball, was a widening in the sidewalk. Every cellar on their block reeked of standing water, and the fire escapes rattled against their walls, the bolts long since fallen away.

But these temple grounds, the way they rattled him was another thing altogether. Even tonight Fabbrizio would gladly have set aside other plans for a while in order to lecture his Playmate of the Month. His Priestess of the Moment. The sanctuaries indeed had consecrated the entire surrounding area to a woman, the proto-Madonna. From here to the former Neapolis you could turn up bas-reliefs of Queen Hera on her throne, a plump pomegranate in her lap—for as the Hag devoured you, she released a hundred seeds to new life.

He could have talked for hours to this mystic wannabe. But he thought it better to let his guest alone, on her first sundown visit.

Fabbrizio left her by the fence while he tucked the bike amid a stand of close-planted oleander. In a careless moment he scraped his knuckles, and the smell of a nearby dumpster cut disgustingly through his honeysuckle scent. Nonetheless he was pleased when he returned to find her dawdling before the fence, each slow step recocking her hips. Italian girls too were susceptible to the spell of Paestum at sundown. The Goddess had to be counted the ultimate Power Wife, didn't she, walloping down with a species-changing crash on all the pretty young things with whom her husband dallied. Even now, an all-night party girl from the nastiest burb outside Naples might take her sweet time at one of the cafés across the pedestrian frontage. Even some Vampire Slayer in a miniskirt and silver platforms would linger over an evening gelato.

Shanti went on staring; Fabbrizio tried to gauge the risk. Her gym suit prevented her from passing for an Italian woman, but there were other foreigners among the evening passersby, and there were other couples who stepped off the pedestrian access in the direction of the new archeological site. Anyone who read the papers knew about the dig, after all. According to the experts, the necropolis might yet prove the richest mainland excavation of the new century.

"These regulations, these laws—Shanti, they are not for someone like you."

She'd said she had a flashlight, in her night-pack of "ritual objects," but they were making their way without it. The girl's teeth, her open-mouthed smile, offered the brightest thing in view.

"The State makes these regulations for others. They fear the true criminal. The illegal immigrants, the *terremotati*."

"The 'earthquaked,'" she repeated. Then: "Oh listen, I know what that's like."

What was this woman saying? "You should've seen me…" some of her words were lost as the two of them rustled past some squat and heavy-smelling tree full of flowers, camellias perhaps. They were cutting through the brush surrounding the site, staying clear of the access drive.

"When I first showed up in San Francisco," Shanti went on, "I was a charity case." Was she actually comparing herself to someone left homeless by the quake? "A sweet little girl from Iowa, all the, all the old structure gone."

He took a moment to frame a careful response, unoffended. "Then you understand, it's a person in a position like that who's the true threat. The earthquaked, in a certain sense, they're also illegal immigrants."

"But, of course I understand, Fabbro. The laws exist for a certain type only, not for people like us."

"Correct. The State wishes no trouble for a person like yourself, a person of culture, with a bit of money..."

Shanti laughed, the loudest sound between them since they'd left the road. "But, only a bit?" she asked. "All us Americans, we're rich, no?"

"It's not a joke, Shanti. In a case such as yours, the authorities would have no serious accusation."

Such formal speech, a touch of bureaucracy in the night. Yet it soothed him, now when they found themselves in Southern Italian jungleland, a rare undeveloped plot, the weeds and berries (he had no idea of the names) in a stinking riot flecked by insects. Explosive greens crowded either side of the dig's rough-cut access drive, which itself lay off a paved but shoulderless byway that could've been laid out by the Samnites. Fabbrizio longed for a church piazza up ahead, or for the usual after-dark diversion of teasing out a place to park amid snug yet uneven brick and steel. When he checked the time again, he squatted by a stand of brush in order to hide any moon-glint off his watch-face. *Carabinieri* were supposed to swing by the drive's entrance every couple of hours, though their rounds too had been complicated by the earthquake. At that the woman with him, older, wiser, put a hand on his shoulder and whispered *Giusto.* "Just:" correct, not crazy—no matter the flutter in his groin at her touch.

"But how, Fabbrizio?" she went on, standing over him. "At least I would be charged for..." he couldn't be sure if she frowned. "For violation of property."

Ahead glowed the lamps above the site's front gate. Nothing Fabbrizio could do about those, and the night watchman couldn't switch them off either, two halogens rigged to a timer and clamped onto poles three meters high. The light set off silent white firecrackers along the fencetop coils of razor wire, and it left leaf-shadows spattered across the unmanned security trailer.

"Don't worry," he replied. "Don't worry."

"*Sicuro.* A person like myself, all I need is my big American smile."

"In fact. They'll only pinch your ear."

In fact. He wasn't nearly skilled enough as a seducer to dream up a lie like this. He'd seen her student card from some place called The New School, the words *Adult Learner* in boldface, and he knew what her passport must look like, indigo blue with a golden eagle. This woman would have no trouble talking her way out of any police station from here to Rome. Fabbrizio, on the other hand—him the *poliziotti* would hold onto. Him, they'd put the screws to.

He turned and hacked once more into the brush. He put some shadow between him and Shanti and the moon's incandescent twins, strung up over the gate. That gate remained locked, to be sure. The night man hadn't done anything so blatant as leave the door open. Leave that open, and even if Fabbrizio and the American came and went unnoticed, by morning the centuries-old graveyard would have a dozen latter-day sleepers. *Terremotati* and other illegals, looking for a decent overnight.

Refugee Centers had of course sprung up, sponsored by the UN and NATO, staffed largely by foreign volunteers. But well-meaning volunteers from New York or Munich, along with valley-spanning tent cities—as big as the Paestum ghost-town, one or two of them—weren't enough to handle all the homeless. The church shelters in the city too remained overwhelmed. The very day of the quake, a day when the papers estimated that twelve thousand of Fabbrizio's neighbors had lost the roofs over their heads, it had been business as usual for smuggling in tomato-pickers, house-cleaners, and nannies. And none of these *clandestini* had homes to begin with.

In the undocumented-worker business, just like in Fabbrizio's business, they took advantage of any disruption in civil order. They sent their people to the tent cities for the quake victims, slipping them past the registration process inside laundry carts or vans full of food. Also the off-the-books newcomers had continued to pitch their squats in any undisturbed corner of the local woods they could find, by day making their way into the fieldworkers' camps or the inner-city "black blocks." Along a couple of these country roads, too, a man had his pick of prostitutes. The women usually worked out of a pop-up tent set off the roadside, behind the ground cover. Young and nameless women, skin and bone most of them, half-clad.

Not that Fabbrizio had any reason to think about prostitutes. Not when the first order of business was to find the section of the site's fence prepared for him, bent back by the amenable security guard, and the second was to shimmy inside. Fabbrizio needed his penlight, the only tool he'd brought, a light that fit one of the slit pockets at his groin. In the other pocket he had something smaller still, nothing you'd call a tool. Under his narrow beam, along the bottom of the reinforced chickenwire, he discovered finally what a careful job he'd gotten out of the security guard. Out at one of the farther corners of the site, the watchman had pried a triangular gap hardly wider than the span of Fabbrizio's own jewelsmithing hand. Better yet, in order to free the fence for bending, the guard had clawed out no more than a couple of the u-shaped fixing nails along one of the corner posts. The splintery upright itself remained solidly planted. At first glance, at second, it would look as if the break had been made from outside.

But Fabbrizio also spied, under his light, evidence of somebody worming into the dig ahead of him. He saw a broken plant-stump or two, a red flower ground to shreds. No mistaking the scraped earth either. He blinked, blinked again, and with each new glimpse the divots left by sandals and belt-buckles appeared more clearly. Someone else had taken advantage of the sweet work done by the security guard, and more than likely during this same first hour since late June's late sundown.

Shanti and Fabbrizio would have company in the old graveyard.

Now what was he supposed to do? What, after he'd come this far?

Was he supposed to turn timid all of a sudden, Finicky Fabbrizio, here on the verge of a fantasy he'd been nursing ever since he'd learned what sex was? Was he supposed to act like he was an old man and all through with risk? 54, instead of 24?

Roughly he told himself—a syllable or two emerging aloud and drawing a glance from his still-smiling companion—that anyone who'd gone under the fence wouldn't be police. Just the opposite. Whoever had snapped that gardenia could only have been another illegal, a *clandestino*. Whoever had trespassed would want nothing to do with two document-bearing citizens, and nothing more out of the necropolis than a level place to sleep. In the next moment Fabbro had his face and belly down against the raked-up earth. The warmth didn't surprise him, he knew how the heat lingered in this soil, but he felt shocked again at how utterly wrong his pants were, these disco suedes that held every smear. As he wriggled under the wire cross-hatching he had a quick unhappy vision of his father, his corpse-face full of dirt. Look what old Babbo was smoking now.

By the time he made it back on his feet, inside the restricted area, Shanti too had slipped under. He got an eyeful that a few minutes ago would've put him into another dream: a woman of the world on her knees before him, smirking as she brushed off her top. Yet just now all he could think of were the prostitutes again, those battered and anonymous types who waited through the night by the local roadsides.

Fabbro couldn't claim much of an intimate life. Among the young people he knew, nine out of ten had paired off quickly—it seemed almost a part of learning to drive—with a *fidanzata* or *fidanzato*. Nearly all these boys and girls still lived with their parents of course, but one way or another they managed regular trysts. At times the lovers went so far as to plaster newspaper up over the windows of a Fiat, more or less privately parked. Fabbrizio however had never bound himself to such a drawn-out trial of monogamy. If someone asked him about it, he'd say didn't feel that lonely. He did find himself wondering if "lonely" weren't some kind of code, in the language of the lovers' Camorra, for needing an everyday ego-stroke. He had to wonder, the skeptical Secondigliano. What was the more complicated ritual of commitment going to give him that he couldn't get from the dozen or so phone numbers in his cell? He had plenty of opportunity, girls he knew from the nightly *passagiata*, the nine-to-midnight stroll along what passed for a boulevard in his neighborhood. He'd met some moneyed types while he was attending the university, and there were clubgirls, too, who came drifting his way, vodka in hand. They would tug at the curls over his forehead:

But look, what a monkey…

A monkey? A pet? So many of his friends had resigned themselves to that kind of thing, a life in the stainless-steel cages of the better cafés and clothing stores. All that dawdling around on the rings and trapeze! All those cooing negotiations which arrived at so little! Fabbrizio couldn't understand why they didn't prefer simply to dance, like he did, and to swivel dancelike from one appointment to another around the greater Gulf. Why carve out more work for yourself, in what little unconstructive time you had? That was at the heart of his holding back, *sicuro*: the work he come to lately and what it took out of him. What room did his black-market runaround, going contract to contract, leave for anything like a wife and in-laws? What, when he was the only breadwinner for the family he'd been born with? His father had been gone nearly two years now, and in the first few months after the old man's passing it had become obvious that Fabbrizio's mother couldn't begin to make ends meet on the few monthly drops out of the government's faucet. Then there was Uldirico, melting into raindrops up in his cloud-castle. 'Rico was nearly as old as this Shanti seemed to be. The *primogenito* had the look of a leader, too, the beard and curls of a prophet fresh in from the Negev, and he was built more along their father's fireplug model than 'Brizio. But over the last eighteen months Uldirico had lived ever more within the narrow circle described by his own two arms, the distance they could reach from his desk chair: between his latest pack of Nazionales on the one hand and whatever research he could tap out of the internet on the other (the computer and hookup had been the family's one substantial purchase with the lump-sum settlement following Babbo's death). Over eighteen months and more, Rico hadn't so much as caught a Metro downtown in order to meet with a professor.

For Brizio the upshot was, he had neither space in his heart nor time in his calendar for catching a *fidanzata*. This when the mating game already seemed dubious, first the chatting up and then the nailing down. Yet he had also never found his focus shifting to a mere drive to score. Not for him the nightly sniff-sniff-sniffing around, among the girls of greater Naples, and the cutting of one ugly notch after another into a belt of perfectly good Campanian leather. Rather, his intimate life had shriveled o something pretty limited. Since he'd taken up his current business, Have Loupe Will Travel, he'd enjoyed nothing beyond the overnighters who could be plucked, now and again, off the club floor. Now a Milanese insurance woman looking for southern adventures, now a rich man's daughter down off the heights with a desire to expand her vocabulary. Now a groping and sucking in somebody's unused front parlor, now a seeking under clothes against the slapped-shut door of a hotel room.

What struck him most about nights like these was the joy in them, each catch of breath infused with a happiness out of nowhere. Fabbrizio and whatever woman had invited him indoors would play together in ways that never smacked of grim consumerism. He surprised himself, with his lover's touch and follow-through, cultivating his pleasures and hers with all the more flexible tools at his disposal. He was happy to have at it as often and as profoundly as the woman appeared to want it, taking his cues from her wet, her throat-work, and the openness of her smile.

So too, he'd had only one prostitute.

A looker, actually: a well-put-together whore of about eighteen, with a touch of the oriental about the eyes and cheeks. She'd arrived recently from some Balkan trouble-spot, the name of which he never got straight. Yet the fine shape on this working girl, the sweet angles of her eyes and her willing though broken Italian, all these had the opposite effect from what a man would expect. Or from what the man who'd brought Fabbrizio to this house must've expected. His host was that evening's buyer, a high-roller who'd believed his skilled young accomplice would enjoy an introduction to this downtown "parlor." Once Fabbro and the Balkan girl had been shown to their room, she'd gone down on her knees before him. Like Shanti, yes: Shanti now, on her knees and wearing a naughty smirk, just after he and the American had trespassed onto government property.

Back at the whorehouse, with the spray-scent making his nostrils wrinkle, with the rips in the gypsy's lingerie making his head-muscles tighten, Fabbro had collapsed into the chair. The unhappiness that sapped him seemed foolish even as he thought up the words for it: she was so *young*, so *helpless*, so *far from home*... Foolish sentiments, the sort of thing he'd known long before he got here, and yet it was precisely such sympathies that left him wilted, muscle and bone. The poor girl... Fabbrizio could do nothing but look her over, slumping ever further into feeling sorry, eventually giving voice to a schoolbook offer of help. At that, however, he'd detected alarm in those tweaky eyes. A half-frightened puffiness came into her face, and brought out, despite the eyeliner and blush-on, its childishness.

The girl hadn't run into this kind of client before. She hadn't yet learned what to do with the likes of Fabbrizio—but she did know exactly what would happen if it appeared she hadn't done her job. She knew just where she'd be clouted, and by whose big hands. As he sat and read the changes in the bare-bottomed youngster, he realized that he wasn't the first of her Johns to suffer pangs of remorse, either. There must've been others like him, polishing up their self-esteem with the rag of their pity.

The only thing different about him was, he'd said something ahead of time; he'd let conscience get the best of him before they'd taken care of business. So Fabbrizio asked for a handjob, right there in the chair. Beh, a bit of mouth too. With the help of a well-worn fantasy about a pampered and lascivious American, he got through his end of the transaction.

Afterward he counted off the Euros carelessly, as if he were drunk. He was carrying a good thick roll, thanks to his work earlier that night, so it was easy to make the extra he handed over seem like a mistake.

Shanti sensed his disquiet, as they moved away from the fence and into the excavations. He avoided her gaze, putting away his little light. They needed no help to spot the graves flagged with strips of white cloth, markers that glimmered under the moon, more false silk. The cloth was tied off at each corner of the tombs' grids, the twine checkerboards by which the dig crews kept track of their progress. As for Fabbrizio, he carried nothing like that, no measuring-stick for his own lower levels. Nonetheless *l'Americana* was sensitive enough to stop beside the first grave they came to, clasp his hand firmly, and go into prayers for a safe night.

"Great Mother, Maker of the World," she said, "watch over us we pray."

Again her touch went right up his spine.

"Watch over us, in this sacred space," the girl went on. "Here we feel especially close to You, Great Mother. Here the spirits consecrated to You remain fresh."

She raised their linked hands to head-level. The night breeze under his arm, hardly cold, gave him gooseflesh nonetheless.

"We feel close, so close to You."

Shanti used the formal *Lei*, but her head was back, her mouth ajar, her eyes shut. "We thank You for this presence in our lives. We thank You for this man—" she reopened her eyes and faced him—"this one who brought us to You."

Still with the open-mouthed smile, she let go of his hand. Fabbrizio was left once more incapable of a clear thought, so badly off that he brought out his own guardian angel. This he kept in the other pants-pockets, the one not holding the penlight. A small piece of old bronze, knobby, spidery: his Penates.

Shanti's smile narrowed, her eyes too. Fabbrizio worked up a quiet chuckle. "My Penates," he said.

In fact according to the professor he'd consulted—a man willing to look past issues of provenance—the figure in his hand might instead be a Lares. You could find isolated Lares, though the classic arrangement called for pairs or threes. Anyway by the time of the first Caesars, in all but the most ostentatious villas, Lares and Penates had become an interchangeable set of household protectors. Still Fabbrizio preferred to think of his godling as the lone-wolf warrior, Penates proud and solitary, and bearing an immense erection. The way the phallus pronged out from the trunk, a bulb-tipped crosspiece between the near-featureless head and the legs in attack stride, the charm created a kind of K—a letter unknown in Imperial times and absent from the Italian alphabet still. A mystery character, illegible as the spelling of good luck and bad.

"It's authentic, isn't it?" Beside him in the dark, Shanti's crescent of teeth revealed their American bleaching. "Fabbro, it's Roman era."

He wondered about his own smile. "Nothing special."

"What, nothing special? It's two thousand years old."

"Listen, here everyone carries a piece like this."

"Fabbro. They carry the *corno.*"

True enough; most of his friends had the twisted red thing, the shape of a crippled bull's horn and the color of a tomato. They wore it with their keys or hung it from their rear-view mirrors.

"A piece like this—" she indicated his green-brown demigod—"you don't buy it at the cigarette store."

"Beh. In many families, in years past, there might have been some old grandfather who was in the army, he might have found a piece like this."

"Oh. Some old grandfather, in years past."

"Many years past, Shanti. Nowadays all antiquities are part of the national patrimony. To take something off the ground would be outside the law."

"Oh, outside the law. *Sicuro.*"

No doubt Fabbrizio had a *corno* somewhere, perhaps in the bedroom desk that now become a permanent parking spot for the rusting Uldirico. But he preferred the Penates. The twisted horn struck a different attitude towards the supernatural, a defensive posture. Every time someone stroked the blood-colored corkscrew, or gave it a tip towards some unseen threat, they were playing a kind of Keep Away, warding off misfortune. Himself, when it came to fate, he wanted better. Fabbrizio wanted a hook to catch the good out there, not just a lightning rod to throw off the worst. Besides, in the American *Playboy* (you could always find such magazines, filched on their way to the NATO base up in Aversa), he'd seen advertisements that featured a cartoon Mexican pepper of some kind. A *jalapeno*, he believed this little vegetable was called, and it appeared the same color and shape as the *corno*. In the ads, the cartoons, the thing was wearing a sombrero. Fabbrizio expected to be working with Americans before he was through, hand in hand with the real money-people, and the last thing he needed was some little token that they would find laughable.

But then again, if Shanti was in any way typical, when it came to Americans he still had a lot to learn. A few feet farther into the site—abruptly cutting short her next prayer to the Goddess—the young woman caught her breath and jumped down into an open tomb. She jumped, an arm- and jacket-lifting movement that wound up leaving only her head and shoulders above the ground level of the necropolis.

The lower space appeared half-excavated, if that. When Fabbrizio followed her in he skated down, almost losing his feet on the tumbled heaps of dig-work.

The tomb was, like the one or two others he'd seen, considerably larger than the corpse required. Fabbrizio, his thin socks torn and taking on dirt, had room to extend one arm for balance while closing the other fist around his poky charm. A dark thought: he'd fucked in hotel rooms smaller than this. Then Shanti was hauling out her own flashlight, larger than his and, now that he got a look at it, an odd accessory for someone trying to reach the Invisible World. Quickly the American swept the gravesite, picking up what few details the moonlight didn't illuminate. Across the two uncovered walls spread frescos of dancing girls, dancing at play, rather than in the more serious poses of ritual. They wore loose-pleated dresses with high, unostentatious belts, and the breasts of one girl had come unbound, innocently. The few pieces of tomb furniture that poked up from the uneven earth included no weapons, no Olympic equipment like a discus or javelin. Fabbrizio saw only the goods of kitchen and bedroom. Among these however was a knee-high krater, an item the crew should've archived and put in storage before abandoning the site for the weekend. The vase remained almost upright, its base sunk in the dirt. Shanti kept her light on the thing long enough to reveal a bright black and orange picture of two more dancers, or possibly wrestlers. You saw a lot of that, two women grappling, one going down; the story always had to do with a mortal who'd challenged a god. Stupid mistake.

Fabbrizio shook his head and turned to the skeleton. No question about the gender, but the tomb kept throwing off that sort of logic, conclusions drawn from evidence. Rather the space seemed to tremble with the love this girl-child had enjoyed. Family feeling glimmered in the very pigment on the walls, powder that had turned wet as tears when dabbed onto the fresh plaster. The decorators, these ultimate interior decorators, had depicted a playtime so heady as to pick up, twenty-six or -seven centuries later, at the very point where it'd left off. The artwork in here might itself be the Goddess that the American had hoped to raise, a celebration that stone could never suffocate. And as for this skull and bones at Fabbrizio's feet, they mimicked the temples at which Babbo and Mama had prayed: oriented towards sunrise. The girl lay on an incline, a pallet beneath her head and shoulders, comfortable. Across her still-buried lap, no doubt the dig crew would turn up remains of the pizza-like cake, the scattered seeds and petrified honey, intended to pacify the dogs at the gateway to perpetual sunrise. Inside her tongueless mouth, perhaps fallen through to the upper links of her spine, they'd find the coin to pay the ferryman.

And the corpse wore that necklace. Shanti let her light linger a while. The gold was unmistakable, shining almost white, and starlike speckles burst on the amber, and on what Fabbrizio now saw was carnelian. Carnelian, he knew these things. He narrowed his eyes, working against the bloodrush in his temples, making a mental sketch of the piece. He saw the pattern; he could knock off a saleable copy.

Then *l'Americana* swapped the light for her needlenose pliers and dropped into a crouch. He couldn't be sure what he heard—a clicking, a scratching—until she spoke that English word, *buyer.*

"Are you... crazy?" Prompted by the *y-r* growl, he was trying her language. "Is this... your idea for how to do business?"

Her smile was visible again, now that his eyes had adjusted to the dark, but it no longer seemed at all sexy.

"Can you, are you…" He tucked his godling back into his pocket, then switched to Italian: "I don't know what you've heard of me, but I'm not the Mafia."

"Fabbro. Also myself, I'm not the Mafia. These days there isn't a Mafia."

He exhaled, lengthily, pinching one tight pants-leg down above the knee. The charm at his groin was prickling oddly, static electricity.

"The Mafia," he began, "I mean the Camorra—let's not talk like children. The Mafia can never be destroyed. Here it will always hold power."

"But that's just what I'm saying, pretty boy. One can always find a market for a piece like this." She waved the necklace. "One can always make an arrangement."

The way he was shaking his leg, Fabbrizio realized, was an American touch. Elvis.

"And Fabbro, making an arrangement, that's what you do best."

He shook his head. The Roman dingus went on tingling, but he let go of his pants, needing both hands against this woman.

"But, you said it yourself." She'd lost her smile. "Let's not talk like children, you said. You're not an archeologist."

"Okay, okay."

"O…kay?" She worked more slowly in English. "Are you saying, you are ready to do business?"

"I am saying, I have work in the business. But in this business, to sell for you, to sell only for you… this is not possible."

"My buyer is discreet. You understand, discreet? He prefers to work privately."

"No, no. Is not possible."

"He has money, Fabbro." Back to Italian: "He has a sack of money."

"But why can't I succeed in making you understand? Do you think I'm one of these big shots, a person of power?"

She'd kept her hand in the money-gesture, her index finger across her thumb.

"Do you think I'm another Don Corleone? Shanti, if I were to make arrangements on my own, I'd be cutting my own throat."

"Ah, you don't give yourself credit, *bello*. This place, in all of Italy there may be no site more famous. And nonetheless it was Fabbrizio who found a way in."

He shook his head and leg both. The American still didn't get it; he had no leverage at the national level, the *carabinieri* or the bureaucrats in Antiquities. One or two of the local cops knew him, o-kay, but the most they'd do for him would be overlook a stray gram of hashish. And as for tonight's security guard—Fabbrizio shrugged and told her. No MasterScam, here, Shanti. Nothing but a bundle of cash and a friend who had reasons of his own for visiting the southern fringes of the periphery. "And even this little, before the earthquake I could never have done it."

Tonight's lone rent-a-cop had no "respect," a word Fabbrizio threw in for the American's sake. "A man like that, he'll talk just to keep his job." He found himself angry at having to spell it out. "If the *caribinieri* come asking questions…"

At least she wasn't smiling any more. "Beh, by the time he starts talking, you will have three thousand more Euros in your pocket. I'm saying, three thousand and perhaps even more."

He found himself stilled, a rare thing even when he wasn't bothered by static electricity. He let his hands drop and drew together the heels of his loafers, there on the uneven grave floor. So much? And all of it his alone, not one penny kicked upstairs to some *Camorrista*? Again the American had him struggling for brains.

"Three thousand for me." He tried to growl. "And how much for the lady?"

Her curling smirk gleamed icelike, under this moon. "Oh, my *settebello*. Truly, you don't give yourself enough credit."

"This piece, it's worth a lot more than six. Somebody would pay six just for—" he jerked a chin at the standing krater—"for that one there."

"I said you might get more, *caro*."

"This girl's piece, the necklace, it could be in a museum. A true half-and-half split, I'd say that would be three times three."

"But who said anything about half and half? Fabbro, don't talk like a baby. What, you lay your eyes on a, on a few old stones and metals, and you believe they can change the whole world?"

Or: what, he believed his night's stupidity had ended? Shanti's question flattened his gesturing much like his daily communion wafer used to, back in his 11- and 12-year-old season of intensified churchgoing. Back before his chest hairs had sprouted, he'd spent several months convinced that he would become a priest—a not uncommon phase, so he'd come to understand, during Neapolitan male puberty. In Fabbrizio's case, throughout that God-struck school year the wafer's white fiber, about to turn to God-flesh inside him, appeared to glitter like snow, or like he imagined snow would glitter, since at that age he'd yet to see any snowfall that lasted longer than five or six minutes on the ground. He'd yet to travel up into the mountains. Tonight, his brief re-shuttering in priestly calm allowed Fabbrizio to calculate a few of the things he could buy with 3,000 Euros (and so long as he was behind the shutters, he could admit the number was no small one, for him). He figured the cash would be more than enough for the required tests on his mother, heart and lungs both. The woman's case would be given top priority, too, because payment would be private rather than part of the national program.

Mama would have her own room at the hospital… he'd take her in an Audi with a full back seat…

Yet as this still moment extended, over the real bones and the imaginary money, Fabbrizio also recalled the serious chill that had seized him at his first glimpse of real snow. Nothing like a communion wafer, snow had revealed itself as raglike granite-bordered crusts, devoid of glitter and dirtied by shivering sheep. Now in full summer Fabbrizio shivered himself, dumb as a sheep, and recognized more fully than ever the deep grip of his idiocy. The grip of this woman, this American. Every figure she threw at him was a fantasy.

"Cutting my own throat." The words came as an impulse out of his chill. "No more sense than a three-year-old."

Though when he was able to bring his better judgment to bear, Fabbrizio understood that she too must've had some fantasy going. Shanti too, prompted by whatever little she'd heard of him, had imagined he could deliver more. She'd fallen prey to the usual American delusions about southern Italians, believing he had a naturalborn gift for the nocturnal and corrupt. As if everywhere south of Rome the babies emerged with an unfiltered cigarette dangling from their cupid lips. Fabbrizio didn't know which was worse, the Mafia myth out of the States or the racist slurs out of northern Italy: *Everything south of Rome is Africa.*

This New Yorker tonight, so breezy about the worst lawbreaking he'd ever done in his life, he'd like to see what she made of a bookworm like Uldirico. Though naturally Fabbrizio hadn't mentioned his brother around this woman. Likewise her *settebello* still received official university mailings, himself, but he hadn't breathed a word about that either. Fabbrizio had done nothing to discourage whatever Hollywood folderol Shanti had in mind. On the contrary, he'd thrown himself into the role, trying to bring off a hip-hop update on Mastroanni. Tonight he would've lit a cigarette, accessorizing, if he hadn't lost all taste for tobacco during his father's final hacking months. The upshot was, even now as they made faces at each other over this girl who'd long ago lost her face, the out-of-towner had trouble understanding that he wasn't King of the Cats. Couldn't "Fabbro" cut any deal he wanted?

"But this is Naples," she was saying. "Here, everybody's always making arrangements, isn't that true? Here, nobody's stupid."

Stupid, *fesso*, of all the slang to sting him with. "Listen, you know what would be *fesso*? To take something out of a place like this and try to sell it myself. Truly."

She showed him a fresh glint of peroxide teeth. "But it's not possible. The Camorra don't know everything."

"But who's talking about everything? Tonight is a business of myself and yourself and one piece alone. It was you who said that around here everyone knows Fabbrizio. It was you who said this site was the most famous."

"You're exaggerating. You talk as if it were the entire American Army after us."

"Shanti, it only takes one to cut your throat."

In talking so openly, he had to work against a stubborn tugging from the back of his head: his lingering yen to seduce the girl. It wouldn't let go, the tidal pull of the fantasy in its orbit. Didn't *Baywatch* in fact come to Italy via satellite? "But don't worry, they won't involve themselves with you." He put some bite into it. "Not you, dear. They won't touch an American."

"Beh, another fairytale. All day this was precisely what you were hoping to do, touch an American."

His hands dropped, his face flattened.

"Truly, *caro*, you're exaggerating. You've got a, a certain American Empire in mind. The regime no one dares to overthrow. But my country isn't so stupendous, these days. This isn't the '60s. These days, if one of these bad guys wants to kill an American, it's only a question of money."

Now what? Had Fabbrizio started to smile?

"*Giusto, no?* I would make a beautiful corpse."

He'd started to smile, small and frank. What, hadn't he been enough of a sap already? How could he possibly trust what he just now sensed—some better give and take emerging between himself and this pseudo-Hindu? But the woman had played him so brilliantly, she'd made such a fool of him. You had to admire a person for that. You had to imagine that two such as them might yet discover some more honest variety of seduction. After all, she'd let him know what the game was before it could do him any real harm. And Shanti hadn't lost her good nature in the process. Faced with two versions of empire, the black market and the White House, either of which could break her, this might-be-thirty-something had simply shrugged, her windbreaker slipping down one shoulder. A fine shoulder, in this dark. Its Arabian bones cut a sculpted contrast to the pearlescent and faintly furred spaghetti-strap of her top.

"But really, Fabbrizio." She lowered her necklace-hand towards the corpse. "This lovely girl here—I've known from the start that I could end up like her."

He shifted his stance, peering out over the rim of the grave. In his head the looping wouldn't relent: three thousand... touch an American... The greater necropolis presented a Stalingrad-scape, with shrapnel glittering here and there among the uprooted, the pockmarked, the jerked-around. One or two of those gleanings might have value, to be sure. The krater by the girl's feet looked like nothing special, or not without a decent cleaning, but Fabbrizio hadn't exaggerated its price tag. Museums tended to clear off shelf-space for any item of that age, especially one still largely intact. One of the other graves might turn up a pot-shard bearing the name of a king, a scrap of ID for the scholars. But what were the chances of finding another piece worth what Shanti could get for the necklace? The right buyer, the right auction, and the boy from Secondigliano could triple again what he'd suggested for his half of the deal. Then what were the chances of coming across another piece like that, even if this dig went forward without further interference, if they emptied every grave without another pickpocket dropping in? Not much, *caro*. Over in Mykenos the burial chamber of Agamemnon himself had yielded next to nothing besides the famous death-mask.

In other words, Fabbrizio's stupid mistake wasn't the first to be made in this grave, today. Whoever had initially brushed the dirt off this necklace, no doubt just before quitting time at 18:00—that person too was guilty of no small oversight. They hadn't realized what they'd found. They hadn't called for the expert onsite. Though perhaps the fault lay with the *Signore* in Antiquities, whatever you called him; perhaps he'd gone home early. The local "technical staff," the ninety-caliber folks who kept their hands clean, they too had been worn out with additional running around since the quake. The Paestum specialist wouldn't be the first to award himself an extended afternoon siesta. It was Friday, after all.

People got tired; people got careless. You might say this was the very underpinning of Fabbrizio's economy, the human animal's unwillingness to take the trouble. This necklace here must first have been discovered by another kid on a miniscule research fellowship, one of those paid per diem, with no reason to hang around and catalogue his find properly. Another one like the many boneless schlubs that Fabbrizio had seen occupying a desk at the university. In fact he'd heard of worse cases than tonight's, one-of-a-kind pieces left lying unprotected on the ground. There'd been that solid-gold libation bowl, over by Brindisi; there'd been that bronze androgynous head down by Mt. Aetna.

A hell of a place to start searching for clarity: a dump of human frailty; a corpse-pit in which more than one brain had been riddled with rat-tunnels. As Fabbrizio made out more of the half-undug spaces around him, it called to mind nothing so much as the mess he'd seen on the news after the quake. For video from the epicenter, editors had chosen the worst: the bridges buckled and wrenched into the valleys they'd been built to cross, the stone-toothed gaps of piazzas torn in two, the toppled shafts of defining churches. In one memorable close-up, the cone-tip of a steeple poked at a sorry angle from a rubble of broken paving and upended cobblestone, and you could see the cross had taken a whacking from both sides. Its horizontal bar bent up at either end, resanctifying the icon, turning it into the trident of the Ocean God.

Some awful power had been unleashed, no small tempest. And three thousand was enough to buy his way out, to escape the worst, him and Mama both. The score of his life on the first, perhaps the only serious crime he ever committed.

Out in the graveyard, out between the winking bits embedded in the swill, he saw something move. Another variety of glimmer—the ripple of hairless skin.

Fabbrizio made adjustments in order to get a better look, wincing as he poked one knee into a cracked chunk of gravewall. He might've kicked something, too; he might've heard a clatter of bone.

Then he was telling the woman behind him to shut up. He was whispering, so harshly he wondered if he'd gotten dirt in his mouth.

"But, what?" Shanti, smart girl, had dropped into a squat at his feet.

"There, yes, there, I see you." Why was he talking like this? "I *see* you."

The glimmer of skin, and of eyes. The moon kept playing its tricks of course, so that the best he could make out was the on-again, off-again play of a figure behind a scrim—a large man, possibly shirtless, possibly black. The guy might have been trying, like Fabbrizio, to see without being seen. He'd drawn himself into a crouch, behind one of the few patches of shrubbery still leaf-side-up. But the distance wasn't much, no more than five or six strides if you didn't count the holes in the ground. Fabbrizio kept his knee in the broken stone, the pain helping him concentrate. He heard whispering.

Now if someone was whispering, who was listening? How many Peeping Toms had Fabbrizio turned up? They had to be peeking and hiding, in any case, no matter what their number; they had to be outside the law. If they'd been police, Fabbrizio and Shanti would've been wearing handcuffs by now.

"Don't be frightened." He was glad for the roughage in his voice. "The police, if these were police—"

She was ahead of him. "And if it were someone who worked for the dig, he'd have a walkie-talkie, a cell phone. We'd be hearing sirens."

She kept herself low, her voice barely audible. Fabbrizio found himself thinking for a moment beyond an arrest. He started imagining that the cops might offer him the same thing Shanti's buyer did: the chance to make his life over. The *carabinieri* could put him in witness protection, with fresh-minted documentation. Italian authorities had started using this tactic, *moda Americana*. And these days there were all sorts of substitute identities to be had, what with the temporary Earthquake I.D. in circulation. Why then shouldn't Fabbrizio get a fresh new identity, under the twinned letterheads of NATO and the UN?

But the cops only made such an offer when the case was important, the trade worth a new life. Fabbrizio, hunched at the grave wall, shook head and shoulders both.

"*Clandestini*," he whispered. "Looking for a safe place."

Any name he had to give the authorities would prove about as useful, in the long run, as those documents printed out after the quake. Earthquake I.D. would be valid only for another six months or so. By then the authorities were bound to have reconstructed the files damaged in the electro-magnetic pulse. They'd've counted all the dead.

"*Clandestini*," he repeated. "Africans, if I'm not mistaken."

He recalled what he'd seen under the opening in the fence, the broken gardenia and scraped earth. Somehow this gave him a better hold on himself. Reaching into his pants pocket, his voice at conversational level, he declared "This should get rid of them," and brought out his penlight. Shanti, at his feet, appeared to shrink into herself. If she were any other woman, he would've said she looked nervous, and she gave a breathless peep that—more madness—left Fabbrizio thrilled. He drew himself upright, shook his head differently, switched the thing on.

More madness: how many of them were there? Three, four?

The man he'd glimpsed in the dark was only the largest, the one the others had put on lookout. Those in the background weren't much visible, since Fabbrizio's skinny beam was more suitable for searching a closet, but insofar as he could see anything, he didn't like it. A cluster in a squat, a staring pair of eyes here and an unsmiling wedge of a face there. The big one out front was bad enough, him without a shirt on. Whatever day-labor this man had found had kept the muscles of chest and shoulders sizeable, a snug brown sack of Sorrento melons. Yet the head was skull-like, with deep balding scoops at either temple, drawn and weary features that suggested the former Italian territories in East Africa. Somalia, Eritrea: some shot-up countryside where God knows what it took to get through the night.

"Blacks like these," he said, "who knows?"

"What?"

Shanti might've gone on trying to talk, or perhaps he only heard her scuttle across the grave floor. In another moment she took hold of his ankle, and he might've felt her fingers trembling before they closed around him. But he couldn't stop frowning, the bloodrush back in his ears as he peered along the light beam.

"So many of them," he muttered. "So many like this, I don't know... a family?"

"What? What does that mean?"

"So many blacks together."

"Fabbro..."

What had happened to the tingle he'd once enjoyed each time she touched him? What kind of bad new jolt had got him now? Fabbrizio tried a gulp of air, but tasted a stench he hadn't noticed before, perfume gone sour and flesh gone to muck.

Foolish as he'd been, breaking and entering with a woman like this, he'd never have done it if he'd believed they'd have company. Never; not possible. It was the little god in his pocket who was led around by his cock, not Fabbrizio. But you make one mistake, and before you know it, the complications tangle and multiply. It appeared there were children among the *clandestini*.

Fabbro's light wasn't so feeble that he couldn't tell a child's arm when he saw it, sidling up out of the shadow to hug the big bodyguard in front. The thin preteen hand had darker skin than its father's—surely the man in front was the father—and the pink fingertips reached not even halfway around the solid adult belly. But the kid hooked on tightly. There might've been a child's voice too, a bedtime complaint.

L'Americana had let go of Fabbrizio's foot. She sounded as if she were finding a better place to hide, more scuttle and clink, but if this heavy-muscled man across the necropolis were a father, and if that just-visible face behind him belonged to a mother... It was a woman anyway, over there in the dark, with gloss on her lips and a barrette glinting in her lopsided Afro. Plus, did Fabbrizio see another child over there, another extended limb? Or was that a machete? Sometimes the day-labor for the local farms stole a tool, a knife, a bigger blade...

"But it's a nightmare," he said into his fist. "Who knows, with these blacks?"

The light went back into his pocket. With a tiptoe thrust he pitched himself up the slope of fallen dirt, in his suede and summer cotton; he flung himself full-length across the muck, reaching out for whatever remained of the 21st-Century ground level. He needed to get a grip, a root, a hunk of something solid. He'd never have gotten off the highway if he'd thought for a moment he'd come up against this nightmare: so many, nameless and savage. The monster in front looked to be three times Fabbrizio's size. The man squatted nearly naked, bug-eyed and protecting his young, and for all the white boy knew there could be a dozen more. They could be all over this dead-man's land.

And the same dread had Shanti scrambling, a changed woman herself. She propped her linked hands beneath one of his loafers, a boost up. He caught hold of a jutting something or other, perhaps a chalky piece of another tomb wall, and belly-crawled up the loose earth. Meanwhile the American was thinking aloud, saying the same sort of things as Fabbrizio had going on in head.

These people... no telling...

Not that he was about to waste time with a reply. During the panic that carried him out of the necropolis, over the next two-three minutes, Fabbrizio had only a single bubble of clear thinking. This came while they were still in the grave, when he couldn't quite get his legs up and slid back down the heaped dirt to land on the American's foot, on her sneaker. Then as he steadied himself he got her a second time, crunch, his hard leather heel across her cloth-covered toe. He knew what he heard then. She erupted in a shout, the loudest noise of their entire visit to this supposedly protected dig. But he couldn't take time with it, couldn't give it a thought, not till after the two of them had scuttled back under the fence and away through the surrounding brush (and any shadow in there could be another one, an alien, dark and impossible to talk to). Only after he'd once more straddled his motorcycle and begun squeaky-wheeling it, stiff-legged, backwards out of its hiding place—only then did realize just what he'd heard. Shanti had yelped in pain, sure, but she'd also delivered something like the slap you give a person who's gotten hysterical. In his ear, she'd shouted:

"Fabbrizio!"

His name? She shouted his *name*, right there in the open grave?

It took Fabbrizio the better part of the trip back to Positano to assess the ramifications, the dread continuing to rack him even as his Suzuki wheeled, no longer impeded by traffic, through the hairpins above the coast. Only during the last loop down towards the tourists' seashore did he succeed in getting his mind around this fresh reason to worry. She'd been loud enough to wake to the dead!

After they'd dismounted, he had to ask her about it. He tried to calm himself, drinking in the scent from the hotel kitchen, roasted garlic tonight. But as soon as he brought it up, her shouting his name, they might've been back in the reek of ancient bones and oils. They might've been arguing about the black market again.

"Fabbro, two times you landed on me." Shanti shrugged her bag up her shoulder. "With all your weight, two times in less than a minute."

"All right, I'm sorry. But why did you need to, so loudly like that—"

"But what do you mean, so loudly? It only seemed that way because you were close enough to step on my foot."

He threw in a gesture, thumb-to-fingertips, where's-your-head. "You saw those people. You know what will happen if they're caught by the police."

"People like that don't talk with the police. And what's more, people like that, the police don't listen."

The hour's ride up from Paestum, the session inside the sensory deprivation tank of her bike helmet, had apparently brought the woman back to herself. Anyway it didn't take someone like Shanti, the unflappable Caper Queen, to figure out that the *carabinieri* might not waste time with tonight's gang of illegals. Nor could you count on the interrogation taking place, to begin with; chances were, tonight would be no different from every other night, and no one wearing a badge would come near the family. The *clandestini*. But even if these blacks fell into the hands of the state, Shanti was right. More often than not, the best an African could expect from the police was a shakedown in the station and a quick trip to the deportation camps.

She didn't need someone to draw her a picture, this American. You had to admire a person for that. Meanwhile she continued her assurances, pointing out that her people in New York had a contact with the local police. "If there were something we needed to know, they'd get a call."

"Shanti, what? A contact...?" But Fabbrizio had begun to notice how the ride had left his collar twisted, his shirt pinching under one armpit. The grave-stink that'd assaulted him earlier might've been his own: his honeysuckle gone rancid and his patches of smeared-on dirt reeking of sulfur, gumming his throat.

"Fabbro, how do you think I knew about the Café Sempre? Think about it, in America they've got the money and here they've got the, the graves."

The thought seemed to make him stink worse. With a thumbnail he picked at the gunk inside a shirt-button. Might've been him working the tomato fields tonight, another subsistence grubber, a slave to the bank till they put him in the dirt. But now Shanti was speaking to him differently, quietly. She offered a drink and a shower.

"They close the bar at two," she said. "But I have a fridge in the room."

He might've been working the pig farms. To get out stains like these, he was going to need his mother.

"You still have a long way to go tonight, yes? Another hour more or less, back up to Secondigliano?"

That brought his head up. "But how do you know about Secondigliano?" Even Italians tended not to have heard of his neighborhood, and those who had generally avoided mentioning the place.

"Calm yourself, *ragazzo*." She reminded him that, as soon as she'd begun making inquiries, everyone had been talking about Fabbrizio. When he didn't stop frowning, the woman told him he should be proud.

"The way they spoke of it, this is a thing of value, to be a man of Secondigliano."

He still had his thumbnail in a button. Dropping the hand, unknotting his features: "All right, something to drink. A good vodka."

"The shower first, Fabbrizio. We don't want anyone thinking you're the *clandestino*."

The place had the sort of elevator he loved, an elegant cage from between the wars, but he and Shanti rode it wordlessly. There was the heaviness of their night-odor, plus the stray glacial blocks of leftover fear, grave-and-shadow fear. In Fabbrizio's case, besides, he found himself contending with yet another round of sighing fantasy. The high heels and lingerie in his mind's eye seemed like stale stuff, catalogue stuff, when for a moment he could stand back and consider them. But to keep them down was like trying to contain smoke with his fingers.

Shanti was the one to put a lid on it. Between elevator and bedroom she broke the silence in an accent that revealed her fatigue, a more American sound than earlier. She repeated that Fabbrizio was going back to Secondigliano tonight. As she fished her key from her gym pants, she added that she'd have him on the road again in no time, and inside the room, her first move was to unsex the bed. She dumped her bag in the center of the coverlet, sprinkling dirt across the rose and lace. The move also put the night-table between the two of them, so that as Shanti ducked into the bathroom (not even bothering to slip off her windbreaker), Fabbrizio was left studying her bedtime book. The dust-jacket cover depressed him too, a grainy photo of the sort of apartment project you found all over his home blocks, one of those penitentiary-style prefabs, the workmanship a good two-thirds outside code. The author's name was unpronounceable too, Al D'la something, one more Arab touch to the woman renting the room.

Fabbrizio opted for the balcony, the timeless low chuckle of the fishing boats in the harbor. The thought came to him that he might have a look in her bag, but he lacked the heart; the last thing he needed was additional aggravation. Then the bathroom water stopped running, and in another moment Shanti was out and squatting before the room's little fridge. She'd left off the jacket, this time, but with her chin in her chest she appeared as neutered as a troll. Flatly she announced that they had no vodka.

Fabbrizio looked again to his shirtfront. Filthy from collar to hem, and his pocket had been torn away.

Just a Coke, he said.

This drew a more humane look. Shanti didn't quite smile, but her freshly scrubbed features softened, and this was enough to make him recall the one other moment of honest feeling he'd had from her, a feeling that seemed the defining reverse to this one. He remembered the hard, hurt wanting the woman had shown him, for just a tick or two up in Piazza Bellini, while she'd been teaching him a new obscenity. And now he was facing the same honesty, the elemental Shanti, for a tick or three. He hadn't gone through a night like this, reduced to pure nerves hardly an hour ago, not to know the real thing when he saw it now. But there before the open mini-fridge she was quick to adjust her face, her mask; she gave him no time to make sense of this sympathy tonight or its negative two days earlier. She pointed out that they had limoncello.

Fabbrizio could see the liqueur from where he stood, two hand-high yellow bottles in a crescent-moon shape. That moon wore a Disney grin and the whole package seemed suddenly contemptible. It struck him as the worst kind of tourist frippery. Whoever had come up with that design had the innards of an accountant.

Shanti didn't fail to notice his frowning. Quietly she again offered the shower. "Take as long as you like, Fabbro."

With pleasure, *signora*. The loud cascade of water, plus the fingertip-shadings of hot and cold you got in a four-star place, seemed to rinse the shit off his feeling and thinking. Afterwards he spent several minutes bent over the sink in his bikini briefs, scrubbing his shirt and pants. He came to see that his bellyflop onto loose earth hadn't lasted that long, or done that much damage, and even the suede would air-dry quickly on the ride home. Terrible as the stains had looked out in the bedroom, in that indirect lamplight, now it seemed like he might not have to burden his mother after all. He didn't want her worrying, even if it meant he had to learn how to sew on a new shirt-pocket.

Also he poked around a moment, just to see. But what could the woman hide in a closet like this, the barren porcelain and steel? A bottle of lavender body lotion, what could that tell him? Rather the rubberized thumb-small container helped Fabbrizio understand himself, as he massaged in a dollop of the lotion. He realized he'd gotten past the wet dreams, the lascivious kidstuff that had preyed on his mind since he'd met this woman. It had something to do with that look Shanti had just shown him, spilling the damp green complications of humanity across the airbrushed flatness of his mental centerfold. Now he was checking his own look, in the mirror. He'd been hearing for years now that he was something of a *settebello*, his eyes so dark and his bones so light. But just this minute the idea only added to his aggravation, it felt like one more piece of Disney, and he let go a groan that rang faintly off the mirror's steel frame. The flimsiness of it: that a mere few layers of skin had played such a part in a night so shameful, so full of threats.

He dropped his gaze and shook his head. A stray thought of his cell phone, still locked in his bike, reminded him that there remained a few hours before daylight at least. There remained time yet to handle himself with something like decent sense, whatever else the American might offer.

He returned to his damp clothes and emptied his pockets. He pulled out his priapic godling, his lucky K. Picking dirt off the bronze, he noticed again the flecks of yellow in the metal's toadlike color. As he cleaned the thing, it occurred to him that back in the gravesite, a bit of gravel might've gotten in with the statuette, a piece of grit that had since fallen out again.

Yes gravel, it must've been, prickling so strangely...

Then as he stood cradling the poky antique, against the spattered sink and faucet and mirror appeared traces of rainbow. Some kind of refraction came into play, must've had to do with the water everywhere and the lights of such a hotel, and Fabbrizio liked the effect, the multi-color speckles afloat somehow amid the porcelain and chrome, like a touch of that Russian Jew—or was he French? or American?—a touch of that Chagall, something better in his mind's eye, something to replace the soulless limoncello bottles. Also he found a moment's pleasure in the music Shanti had put on, out in the bedroom. On the radio, perhaps, she'd found some pop thing in English, he'd heard it before.

...you say, go slow... the second hand unwinds, time...

An American tune, afloat on the supernatural enhancements of those studios in New York or Los Angeles: glut and innocence at once, the honest tremors in the girlish outcry reinforced somehow by machinery laden with a thousand knobs. He had to shake his head at the contradictions, he had to blink against the scraps of silent fireworks on the bathroom air, and when he closed both hands prayerlike around his charm, his Penates, he suffered again the indefinable electricity that had sent its jolts through him in the half-undug tomb site, jolts that now suddenly and without his willing it made his grip close still tighter around the two-thousand-year-old bronze. After that, a voice.

...my necklace... my father... the truth in how he fastened it around me...

A voice, or perhaps a kind of discharge, up the arm on a direct line to the ear's innards. He shivered but his grip wouldn't release; the reptilian bronze, the triple-spiked deity, seemed sealed between his palms.

...my father hooked it around my perfumed neck... so much truth in his farewell... and death as ever so near...

Around him colors kept popping and wheeling. He was blinking, his head lolling, yet that had nothing to do with these insubstantial sparklers in their uproar.

...the fastening greased by the oils... my breasts still unformed... and death now again so near...

His control was letting go up and down his body, though by this time he knew what he was hearing, whose voice had penetrated his nervous system. He staggered back against the sink, forward into the curtained tub, the mirrored door. Hail Mary, full of grace—but what good would it do to pray to Mary? If Fabbrizio were in fact praying, if those words had started to sound in his unshaven throat, what help could he expect from so young an immortal? The spirit who spoke to him in this bathroom, spoke to him or through him, she'd lived and died half a millennium or more before the mother of Fabbrizio's Savior first saw light. The dead Greek girl, still more than half buried—that's who called the shots in here. The very fact that her would-be grave-robber had managed to begin his pitch to the Queen of Christian Heaven, even in a mumble, must be proof that whatever remained of the youngster from Paestum had finished its say. Yes, the séance or whatever you would call it had run its course. Fabbrizio felt the bronze-conducted electricity ebbing back down his arm, his grip relenting, and after that the brightest colors visible were the dark pink dots where his Penates had bitten into his unclasping palms. In his ears, only a seashell roar.

Not that she'd left him the way she'd found him, this stuttering ghost. For a long moment of fading buzz, of blinking into corners, Fabbrizio could be certain only of who'd set off the noiseless fireworks and put these long-past-midnight warnings in his ear. He hadn't lost the centering he'd gained between Shanti's face before the mini-fridge and his own in the bathroom mirror. He could understand, still, that if he came up with some other rationale he'd only be lying to himself again. No choice but to blink and bear it: this had been a voice from beyond. It'd been the girl from the half-open tomb, the *Greca*, her with the "breasts still unformed" and the father hooking on her necklace. Plus she'd also shown him a bit of the busy color of her astral landscape.

No choice but to take it on faith and see what if anything the girl might've meant. For wasn't he the artist, wasn't he? Born to go on faith, on hunch?

Uldirico was the one who needed hard data, and look where that had got him.

Not that Fabbrizio didn't have second thoughts. Thoughts like, he might only be making something supernatural out of ordinary mental instability, a "dissociative break," stress-related to be sure. Or then again, laying these after-shower shivers off on la Greca might be a simple matter of falling back on the first notion that came to mind. Only natural to follow the line of least resistance—it wasn't as if he had much else to prop him up. His knees felt as though they'd give any minute and no midnight refresher had ever made him so dizzy. No vodka, no hashish, nothing had put such a wobble into Fabbrizio, and this on top of plain weariness on top of the evening's earlier hoodoo terror. All of it heaped up along his spine, it almost pitched him into the tile walls, the very surfaces he was still trying to bring into focus. Checking his fall, practically toppling over the other way, he found the doorknob and lunged or fled finally out of the bright water closet. In his bikini briefs, with the cock-high figurine dancing in his loosened hand, he reeled up against the foot of Shanti's wide bed.

Shanti's, yes. The American had reclaimed the bed, brushing the dirt off the coverlet, off its doily trim and rose decoration. She'd put the bag away somewhere, he couldn't see where. He couldn't take his eyes from her, a good-looking woman laid out before him in nothing but panties and a complicated old necklace.

"But what?" she asked after a moment. "Don't you like this combination? Don't the colors go well?"

Her smile alone was a skin magazine, red and indulgent. The panties, tight and narrow, had that cloudy off-yellow called *oro sommerso*, submerged gold—and in fact matched the necklace.

"You see the, the underwear," she went on, with a languorous flip of the wrist. "You see the gold at the neck, yes?"

At the neck. What else would this princess of trickery wear to cap off her evening except the piece of jewelry about which Fabbrizio had just been receiving mystic bulletins? Or mystic only maybe, only possibly, what difference did it make now? He couldn't look at anything else, even with the pale petals of her shoulders shifting, the brown snouts of her nipples hardening? Even so, the necklace fascinated him most.

That stone in it, that variable green: not just Russian amber, but also carnelian all the way from India. And the gold shining, now that the whole piece had been wiped down (could Shanti have had some cleanser in her bag?). The design followed the fashion you saw around highborn Mediterranean necks for over a thousand years, from Mykenos through Pompeii. The stone, shaved and sculpted, provided the design for the ornament. In this case it called to mind one triple-layered corner of a gameboard for Chinese checkers, or perhaps an inverted pharaoh's pyramid, striped by three successively smaller bands. Around those, enhanced by those, the more precious metal added highlights and trim. To Fabbrizio old gold like this always had a touch of the animal about it, the yellow of a monkey's eyes. The bright stuff dangled in tails, too, here and there along the bottom rung of the necklace. Woven string-lengths of gold hung down an inch or so, each holding at its tip a caged nugget of amber, the stone in this case pale as lime. The central hanging strand lay now between the woman's breasts, down over her heart: a monkey's tail in the shadow of a pyramid.

"*Ra-gaz-zo.*" Her tone suggested the five or six years she had on him. "Again this face of surprise. But I see I'm not the only one in my underwear."

He dropped his eyes, finding his flat waist again in a model's pose, stippled by trails of shower-water. Never before had the momentary arrangement of muscle and skin seemed so stupid, so vain.

"If you've lost your tongue, I'm going to be disappointed."

It came to him that, this entire time, the radio had remained on. The current song too was American: *...such a night... sweet confusion....* At this hour you could pull in the U.S. Armed Forces Network, faraway stations. But what station had Fabbrizio been tuned to when this woman had slipped the green-and-yellow treasure into her ditty bag? Hadn't he had eyes or ears for anything beside the half-lit blacks across the necropolis? Fabbrizio began to gesture in disgust, but the movement made it look like he was waving his own ancient token at her—erection first.

She chuckled. "He's got the right idea, that one."

"The necklace," he managed, "it was, it was a gift. From the girl's father."

Her look narrowed, and he noticed she'd freshened her makeup. "You know this? You can be sure the necklace was, was something for the burial in particular?"

When he shook his head the spatter from his hair, its tips still wet, took him by surprise. A few drops landed on Shanti's naked feet, and when she kicked, startled, her reopened eyes revealed another flash of something more mottled than the hot-momma brass she'd shown him since he'd come out of the bathroom. She had some rage in her, this still-young woman, some score perhaps that she had yet to settle. But

Fabbrizio was shivering differently. He had cold spots in his thinking. How could he tell this playgirl about the wildly different signal he'd just received, the seemed-to-be spirit guide, when front and center before him she'd plumped up a flesh-full bag of candy, *oro sommerso?* Come and get it, Secondigliano. Come celebrate, and never mind any private motive the party might have. But how could he, when he was the one to've actually brought off the phenomenon about which she'd been giving him a line of talk?

He'd done it, New York. He'd summoned a spirit. And even if he hadn't Fabbrizio could no longer spare the energy for the doubt, for thoughts about how he loved the old jewelry and he knew every piece up in the Museo Nazionale... Such logical rags were no use against the fingerprints on his spinal column now. Wherever the touch came from, it took the strength right out of him. Anyway what had the voice in Fabbrizio's head, in Shanti's bathroom, told him? What was his inside information, if not bad news? Insofar as there'd been anything like spectral communication, insofar as the burial necklace and the household icon had functioned as transmitter and receiver, the message that had come through left a cold spot. Someone was dying, was the message. Someone close by was also close to dying.

"You're sure about this?" Shanti repeated, a finger trailing lightly along either the lower edge of the necklace or the upper curve of a breast-tip.

"It was—the custom. An offering for the dead."

Fabbrizio fortunato, they called him around the neighborhood. He was smarter than most of those working off the books, taking advantage of his unfinished university program, plus his knack with eye and hand. *Fortunato*, he'd wangled entry into one of the least exposed of local "irregular economic activities." Then there was his Penates, another example. Who else could've caught such a break, happening onto a professor's unlocked storage cabinet on the very first day of his intended conservator's program? As for tonight, 'Brizio knew what the boys down the block would think. He had no trouble picturing their faces, their lips puckered with jealousy, with fantasy. Listen, guys—what you're thinking, it's nothing but fantasy. Nothing but thin air. The reality was, faced with a stolen *Playboy* come to life, their buddy felt the opposite of his little bronze sidekick with the permanent hard-on. Whatever sexual overture *l'Americana* might play, he was in no way ready to hum along. Whatever luck-muscle Fabbrizio might once have flexed had tonight been left limp and exhausted.

"But then...," the woman's hips stirred as she spoke, "what offering remains for us? For us the living?"

Fabbro cast another look down at his midsection, shapely but pointless.

"What are you looking for, *settebello*? You know with a woman like myself, there's nothing to worry about. I've had a, an operation, you understand?"

"Listen." He might've picked up a hesitation in what she'd just said. "Listen, Shanti. Let's talk a moment..."

Yet perhaps the young man remained a *fortunato* after all, even here in a hotel for tourists, with his seducer's outfit wrinkled and dripping into the tub behind him, and with his charm-piece looking, in this light, like a brokeback praying mantis. Even so, at that moment the woman's phone rang. The room phone not the cell, a ringing loud and direct rather than some electronic fugue.

One ring was all it took; Shanti's horizontal posture went through a remarkable quick-change. Remarkable but hardly mysterious, or not to Fabbrizio. He had so little trouble reading the body language— "back to business"—that he found the experience reassuring. He hadn't lost the knowledge of himself and this foreigner that he'd come to in the bathroom, back before La Greca had butted in. He hadn't been so damaged. Shanti's candy-bag had knotted shut again, at least for the duration of the call. Back to business, and it took no playacting for him to make the same adjustments. Fabbrizio started to frown, honestly. But, what? At this hour?

The woman was sitting up, the necklace hanging now over her nipples. After the second ring, she spoke in English: "Fuck me. It's got to be the States."

Fabbrizio wasn't so damaged. In New York, he recalled, it would only be the American early dinnertime.

"*Fuck* me." There was her anger again; she hadn't wanted to say those words in this way. Then she put on a joke face, a child's pout. In Italian: "Fabbrizio, what a shame. This must be my friends from New York, and I must speak to them."

Signora, believe me, the last thing you need to do is apologize. Nonetheless while she took up the receiver, this fleshy looker who'd led him astray so sweetly, this quick-blooded stranger now tossing her bed-ratted hair off one ear as matter-of-factly as a receptionist—while Shanti did that, Fabbrizio went into another kind of game. He kept his frown in place, straightening his back and shoulders with the better judgment of someone who'd been in this business longer than she. He'd been in the Naples branch longer, at least. And he gave voice quietly to an old hand's disapproval.

Beh, these Americans. They think they can shit where they eat.

He returned to the bathroom, taking up his pants and shaking them out. When the suede's wet heaviness made him grunt, he used the grunts to add emphasis to his disdainful muttering. This wasn't professional. The woman wanted the some kind of schoolgirl thrill, he grumbled, when what they needed to do was to hammer out on a story for both the *carabinieri* and the bad guys. The whole night had been like this, one wild scene after another...

Naturally Fabbrizio also kept an ear cocked for whatever he might be able to translate of the overseas conversation. Shanti jabbered rapid-fire, and there was a lot of slang or shorthand. But he got the gist, even as he yanked his damp, chilled pantsleg back over his now-aching knee. He understood that matters had taken a bad turn. Serious trouble had erupted, somehow, trouble enough to make Shanti draw her knees to her chest and hook her arm around her shinbones.

Was this what his Greek visitor, tonight's friendly ghost, had been warning him about? "Death" in some other sense?

He left off shaking out the shirt. He stopped his toughneck muttering. Insofar as he could understand the English, he could tell that this was about the police. He knew the word "arrest," he knew "suspect" and "jewelry" too, all practically the same as the Italian. He recognized "dig," naturally, and Shanti also made mention of *clandestini*. The cops had rounded up a few people for the break-in, sounded like, illegal aliens, sounded like. And already some kind of bad news had come out in their interrogations, something about some jewels.

The next time Fabbrizio met the woman's look, neither was putting on an act.

Second Evening

His poses had no effect on the *Greca*, either, the animus somehow made talkative again after three thousand years. One night wasn't enough for the girl to have done with him. Hardly more than a week later Fabbrizio stood confronting her skull again—it could only be hers—and the sight set his adrenaline spiking as wickedly as it had down in the Paestum grave and over the Positano hotel sink. Indeed a week ago, best he could recall, he hadn't been so afraid. Or his fear hadn't had such blunt, cold clarity. This time, his pretty face might end up looking like hers. The skin fell away quickly enough, when a person was planted under a layer of lime.

Today he stood faced with her again thanks to two *cammoristi*.

One of the gangsters had propped the skull upright playfully, using an extended middle finger to keep the point of its jaw balanced on a tabletop. A difficult thing to balance, a hollow inverted pear. Until they'd shown him this, bringing it out of a burlap sack they'd stowed under the hatchway stairs, Fabbrizio had felt glad, more or less, at finding himself back in this basement. Back to finish the job—a job that must've taken the original Paestum shop a week, while the man of Secondigliano required only a pair of overnight sessions. Plus the workspace was familiar, the same as he'd used the last time he accepted an assignment for these two so-called friends. Upstairs in the coffee bar, they'd flashed a billfold more than fat enough to cover the promised payment.

Beh, promised. Now the other bad guy kept an elbow crooked inside one of Fabbrizio's, as if propping him in place too. This closer one was making remarks that he seemed to believe were funny. "A pretty little thing, this one."

The other thug was the larger, with an upper body that called to mind the stuff of monumental frescos. A brute out of Caravaggio, looking on as a saint was flayed alive. When this guy laughed, in so airless a basement, the sound itself seemed made of muscle.

"She likes you," said the one in a better position to slit Fabbrizio's throat. "But look, she likes you!"

The big one preferred the name Treno, and he wore his hair in a weightlifter's buzzcut. He was making the bony husk nod, on the tabletop.

"Fabbro, how can you ignore a beauty like this? You're hurting her feelings."

"What she needs," grunted Treno, "is a man with a good fat dick on him."

Fabbrizio kept his look in place, a limp and puzzled smile. With his free arm he touched the cluster in his pants pocket, his lucky Penates. But why did the camorrista at his side have to wear so heavy a scent, a musk? Fabbrizio had the thought that if anything here would start him screaming it would be that darksome odor, one of those herbal oils out of Africa. What was it doing in this basement, where the local volcanic mulch was oppressive enough? His could-be murderers also hadn't bothered to switch on the bulb that dangled from the center of the uneven ceiling.

At least there was a bit of sun. This late in June, even a low basement window caught its share of slant six-o'clock rays. Not that the window offered much. Fabbrizio found himself thinking suddenly of the older Americans on their "art tours," the sixty-somethings with nothing better to do than prove how sensitive they were. One of those biddies, getting out her watercolors to capture the beauty of sundown on the Mediterranean—beh, she wouldn't look out *this* window. Outside the heavy-duty glass, unwashed for ages now, all you could see was a scrap of a shared lot. An alley really, with only one way in or out.

Around here Salerno was light-industrial, shops mostly closed for the night already. Now that Fabbrizio thought about it (and where was his mind, anyway? what were all these irrelevancies?), he had to wonder how the window's sideways rectangle let in any light at all. Yet you could make out the shelves along one wall, with their jumble of coffee-making materials and the stuff of less legal activity. An oblong of sun reached as far as the skull, as well, and Fabbrizio recalled the play of the moon, not ten nights ago, across this same rounded bone. Like the glistening that gathers on a melon as the fruit goes rotten.

It had to be the Greca's skull, and not just because of its undeveloped size or the gender these two kept using. "What she needs, my friend—"

the man at Fabbrizio's elbow sounded admonishing—"is a thing to give her a pretty look. A nice necklace can do so much for a girl."

This lame joke by itself would've been all that a smart *giovanotto* needed to hear, in order to know just who this was on the table, this jug full of holes. More than that, Fabbrizio had read the papers. He'd read his bookworm brother's morning delivery (most days Uldirico himself wasn't awake enough for the paper till noon) over this last week-plus of lying low.

For days, Fabbrizio had ventured out of the apartment only for his mother's sake. He'd visited the hospital, of course. He'd stopped in at the private studio of a doctor who, for a price, could assure the signora of quality recuperative care. Other than that, before the cammoristi had mentioned a figure high enough to lure him back down to this Salerno bar, he'd confined his journeying to a few select areas of the news media. He pored over the *Napoli* pages, the regional coverage, and any articles having to do with the Commission on Antiquities. He couldn't look at all the papers—this was Italy, with thirty parties in Parliament and a rag for every one—but if anything got into the dailies he did see, it didn't escape his notice. And nothing in the papers had made tonight's and last night's Salerno visits seem like too great a risk. What after all did a broken krater and a stolen skeleton have to do with him?

Even the necklace, as it appeared in the paper, had nothing to do with him. When Fabbrizio got a eyeful of the "artist's rendering" in *Il Mattino*, it'd made him laugh out loud. The drawing was based on the recollection of the dig assistant who'd left the piece lying there in the first place. That young man had been stripped of his fellowship and sent back to the libraries in Bologna, back to the city where a wallet dropped on the Communist sidewalks was returned untouched to its owner the next morning. But before the college boy left the South, he'd given the police a description of the tomb jewelry, "artistic" indeed. He'd misplaced an entire band of the green and carnelian, so the striping was rendered out of balance. Worse were the decorative pieces shown dangling from the piece's lowest rung.

Fabbrizio had had no trouble picking out such fine points, the nuggets of caged amber, against the tan-bordered swag of Shanti's breasts. Her breasts were the belled underside of white roses, and the stones prismatic touches of dew. But in the newspapers, the tails that dangled from the necklace's lowest semi-circle hung empty. Rather, at their tips, each one had some geometric form, now a star, now a cross. They might've been hood ornaments.

Fabbrizio discovered too that his very name had suffered a mangling. The *clandestini* on the gravesite had turned out to be a family, just as he'd suspected at his first mind-fracturing glimpse of their skin and shadow across the broken dirt. He'd been right and yet he'd gone crazy with fear—he'd been right, and yet by the time these refugees had fallen into the hands of the police Fabbrizio had been putting as much distance as he could between him and them, his knuckles going white around the Suzuki's accelerator. Nonetheless, once the cops got these blacks into interrogation, they spoke as a family. The husband said one thing and the wife another.

The name the homeless had heard shouted among the upended stones, in the dizzy redolence of lemon, sulfur, and plaster in decay, was another of those fluttery Italian sounds that gave Africans such trouble. Fabbrizio, Maurizio, Federico...

On top of that, this ill-defined array of names had been kept out of the papers for a good three days. This latest grave robbery loomed as a disgrace for all the authorities involved, and so the media had waited till it had no choice except to acknowledge that the culprits couldn't be these first, promising suspects: a family of illegal immigrants rounded up that very night. They'd been snagged on a routine police drive-by just minutes from the dig, three undocumented Somalis walking bold as you please out along the roadside (Fabbrizio, checking one article against another, understood that he and Shanti hadn't been the only ones shaken up by the graveyard encounter). Father, mother, and teenage daughter, these were. Then after they'd been brought to the nearest sizeable police station, the Salerno station, they'd offered the one item of barter they had. They'd seen something.

A likely story, just what you'd expect of clandestini faced with deportation. And they admitted to breaking the krater, too. They'd handled the old wine pitcher carelessly, frightened to begin with and then hightailing it off-site as soon as the daughter had let the thing drop. Nevertheless, in a matter of hours their wild tale of a more significant robbery was confirmed, and in a matter of days it became clear that these blacks couldn't have done it themselves. Even the papers with an anti-immigration platform, even the reactionary *Corriere della Sera*, had no choice except to admit that the funeral jewelry must've fallen into other hands.

Homeless, cell-phone-less, barely able to speak Italian, these original suspects were boat people, in the country less than a week. They'd ridden down to Paestum in the back of a truck, some six hours before discovery. Yet even they would've realized that the necklace was valuable; they wouldn't have picked the piece up just to chuck it into the underbrush. The cops had searched, to be sure, shoulder to shoulder with a swiftly assembled posse of professors and students. Nothing. Then another posse had ridden up, from the direction of Amnesty International, the UN Council for Refugees, and the Communist daily *Il Manifesto*. The Somali family became something of a cause.

It emerged that, while crossing the water from Tunisia, this hand-to-mouth crew had lost another child. A younger daughter had drowned somehow. Fabbrizio didn't learn the details; he'd been skimming the paper for other business anyway, and then once he'd gotten the gist of the story regarding the Somalis' loss he'd let the *Mattino* drop and found himself, after a moment, standing before his mother's kitchen shrine to Padre Pio.

So many families, he found himself thinking, living with a hole in the photo. So many in his city and its periphery, staggering over a cavity, a hollow ...

But while the Africans' tragedy sent Fabbrizio briefly back to God, to the same yearning for the wafer as had staggered him a dozen years ago, the more engagé humanitarians around the country had made an example of the case. This whittled-down family came to stand for all the wrongs against new Italian immigrants. The father turned out TV-worthy, the hairless ovals at the sides of his head nicely set off by wavelets of gray sideburns. In one news sequence he stood paired with the rock star Sting. Also the father had the voice of a griot, the rumble of generations. When this man declared that his family wasn't capable of some midnight deal—they couldn't, that is, have fenced the necklace in the short time before the cops got to them—you believed him. Besides, even if the cameras hadn't been rolling, what choice did you have except to believe him? The shadiest broker in greater Naples couldn't have arranged a deal in the middle of a Friday night. Not for these people.

And there was more evidence, more convincing, that the Somalis were innocent. There was the girl's missing skeleton. The entire short length of bones had been yanked from its grave that same night, leaving nothing but the painted walls, the empty pallet, and the scattered shards of a busted krater.

Now what on earth would a family on the run have wanted with a skeleton? And where would they have put it?

Fabbrizio had no idea. Now that he found himself confronted with the skull, between two guys themselves responsible for a few such skinless leftovers, he'd lost the logic with which he'd collated the stories in the papers. Once again he was little more than adrenaline and wild thoughts, as if he'd tumbled back into the girl's grave.

On that night—get hold of yourself, Secondigliano; think this through—on that night nine nights ago now, his fear had surged up all over again following the madness in Shanti's hotel bathroom. For it was then that the American had passed along the news of the *clandestini*'s arrest. By the time her phone call came in, Fabbrizio would've thought his fright-fuels exhausted. But while she'd talked into the receiver this strange woman, at once playful and careful, had drawn her knees to her chest. She'd armored over her untanned swag. After she hung up she'd frowned at her would-be boy-toy, thoughtfully, giving away none of the secret anger he'd noticed earlier.

What I have just heard, she'd begun, oddly formal, *fills me with fear.*

A fear blunt and cold, of a piece with kneecaps and telephones. Shanti's people back in New York, she reminded him, had a contact among the local police: part of the ruling system, supply and demand. And tonight, the word from the precinct house was, she'd lost her moment. With the arrest of the talkative Africans, the American player had lost the dozen or so hours of relative calm on which she'd counted, the grace period before the authorities grasped the full extent of the crime. Given tonight's bad luck, the cops, the investigators in Antiquities, the security teams at the airports, all these and others were gearing up to question every dealmaker and search every bag. The bad guys would be in on the hunt too.

"A face like that," the gangster at his elbow was saying. "Certainly she needs a little decoration."

"A choker." Treno slid his other meaty hand up against the chin, thumb curling around one side, fingers around the other. "Make a good whore of her."

Fabbrizio tried thinking of his mother. A heart attack, he reminded himself—Mama had a heart attack. That's what this unquiet Greca had been trying to tell you. And that's why you came down to the Café Sempre for a second assignment. A good son has to make every last effort he can, when his mother requires the sort of therapy that only a private studio can provide.

"What she needs, my friend, is something classic."

This gangster at his elbow went by a name likewise overblown: Nerone. He wore his own hair long, hanging well down his collar in back and in front swept up into paired black frames for the corners of his brow. The vanity seemed in keeping with his overripe smell. And while Nerone lacked the heft of his partner, when he nudged tonight's contractor in the ribs, Fabbrizio felt it in his pants pocket. His Penates was once again conducting an electric prickle. At least he'd left his suede pants at home this time, selecting instead something looser, though of a flashy salmon color you wouldn't generally wear for craftwork. His shirt was unlikely as well, a butterfly lilac.

"Secondigliano? Eh?" Fabbrizio couldn't risk avoiding the man's look. "Something classic for this pretty little one, don't you think? A piece like the Roman ladies used to wear, eh?"

"But, it has to be Greek." Treno let go of the jaw to make the you're-an-idiot gesture, amiably. "The thing that concerns us, it's from Paestum, it's Greek. No? It's for that we brought in this faggot."

Mama had a heart attack, Fabbrizio reiterated silently, and you weren't there to help.

"But, Treno. What an ugly word."

In fact, he didn't mind that these two believed he was queer. Among the roughnecks with whom he usually dealt, Fabbrizio's area of expertise alone was enough to stamp a man as femme, and in this case he'd played to the misconception. He'd come in rolling his narrow wrists and wearing the colors of a hothouse flower. The less this pair understood him the better.

"This type here," the one at his elbow was saying, "is our friend. Eh, *settebello*, isn't it true? Aren't you a faithful friend, a loyal friend?"

He put on an indeterminate pout, thinking: the friend who matters is Mama. After her heart attack it'd taken Fabbrizio the better part of a day to reach her hospital bedside.

After Positano, after he and Shanti had each gotten done with their long-distance messages, Fabbrizio hadn't made it home. The hourlong swing back up the Bay's underside and around the downtown—he couldn't manage it, though since dropping out of the university he'd certainly had longer night-journeys. Also he'd left Shanti's hotel alert, unfucked, and his clothes had dried after the first few hairpins along the near-empty Amalfi Drive. Nonetheless he'd lasted hardly half an hour on the pre-dawn highways. Instead he'd turned off into the city, taking an exit with the design of a locomotive.

Near the central station, among the "black blocks," his friend Monte Zu kept a flat. 'Zu seemed actually to have darkened up since Fabbrizio had met him, to've enhanced his tan somehow, in order to better circulate among his neighborhood clientele. At first glance, you'd think he too had recently arrived from across the Mediterranean. On top of that, Monte Zu claimed his hashish and kif came from Tunisia and Libya—both countries in which to harvest so much as a single cannabis flower risked getting your head chopped off. But if a person couldn't entirely trust the man's Afro-affectations, they could count on 'Zu to stay awake till sunrise. If the dealer didn't have a new girl in, that night, his colleague from Secondigliano would be welcome to lay a couple of pillows on the floor.

So Fabbrizio had pulled over to the beltway shoulder, at the station exit. He'd taken his cell phone from under the Suzuki's seat and, before checking on his downtown friend, tried again to shake his head free of the Greca.

Death so near... Now again so near...

Even riding without a helmet, over this last stretch, hadn't cleared away the girl's throaty whisper. She weighed so much on his thinking that somewhere above Positano he began to realize she'd spoken with an accent. The ghost had sounded Balkan, wouldn't you know it, her vowels baggy in the way of refugee Albanians and Kosovars. So his doubts came on, forcing him to the highway shoulder, fracturing the certainty he'd felt down in the hotel bathroom. Had he merely imagined the phantom in his ear? If he was going to call himself an artist, a man who pulled stone and metal aggregations out of thin air, he'd better acknowledge the danger for a case like this. The vulnerable side of the sensibility. Compared to most of the boys on his block, minor-league headcrackers who'd never come near the university, Fabbrizio was as dreamy as his brother. And in fact tonight's magic had come to him in an accent he'd long since learned to recognize. His lone prostitute, the schoolgirl he could barely stand to touch, she might've spoken with precisely that accent.

So the trip up from Positano became too much. Fabbrizio couldn't even seem to shake the static out of his Penates. The bronze K felt permanently destabilized, in his slit pocket. Granted, it no longer carried the voltage he'd felt in the graveyard or the bathroom. But the piece still itched against his thigh, just as the girl's admonitory fragments continued to echo across his head. Whoever it was up there, la Greca or merely *la trauma*, she'd kept hold of him as tightly as these two bad guys did now, chuckling over the remains in a Salerno basement.

...so near...now again near...

She'd been right to warn him. Nine nights since then, and on every one of them he'd felt ashamed. He hadn't realized that the girl was speaking of his mother. Once he'd gotten his telefonino out from under the bike-seat, there by the station exit, he'd discovered that someone at home had tried to call him—but he'd never made the connection to his earlier message, the one via special remote access. He'd left the Secondigliano call unanswered, and fifteen minutes later he was chaining down his bike in a black-blocks alley under Camorra protection. When he woke the following noontime, tasting the dust off Monte Zu's floor and switching the cell back on, even the second call from home seemed like nothing to worry about. Just the opposite, as the little screen lit up again, he found it encouraging. That familiar lime glow, riding the phone's body like a postage stamp on an extended tongue, meant he'd made it through the night with the same tools he'd had when he'd begun.

Likewise, it wasn't difficult to guess what these calls were about. His mother and brother must've heard some dark new rumor about his work. They must've stumbled across some fresh reason to berate him. The younger son's best move, in such cases, was to leave the phone alone and handle the hard business face to face.

"Eh, pretty boy? Aren't you loyal?"

L'Americana, he thought. Put the finger on her.

"Aren't you faithful to a pair of friends who've given you work?"

Blame Shanti and promise these two the necklace, that was his out. He believed he knew where the woman had gone, "playing it straight for a few weeks" as she'd put it. Once Fabbrizio passed that information along to the cammoristi, surely he wouldn't have to die with this buffalo stink in his nostrils.

"*Sicuro*," he declared. "Those friends who have helped me, they may count on my complete loyalty."

Treno gave a grumble and let go of the skull. The thing made no sound, rolling over as if on a pillow.

"But, what?" Fabbro worked up a passable self-righteousness. "Whatever you have asked of me, I have done it with respect. I know well that with Treno and Nerone, I am among men of honor."

"Fabbrizio." The crook beside him gave it a slow enunciation. "Fab-bri-zi-o."

Couldn't risk not meeting his look, and couldn't risk pulling away.

"Have you been reading the papers, my friend?"

"But, what?"

"Been reading about the Africans, the ones they caught? Those blacks? You know what they're saying?"

"Naturally I know." He threw in a bit of a lisp. "All my friends back home ask me where I've hidden the jewels."

"And you won't tell us either?"

Treno gave another of those side-of-beef laughs. He'd ducked back beneath the stepladder staircase that ran up to the hatchway.

"You know," continued Nerone, "down around Salerno here, this zone around here, this is ours."

The other one again hoisted the burlap sack from which they'd taken the skull. Fabbrizio heard a low rattle.

"This is our neighborhood, Paestum too. My friend, you can imagine how we feel, when we learn of strangers here, strangers who take what doesn't belong to them."

"But… strangers?"

"Eh. A disgrace. There was a party, all strangers, there in that graveyard."

"A disgrace," Treno said.

Fabbrizio looked to the worktable, the pieces he'd prepped and finished during the long session yesterday. No advantage revealing anything more before he found out what they had in the bag.

"Now then, the police," continued Nerone, "they have the Africans. You read the papers, Fabbro, you know these things. But let me tell you something nobody knows. We have one of the others."

Treno slung the brown sack on the table. Fabbrizio couldn't make sense of the noise from inside, but he knew when a man was throwing his weight around. The Greek girl's skull was left wobbling.

"A dick of a thief," the big one said.

"We've got him," Nerone went on, "one of these who thought they could have a party behind our backs. And this one, he'll give us everyone."

"But look." With another rough move, Treno emptied the bag. "Look at the shit he's trying to peddle."

As the stuff clattered onto the tabletop, Fabbrizio at last let go a flinch. And another, and another: he shuddered, whole-body. Not that the bag held much, and not that Treno was entirely careless about it. The mobster knew better than to knock last night's work off the table, and what he poured from the bag was little more than gravel. When Fabbrizio at last got a decent look (ignoring the amoral squint of the man holding him, his pleasure at a captive's show of fear), he could see at once that whoever had fallen into the cammoristi's clutches was merely a scavenger. This new scrap could only have been collected by someone who'd come along after he and Shanti, the same person who'd grabbed the skull, more than likely. Whoever he was, or she, at least he'd known precious materials when he saw them. In the fresh heap on the table, Fabbrizio spotted a macaroni of gold, a flinder of amber or carnelian. Rubble of some quality, though nobody sold this kind of thing by weight.

The skull, on the other hand, could bring in as much as three dozen Euros. Such things had a ready market, if the word were put out with appropriate discretion. Fabbrizio was past his flinching now, sizing up the evidence. Treno and his longhaired boss exchanged another filthy wisecrack or two, but these didn't keep their loyal friend from reading the message in this bone and stone. The graveyard bits and pieces would bring in pocket change and the skull, considering its history, might pay for a week's groceries. The skeleton, the whole, could command serious cash.

Nerone's grip was starting to feel ordinary. Fabbro pulled free.

"*Madonna mia.*" He bent over the winking scrap-heap. "What type of creature would steal a girl's corpse?"

The big man across the table, over his head, erupted in a soulless bray.

"It's him who gave you this, this garbage here." Both Fabbrizio's small hands were at work by now, sorting the gold from the rest. "That type who took the skeleton."

Nerone gave an extravagant sigh. "Imagine. He thought he could steal from us, then sell to us."

"O-kay." The American word had a businesslike bite. "With this stuff tonight, we don't have the problem of yesterday. Or we don't, if you also have the other?"

The nearer crook allowed himself a nod.

"Then I think yes. You'll have your fake tonight."

"A lovely fake, Fab-brizio." Nerone still toyed with the name. "We have the picture from the paper, you know?"

He answered nod for nod, setting yellow with yellow.

"But perhaps you got a better look than that. Eh? In the cemetery?"

His nerves remained in check. Tonight was no different than last night after all—these two still wanted nothing more than a counterfeit antiquity for a gullible collector. It was just as he'd suspected when he'd first learned that Nerone had placed a call to one of the gofers up in Secondigliano. The way they'd batted Fabbrizio around, these last several minutes, amounted to no more than a game. Cat and Mouse, or Freak the Faggot.

"But are you truly our friend? Or instead, did you lift that necklace?"

Of course the game had a purpose too. If these two freaked him out enough, and if he had a confession to make, they'd hear it.

"With the one we've got," Nerone said, "the type who took the bones, we'll get the others."

"We'll have our own party," said Treno.

Fabbrizio confined his shrug to his eyebrows. Whoever these two were talking about, it couldn't be anyone he'd met. He'd made a point of that, not meeting anyone, not even the site's night watchman. As a general rule he kept away from people who made stupid mistakes such as this. Fabbrizio looked around for his tools and, almost meekly, the larger cammorista fetched the kit.

Hard rubber, scuffed and colorless, the toolbox had nothing of the Mafia about it. What it held had a mundane clatter, comforting just now, though the earlier noise from inside the burlap bag must've sounded the same. Fabbrizio, mincing, asked for the apron. This was a wide wraparound, silvery and plasticized, smothering him from neck to knee and weighing against the spiky thing in his pants pocket. Nonetheless the coverall felt like no great burden, not after what the wiseguys had put him through. He opened the kit with a workaday exhale.

The gold would pose no problem. Plenty of that scattered across the shaky tectonic plates hereabouts, inadvertent discards from as far back as the trader Phoenicians and as recently as the Ugly Americans. His employers were always ready with a few Euro-cents for some hardscrabble type who'd turned up a chunk of the yellow metal. Carnelian too was common enough. The stone had been the chief item of the India trade, back in the years when the skull on the tabletop had known itself, full of prayer and dance. But last night, the green amber had looked to be a problem. For the sake of the sale, Fabbrizio needed to remain reasonably faithful to the "artist's rendering" in the news, contemptible as it was. Nerone's and Treno's buyer expected nearly half a handspan of a stone that, at a time when Paestum was still a one-temple town, had been relatively rare. Fabbrizio would do what he could to lighten the amber's hue, or darken it, whichever was called for. He knew as well the way to shave the stone, the sort of hole to drill and where, and the size and style of pin with which to make the attachment. The toolkit appeared to hold enough iron, copper, and silver (some of it old *lira* coins) to come up with an effect now bronze, now electrum. In layering gold over some other material, too, he'd learned to imitate the Grecian beveling.

Nonetheless he still didn't appear to have enough of the green, just like last night, and he said so.

"Eh. A bit of this, a bit of that." Nerone waved his hefty partner towards another shelf. "It's not a problem for the legendary Fabbro, *certo*. Nobody knows these pretty old things like our friend Fabbro."

Now what cockroach had crawled into the man's ear? Fabbrizio kept his focus on the project: soldering iron, check. Tongs and tweezers, down to needlenose size, and a needle of an awl.

"You know, my friend, we heard there was a woman here upstairs, asking about you. *'N'Americana.*"

Yellow with yellow, green with green. He reminded himself that, beneath any other issue these two might have with him, it was in the nature of crew chiefs at their level to keep a contractor nervous. For up-and-comers like Treno and Nerone, the *malavita* was all about control; the money was merely… o-kay. When they dealt with a freelancer, they couldn't help but bristle.

Treno came back to the table with another small bag, a worn jeweler's velvet. "That dick at the bar, he can't keep his mouth shut."

The other reminded his partner quietly that the barrista's brother was with the Salerno police, a useful connection. Anyway their concern was "our companion here," and whatever he'd said to that American woman.

"Oh." Fabbrizio rolled his eyes, putting some Broadway into it. "But when did I ask for this trouble, another crazy American? I told her she should try the hippies up in Piazza Bellini."

"Yes, Fabbrizio, that's what we heard. You said she should try Piazza Bellini."

They wouldn't let up, would they? As bad as the Greca last week, nagging him throughout the drive home. Fabbrizio jerked his chin at Treno's soft new package, but he didn't even get a chance to ask; again Nerone brought up the piazza by the museum.

"But, of course I know Bellini." Quickly he thought through the reputations of the downtown squares. "My friends, instead, we like Piazza Municipio."

The bigger one gave a snort. "He likes the docks. All that fresh dick coming in off the islands—"

"Treno, eh. What do we need with this? Show our friend what we've got."

Of course the thug couldn't just pour the stuff out quietly. Treno had to sling the bag's contents onto the table, this time sending a small rock or two skittering into Fabbro's arrangements from the night before. It almost made you sorry for the man, seeing him put on display after display. Almost swayed you with the pressure he must feel around everyone except perhaps his own mother—a woman who, whenever she thought of her boy, no doubt came that much closer to a heart attack of her own.

"Pieces of shit," the big man growled. "Look at the *shit* some people think they can pay us."

"A bit of this, a bit of that." Nerone remained at Fabbrizio's elbow, and he took up one of the stones out of the jeweler's bag. "It looks good, this from Russia."

"Ah, yes." Fabbrizio had to admire the selection. "The green, it's… "

"Look how the Russian cunts try to pay us."

"But listen, friend. It's just the price of business, when you work with a place like Lithuania. Sometimes the girls have jewelry."

Fabbrizio narrowed his gaze, struggling against the unexpected reminder of his prostitute, the babyface in torn lingerie. Eh, Secondigliano: it's not going to help her if you can't even look at these rocks. But over the next moment or so he could only see these dark pieces for the petrified sap that they were, a Baltic swampland goo. Also, on a few of the stones there remained gold fittings, plate that had proved too troublesome to yank off. Listen, friend, you don't want to think about that either. And now Nerone had left off talking about his partners in the European Union. He and the other had fallen into a wordless stare.

No point giving anything away. "If I don't discover that I have a need for something else," Fabbrizio declared, "it's a job of six more hours."

"But, six *hours*? What do you think this is, the fucking Sistine Chapel?"

"Oh, the Sistine Chapel." If tonight's shakedown was only about the work, it was easy to meet Treno's glare. "The ceiling alone took three years."

That glare. It almost made you sorry for the man, to see him saddled with so unrelenting a machismo.

"Eh. Let our friend here alone. Nobody knows these old pretty things like Fabbro." But Nerone again took the freelancer's elbow, and made sure to catch his eye. "Also he knows we don't pay by the hour."

Stay with the rocks, Secondigliano. The materials, tools, and techniques. Everything previous had been the hard part, hadn't it, the negotiation via manhandling. Of course Salerno & Co. couldn't simply tell him up front that they'd gotten hold of the mystery thief, the *skeletro-rolo*. Of course they had to sweat him, as if Fabbrizio might've turned police informant in the few hours since they'd last seen him. But the rough stuff was over now, and the running around too for the time being, motoring north and south and back again. Every time you pulled off the road you had to check the cell for calls, and before you called back you had to think a minute about the number. Every detail was another impedimentia, even a phone number the size of black-coffee spittle on a screen the size of a postage stamp.

What remained for him now, however, was a business he'd been born to do. *Sicuro*, and he never tired of saying so, even when he had to affect a lisp for Nerone's sake. Yet tonight his eyes and hands continued to drift unengaged over the half-finished necklace, the pieces for combination. He must've looked as if he were at a séance: Speak to us, oh braceletier for Eve and Lilith…

Perhaps Fabbrizio was only waiting until his two employers' footsteps disappeared from the café overhead. They took time for coffee.

Corretto, he recalled: Nerone added cognac, Treno some sort of flavored vodka. And for men so different in size, the wiseguys turned out to have a remarkably similar tread. The two almost moved in march-step, shaking down dust through the cellar's slant rays of sun. Beyond that down-drifting powder, its twirling membranes, the ragged mortarwork of the scaly wall-stones suggested a tomb mosaic shattered in the latest quake.

Yet even after the cammoristi were out the door, Fabbrizio dawdled like a Roman bureaucrat. Shop conditions here lagged below approved standards, didn't they, especially so long as his only light was the unshaded bulb overhead. His tools, stones, gold pieces all turned garish. What had Nerone and Treno done with the clamp lamp? Also they'd kicked away the matchbook he'd used to prop up the table's short leg; lucky there was a box on the shelves, pack after pack embossed with *Sempre*. Only after his work-surface was level and properly lit did Fabbrizio start to check color, to assess mineral-grains in the amber and carnelian. He took up the magnifying glass and tried not to think about the fittings still in place, the goldplate scratched by a pliers or blade. Scraps now, in a greasy basement bag.

In time the fittings gave him his first actual task. He set aside those he might hammer into lamina, and in the process discovered that two or three of the adhesions revealed traces of silver. Electrum rather than pure gold, this was the more appropriate weld. Mixing the gold with borax might be more common, and it too might go back as far as the Greeks. In Pliny (the older Pliny, the scientist who stopped to get a closer look at the poisoned clouds bearing down on Pompeii—talk about a stupid move) you found mention of this mysterious "Krisocolla." Could be borax, that, and so to choose electrum over borax could be a quibble, finally. But it was just such a quibble that could scare off a buyer. Better to search out the silver alloy, and with that to make at last his actual beginning, his break into some better state of mind than the fretting that had drawn him twice now down into this basement, his ripply but never unpleasant lurch into working, a change in wave-form across his mind, his shoulders, the tips of his fingers.

Fabbrizio got the fire-bowl going, the charcoal, another necessity for a viable *falso*. You needed traces of coal-smoke. Materials, tools, techniques: the more these occupied him, the greater the muscle-engaging ascent into the craftsperson's fundamental reassurance—the certainty that, for these few hours of the job, he remained something entirely distinct from the skull on the table. That dry and meatless gourd, beh, it might appear to sit watching. But could anything watch in a way at once so close yet so far-reaching, the way Fabbrizio himself was watching, moving from finger- and tong-tip up to his mind's eye and the classwork in his memory and then back down again? And could any other craftwork dunk the senses in so rich a wallow? The oleaginous sweetness of the gold as it cooked; the peppery colloid brew, copper and fish-paste at a lower temperature; and the fleshlike changes in the color and patterns as they melted down or re-petrified, as if the very whorls of your fingerprints could change. Now and again Fabbrizio had the notion, while he built a piece of jewelry, that the multi-directional pleasures of the experience were hardly human at all. Rather it called to mind what bees must go through, traveling from flower to flower with paws ever more laden with a bright and yellow softness, then coming home to cobble together a mosaic, a tiny cathedral, built of scented and colorful handfuls.

Such multi-dimensional pleasure—how could his father have let it go? How could the old man have lost his guts, like that? Fabbrizio believed he'd picked up the rudiments of jewelry making before he was six, from Babbo's shoptalk at dinnertime. Problems with the furnace, the electrical connection, the quality of stone or gold. Mama had no trouble holding up her end of these conversations, given her parents' business in shells and corals. Though their shop too, what a shame, had been abandoned.

For little 'Brizio, the upshot was that by the time he first visited the father's workspace, he knew the names of the tools and the sequences of production. The "factory" occupied a garage area, hardly bigger than this basement, off a courtyard intended for automobiles. Many a street-level space briefly housed some low-level business, among the slapdash palazzi off Corso Secondigliano. Even the tottering hulks thrown up after the 1980 quake, when the mob had pocketed two out of every three government checks intended to finance new housing, even these kept sprouting makeshift storefronts, family ventures, shoestring entrepreneurs. Babbo's jewelshop at first had no trouble finding a task or two for young Brizio, the Dellaruba brother with the better sense of size, pattern, and which tools worked best. And when the boy scrubbed the amber, the bicarbonate of soda made his eyes water, but he never felt foolish about it, the way he did over his mother's onions. When he collected scrap the filings caught under the skin of his palms, yet he enjoyed that too, especially the gold, as if he could change into one of the powerful aliens he saw in the comics and museums.

And after the first five or six months on the job, Fabbrizio the fast learner, he'd understood that his father was no craftsperson. Not at heart: not like his son. Even as he came out of his dream of being a priest, still not quite a teenager, Fabbrizio could sense the vitalizing worker's world just upslope, where the jewelers perched on high stools, their breathing satisfied and their smiles supernatural—though the boy understood this last was only a trick of perspective, since he was looking up at their faces through the bright glass of their magnifying lenses.

But his father's expression around the little *fabbrica*, nine days out of ten, was ordinary no matter what the angle. Not for Babbo the orgy that his son indulged a dozen years later, in his counterfeiter's workshop. What had drawn the old man to the Secondigliano business, rather, was the tinkering. Technology in the old sense, gear and steam and timing and tubing, that's what the father liked. Whenever some sign of happy engagement played across his face—the jawline like the fat end of an egg and the beard too stubborn for a razor: looks hard to distinguish from Uldirico's, in memory—Babbo was sure to be poking around in a broken piece of machinery. In apparatus like this, kitchen-sink industrial, the problem would always yield to patient inspection. You'd spot some glitch in the wear and tear, the lubrication, the connections. The father loved that, visible logic, and when he succeeded in getting the equipment operational again, Madonn'. To look at him, you would've thought that this was one contented galoot, and that he was lighting up a fresh cigarette in simple celebration.

Insofar as Brizio and Babbo could claim good times together, they'd been times like these, shop-wise and task-sharing. Insofar as the son had ever worked up, in his mind's eye, a design for a lasting father-son bond, it too had taken the shape of this neighborhood workplace. *Dellaruba e figlio*, Fabbrizio could see that. Also he could see how many storefronts got boarded over again, in the blocks around his home; it looked as if, every time a business got halfway solvent, it had to close up shop. Left plenty of room for Brizio and his old man, didn't it, all this good commercial space going to waste. Babbo would make sure that the equipment stayed in shape, and the son would handle the artistic end. Maybe Mama could help, too, arranging for her old family connections to supply coral. Maybe they could bring in Uldirico for the accounts and the advertising.

But his father had been let go. By then Fabbrizio was a week short of his introductory driver's license, the one for single-stroke cycles, and he could picture a bike with a sign, a little toolkit. But the old man had been literally barred from the door.

And yet the shop, at just that moment, would seem to need every man it could get. One of the brothers who ran the place had disappeared. Disappeared, inexplicably—you would've thought the factory's co-owner had stepped into a hole along the Corso. For the first few days afterwards the man's wife couldn't seem to get off the streets, wandering around till long past midnight and talking with anyone who would listen. She played for them her husband's outgoing cell-phone message, the only response she got when she called the number. At least, she declared, the message was a comfort to their daughter. Meanwhile the jewelers shut down for the better part of a week. The first time Fabbrizio and his father found the place open, the remaining brother (also the younger) had blocked the doorway, his hands raised.

No, Signore Dellaruba. No, impossibile.

Babbo had asked his son to wait in the courtyard doorway, and to the youngster looking on, it appeared as if the two men had discovered themselves trapped beneath a sudden dump of dirt and ash. Their faces, heads, shoulders went down, and as the swill heaped higher it left them only seeming to stand upright, propped in place. Any trembling Brizio detected within their clothes, their loose workingman's gear, was devoid of actual muscle. Rather the repairman and the shopowner might've been two sacks of butterflies. Yet the boy could also catch enough of the grownups' baleful shared gaze to understand that both men had seen this coming, this rain of debris. Neither appeared surprised, exactly; they'd known they lived in a falling-rock zone. And in the father's case, he was pinned for good.

Babbo might look as if he was moving. He might touch his son's shoulder and trudge home. But it took the mother, with a labored shrug which made it obvious she'd spent her life too under that threatening sky, to speak the clarifying word *Camorra*.

Mama was also the one to remind her husband, in time, that there was other work available. She had a line on office work, the mother pointed out, a sister who worked in the national lottery. Brizio must've heard her bring up the possibility a dozen times; certainly he'd heard her the first time, one of the many mornings that Mama had woken to discover her husband asleep in the TV chair, the breakfast news on Mute before him. Brizio had quickly grown used to such mornings. When the TV's sound was off, he liked to squat behind his father's empty grappa glass and study the screen, watching the colors bend, the images split and overlap. Though by tonight, this night in a secret workshop off a blind alley, he'd begun to wonder if there hadn't been something else he was looking for, there beside the immobilized old man (old? when Babbo wasn't yet out of his 40s?). By now Fabbrizio had begun to see another overlap, the image of his father in those days running together with that of his brother in these days: the *primogenito* before his computer, a big man in the prime of life slumping into ever more defeated posture even as he sat trying to get some sociological clue. The mountains of data on the web, the midnight news on TV and the morning updates—why couldn't these so-calls heads of the household understand that the screen wasn't the only shape that could be given this material? That even the talking heads could be bent to their own imaginations? Bent and made manageable? For men like his brother and father however constructing a life had to be according to the directions or not at all. So in Uldirico's case it had to be one exam after another, a university counterpart to the electrical connections in one of his father's repair sequences. So it fell to Fabbrizio, the *secondo*, to carry the dinner plates to the table. As it had been Mama who'd got their father the last job he'd ever held.

When her own family business had failed, the mother reminded her groggy husband, her sister had remembered an old church friend. A local comptroller for the lottery, a man who once might've had a sweet spot for the woman. And after a few years—certainly by the time Babbo had lost his position at the jewelers'—Fabbrizio's aunt had developed some pull herself. Of course the first time Mama made this suggestion, Babbo merely rolled his bleary eyes and heaved himself groaning from the TV chair. But after enough additional reminders, Brizio himself heard a lot of them, the father at last submitted the paperwork, along with an appropriate bit of cash. He wound up in a posting for which he had to shuttle documents from desk to desk. From nine in the morning till dinnertime, he would match one string of digits with another, and the lone piece of machinery he worked with was a stapler.

Whatever few inches of breathing space remained to the father after the dirtfall, he'd blocked it soon enough with tobacco ash. Took him hardly half a dozen years.

After a couple of hours, the Salerno basement had filled with cooking odors, in particular the fish-and-copper tang of the soldering paste. Upstairs, Nerone's and Treno's man knew the drill. He kept up his roasting and brewing, redolent enough to carry for blocks, while underfoot Fabbrizio's charcoal-heated glue reached the point of bonding with the gold. Here in the workshop the joining paste might, by smell alone, satisfy a glutton. And the colors' changes seemed to creep along the surfaces of his skin...

He had to wonder again how people had pulled off forgeries without the colloid trick, "hard soldering." If a granulation pattern were called for, in the old days, counterfeiters had simply brazed the gold filings to the surface. An effect entirely too ritzy, as if everyone who lived under the Caesars or the Athenians had the same money as the royal family. Still it wasn't till the more recent reign of Andreotti the Politico, about the same time as government-funded construction projects like those in Secondigliano became the Mafia's boondoggle of choice, that some Englishman had cooked up a new approach. He'd discovered the fish-paste trick, this Englishman, a technique hard to distinguish from the ways of twenty-four or –five centuries earlier. He must've been a tinkerer, a man not unlike Fabbrizio's own father. Or like he used to be.

How could he have lost his guts, Babbo? Gearheads were always in demand. How could the old man have cut out his heart and tossed it in a desk drawer?

Granted, a technician and fix-it man usually took his pay in cash, off the books. Irregular activity, without a pension—but hardly so risky as criminal activity, the kind of thing Fabbrizio had come to lately: each new contract, so he was learning, increased the danger. Anyway if *Dellaruba e figlio* had become a going concern, the old man would've still been breathing. It could've worked, bent a little, made manageable perhaps by running the business out of the trunk of the old 600. Brizio himself—or *Fabbro*, as he began asking people to call him—had taken on a wide assortment of such pick-ups before he was out of high school. He'd even accepted three or four freelance jobs from his father's former employers. In time the shop off the courtyard had to give it up like so many others, boarding over their doors, but before then the remaining owner didn't forgot the gusto and affinity shown by the Dellaruba boy. As cash ran low the man let Fabbrizio handle more professional assignments, and when the boy hadn't known the technique called for, he'd known where he might go watch it done. Around Naples you could always find another goldsmith, and learn the way they liked their coffee.

Fabbro never allowed these attachments to last. After the way Babbo had let him down, he knew better than to trust in any longterm mentoring. But by the time the fifty-something "old man" first went on a respirator, his younger son had samples and a reputation. He believed he'd go on like that, too, education around the campfire, keeping his eyes and ears open while the braves with many pelts sat and tended to their spears. He saw no need for formal schooling beyond the nine-month course for a certificate. And he didn't figure any loss in the transaction either, any abandoning of the things he loved, such as his abiding fascination for the gold- and silverwork of the Caesars and the Sybarites. His journeyman's life would have room for that, he imagined. He'd buy the occasional day-tour down in Paestum, plus a membership at the Museo Nazionale. Everything in its place for this "Fabbro," a young man with wheels and a job.

Mama however felt differently. To the tip of her onion-chopping finger, wagging in his face, she felt differently. His mother insisted on *regular* activity, professions entirely within the law. Both of her boys were going to start with a proper *lauro*, and the younger would study Conservation of Antiquities.

How could he argue, with her finger in his face, with the oil off the onions sprinkling his nose and lashes?

Brizio, she declared, *Fabbrizio fortunato, this is the one thing I ask You use your gifts to get out of this slum.*

How could he point to his stymied brother, ever less likely to escape the bright, square tunnel of his screen? Mama was maybe the only reliable family he had left. How could he tell her: Nobody gets out by going straight?

Not that Fabbrizio had disliked his days as a "bookbag"—one of the gentler words for it, among his late-sleeping pals along the block. His university career had begun with that unlocked, untended storage cabinet and the Penates now in his pocket. Finders, keepers, and he couldn't help but imagine there might be some better piece waiting for him, around the next dreary sheetrock corner, or beneath the scarred industrial furniture. Plus there were the girls, a good half of whom set him dreaming at a single glance. But the kick these co-eds gave his appetite seemed finally nothing special, not when a young man could sample the eye-candy at any downtown *angolo.* What set his time at university apart were the lectures. Nearly every talk was seeded by some budlike detail that, as he returned to cup it and sniff it over the next few hours, would pop wide open and multiply into a jungle. Fabbrizio discovered himself capable of spending half a Saturday in the library. …advanced filigree enamels, in fine-woven wire, date back at least as far as the founding of Naples (cf., the chryselephantine statue at Delphi)… lion-head finials on a chain necklace characterize the court of Alexander and his descendants (cf., the tombs in southern Russia)…

Finial! Chryselephantine! Like a tickle from twenty-four centuries back, born again to make a young man laugh again, and then seek more of the same for fully half a Saturday. The liveliest examples came thanks to one professor in particular. This was a lecturer well past 60 but still restless, still going back to the dig and the display case; a man whose notes themselves had notes. Yellow post-its curled up from the pages of his spiral pads. The guy had a libido yet, as well, an undiminished enthusiasm for sex man-on-man that came out even as he lectured, expressed as a fine sashay in the timing and choice of his gestures. Tonight Fabbrizio had used the old prof as a model when he'd put on his faggot act.

After all, the Camorra too had a use for his university training. Knowing when to bond with electrum, when to mix up the colloid formula, that's what they paid him for. Tax-free, with both the advance and the final payout running roughly three times the amount of the late Sig. Dellaruba's monthly pension. And Mama, that was the best grade a boy could get this semester. The best way to get back at that doctor last week, too, the cardiac specialist at the hospital in Camaldoli. To hear that doctor talk, you'd think this family was the worst trash on the periphery.

The coronary itself hadn't been so "debilitating," the doctor had said—then paused to see whether the two Secondigliani on the other side of his desk knew the word. Fabbrizio let the expression drain from his face. He'd always found this man's type a bit off-putting anyway, bald and chinny and churning with professional zeal. You could see Mussolini in the way he put the period to every statement, now using his shiny forehead, now his long jaw.

Not so debilitating, the doctor repeated, his chin coming up. But he should add, his brow dropping, that he'd lost patients who'd suffered shorter fibrillation.

Fabbrizio reminded himself how tired he was, with no more than three hours' sketchy sleep at Monte Zu's. He couldn't be sure he'd lost the last echo of the Greca's warnings, either, the sympathetic vibe in the pocket of his unchanged pants. Nonetheless today was better for the meeting with this guy. Better to get him out of the way now, this *Imperatore* in a white smock. Tomorrow, when Mama was allowed visitors, her Brizio needed to have the headaches behind him.

The doctor made an adjustment of a paperweight, a desktop commemorative. To touch the piece fetched a small, proud smile, and he went on to say that the greatest concern was the damage done to the muscles of the ventricle.

An infarction like this—another insulting look—weakens pulmonary action.

Doctor, thought Fabbrizio, what would it weaken if I took that paperweight and smashed it across your face?

But the man across the desk, for all his intensity about trauma and recuperation, looked fundamentally peaceable. His hands would sway with the movements of his meaty chin and forehead, slowing to a stop at each longer word: *cardiovascular, arterial.* Fabbrizio had the notion that what most stayed his own hand was that he didn't want to give Uldirico the satisfaction. He would love to see Little Brother lose it, Rico. Yes, the older son had the stodgier makeup, but that didn't mean he wouldn't enjoy scoring a fresh point or two off the younger. Back when Babbo was still alive, Uldirico had been known to get in his jabs, real zingers some of them, across the after-dinner game of *scopa.* As the cards went around, the *primo* would draw out Fabbrizio concerning the latest regional elections; then he'd pounce on the first proof of how little the younger one knew. In general Brizio could barely distinguish the left wing from the right.

On evenings like those Rico's tone might've revealed a hint of good nature, mere ribbing. But no more than a hint—he hadn't always been this lump of avoirdupois across the bedroom. There'd been a time, in that bedroom, when the brother had nursed such a passion for his Marx and Gramsci, for his daily *Manifesto,* that Fabbrizio had learned to sleep with the light on.

That filament might still burn somewhere within, despite Rico's ever-crazier hair and ever-widening belly. Should Fabbrizio take a poke at this doctor, or heave his desk-piece through the office window, that might well reawaken the old sibling rival. Might bring back the smirk that used to sting him so, across the cardtable: oh, *secondo.* For there was no getting around it, Uldirico was the one who'd been home. The sociology student had been sitting hardly a dozen steps from their mom when she'd suddenly dropped that morning's groceries, her summer-brown arms and legs no longer equal to the last flight of stairs. Another goddamn flight of stairs, the iron strutwork showing through the quick-mix concrete.

The very geography must've seemed against her, the ground pitching in waves fish-hooked to the center of her chest. It wasn't much of a chest to begin with, a narrow and reedy container like her younger boy's. Yet Fabbrizio had been nowhere near. He'd gotten the news first from a ghost and then from the ghost's slightly younger sister, the crone who perched on a chair at the streetcorner by his home. This grandmother sold contraband Luckies out of a box beneath her skirt, and that morning, that late morning following the hardest night of his life (until perhaps this one in the cellar of the Café Sempre), he saw the old woman come out of her chair before he'd even swung off his Suzuki. His first thought was, the cops; his second, the American. The pretty witch had set the police on him...

Then hardly an hour later, with no better cleanup than a splash over a hospital sink, he sat in a doctor's office thinking bloody murder. The specialist crossed his arms, summing up. He recommended a regimen of cardiovascular exercise, combined with changes in diet. "The woman and I can work out specifics."

The woman? Fabbrizio flung himself from his chair, heading for the room's lone window. He let go a slicing sigh, enough to put a stop for a moment to the *medico*'s fastidious patter. They both knew "specifics" was a code word anyway. They could read the code, plain as day, a message that had Fabbrizio slapping the wall beside the window. A slap was okay, though, even with Uldirico watching. A bit of noise only, a slap was the smart move; best to get the anger out of your system here and now. Tomorrow when you see Mama, that's got to be gone, you've got to be Ghandi. Nonetheless the view out the office window offered no relief, only another parking lot, a struggle all too familiar. Cars were crammed in sideways, backwards, frontwards, one or two in spaces you wouldn't have thought possible. No vehicle could budge without the say-so of another widefaced little dictator, this one in blue rather than white.

The doctor began again, his tone careful. Patients have a range of care-levels from which to...

Finally Rico came to life, asking about coverage under the national insurance. Fabbrizio watched his brother in reflection, a heavyset figure pale from his long hours indoors and yet covered in hair. Meanwhile out beyond the reflection, out in the parking lot, a new arrival was ushered into one of the good spots by the door. The driver had pulled in with a hand out the window, a double-fold of Euros between his fingers.

And the next day, Fabbrizio swiftly wound up at the window in his Mama's room. At the window, turned away from the bed, unable to face her. He pored over his pale midday reflection. He sought the good son who'd made the drive back to Camaldoli, who'd shared an unrancorous ride in the old 600 with his brother. A sweet and loving spirit, that son: prepared, in the fullness of his sorrow, to give and give again for the family. But Mama—what could a man give without money? What, especially when his mother lies before him with the very skin of her arms unraveling, the brown wrinkles leaving peelings on the bedcovers the way shavings off his draftsman's pencils used to litter the heavy paper of a sketchpad? And the hospital had put Mama in a dormer, a room with six beds. At least she had only a single roommate, a man who looked a good thirty years older than she. More *fortunato*, the old guy was asleep. To judge from the snoring, he'd left his cares far behind.

Then do the same, good son. Let it go, no matter what she's saying.

"Brizio, death is so near."

Was that his mother's voice, really? Hers, all quaver and murk?

"My son, I know now how death is near. We all know it now. And it's for this that I ask, while there's still time."

She wouldn't sound so otherworldly, he told himself, if his own legs and back weren't so racked with shudders. He hadn't recovered from the night before last, the hard hours on the Suzuki.

"Please, my Brizio, don't turn away. Your mother is asking with death at our shoulders. No more. No more black work."

"Mama," he asked the window, "how can you say such things, 'while there's still time?' The doctors, they tell us—"

"But how? How can this heart of mine ever recover while my boy drifts into worse trouble every day? Just one job for the wrong people, and you will end up with some Camorra man cutting you—"

"But, what are you thinking?" With a glance over one shoulder, he indicated her neighbor. Of course she didn't know any of the names involved, but it didn't take much to make the likes of Nerone and Treno nervous.

"My Brizio. You have no fear for the danger you're getting into every day, but you fear your mother, now? You know how much you sound like your poor father?"

"Mama, peace." Surely he was artisan enough to work up a smile that would last for fifteen minutes.

"Your father too had such a hard head. Till the day he died he refused to call his trouble by its name."

First the Greca, now his father. Fabbrizio was surrounded by ghosts, and the most troubling was this outline on the window before him. Back at the university, the reproductions in the library had seemed more alive. The only feature he could make out was his mouth, the lips he'd been told were pretty. But what he noticed in them at times like these was the African influence, the natural pout that threatened, Jagger-like, to take over the face. Of course the thick and lowhanging curls, the high cheek-squaring bones, these too revealed a bloodline siphoned off the southern side of the Mediterranean. But he saw none of that in the phantom on the glass, only his mouth, made bloody by some refraction of noontime sun.

"Peace," he said. "Enough."

"Such a shame, you won't talk about it. Precisely like your father. He kept his mouth shut even while the *terribilità* was eating him up from inside."

"But will you *stop talking* about my father?"

Wheeling around, Fabbrizio noticed the hitch in the snoring from the farther bed. The old man's eyelids may have fluttered.

"How can you even *speak* of me as if I were that, that, Babbo? I'm a man with guts, with honor."

Now it was his mother checking the roommate. She lay on her side glaring, in fact; not at all the Pio disciple he would've expected. This woman brimmed with as much aggravation as saintliness, and when she flipped over, with a grunt as if the move took something out of her, she frowned at Uldirico too. The older brother was sitting, of course, always the first to find a chair these days—and the last person, Mama, you should look to for help. The wimp had his fingers so deep in his beard, he might've swallowed the first couple of knuckles.

"How could you think," Fabbrizio went on, "I would ever *endure* such a miserable life?"

He couldn't keep still, turning now to the window and now to the foot of her bed, gesticulating whole-body. "You think I would bury myself behind a desk somewhere for a paycheck that barely put plates on the table?"

"He put plates on the table, Brizio."

"Mama. In our building, people can't even pay to repair the elevator!"

And what was this awful confusion in his mind's eye? When his mother rolled on her back to face him, Fabbrizio saw both this shrunken, sunburnt woman in need of repairs, stretched out before him in her hospital shift and—lying at the same angle on the night before last—the plump and smirking *Americana*, in her designer underpants and priceless necklace.

"Beh, the way that man left you…," dropping his eyes to the floor, he shook his head. "You go up and down the stairs, up and down the stairs, day and night. And always with the bags!"

"Brizio, why can't you understand? You are what weighs on my heart. You're the one stuck on the stairs. You could climb, but you refuse."

"I'm the one who has an idea, understand? One good contract, Mama, just one, and this family can start all over!"

"Why don't you see it could also go the other way? One bad assignment, Brizio, and even if no one cuts your throat, your soul could be ruined. You'll be drained of hope just like your father."

"Oh Madonn', my soul? Listen, let me tell you the real danger. If I'd left it up to my father, we'd be living like clandestini!"

"Our father." This was Uldirico at last, his voice for a moment putting the brakes on his brother's aggravation. "Our father, but—he's an old story. We must learn to put that behind us."

"Exactly, Ul-di-ri-co." Fabbrizio felt his nodding in the top of his head. "An old story that can do us no good. You would know about stories like that, fairytales, the way you waste your life reading them."

"Brizio, calm yourself. I'm saying only, the man is dead. He's history."

"Exactly. He's dead and useless, and he was *always* useless! In this family there has *never* been anyone but *me* with the guts…"

Over the days that followed the younger son did what he could to get past this. He did all he could, visiting his Mama every day that she remained in the less-than-private room, each time arriving with flowers and a dependable smile. Before he headed to the hospital he might be poring over the day's papers, looking for some detail that would land him in prison, or in a Camorra limepit, but he left all traces of that anxiety outside the Camaldoli gateway. Just the day before yesterday— the day before his first session on this Café Sempre job—he'd helped carry the woman back up to their apartment. Slung on his bracing arm, she'd let her head fall on his chest, forgiving, and meanwhile up in the kitchen he'd already prepared a heart-healthy salad with octopus. Likewise, throughout this same week-plus, every morning he'd made sure to first visit the blue kitchen shrine to the Capuchin Padre. As he lit the new day's candle, he would speak his mother's name.

But she'd requested also that he pray for the soul of his father. Since the man's death she'd kept a wallet-sized photo stuck inside the shrine's frame. And every morning, including yesterday before his first run down to Salerno, Fabbrizio had tried.

It would've been easy to skip it and tell Mama otherwise, with his new smile firmly in place. But didn't he want to do better? Didn't he, especially, on a day when he was about to go work with murderers? So he'd stood before the little candle with his stomach growling for coffee and whispered a Hail Mary, or most of one, throwing in his father's name wherever it seemed to fit. But these sanctified mumblings too flattened quickly under a fall of stones as ugly as toads, toads that as in the old fable had erupted out of his own mouth. On that first visit to his mother in the hospital he'd flung the opprobrium for his dwindling family so high that ever since, the filth had rained back down and knocked the air from him even as he called on the Queen of Heaven. Life in a falling-rock zone.

And this in a kitchen barely adequate to begin with, where to get to the balcony and sample the morning air you needed to squeeze past the stove. Never mind what might be on the burner. The *terrazzo* itself had room for either the clothes on a dry-rack or a grown man with a cigarette, not both. Fabbrizio's apartment was so claustrophobic that on the very night his father had told him about sex (another rare happy memory of old Babbo), he'd later heard his parents going at it and pictured, with the drudgelike clarity of a schoolbook illustration, his mother taking it up the ass to keep from getting pregnant (something else his father had told him about, now ruined for him permanently).

Oh, Fabbro. Peace and love, hippie boy. It's only the stink of the fake-work that's got you gloomy.

At this late stage in the process, the colloid paste smelled of decay. Naturally the cammoristi had put in a workshop flue, another something to hide the black work, a tube that siphoned the fumes away from those of the roasting and grinding upstairs. Anyway the gold was losing what scent it had, by this time. Both the metal and its attachments to the amber and carnelian were cooling, solidifying towards the point where he could begin the final joinings. For that he'd use mostly the solder, though a couple of the central links seemed right for the more gold-intensive brazing.

As for the unhappy drift of his reminiscing, he'd seen that before. When he was working, in the *artigiano* zen, the business in his head could occupy another plane entirely. In the same way, it didn't matter that the smells down here had gone sour; his fingers and his eye operated as if inside one of those iPod players he'd seen at the discos. A supplemental soundtrack, the Pods played on impervious to the dizziest spin moves or the heaviest bass lines. Now as Fabbrizio laid out the parts of the necklace, taking stock of the different degrees of finishing necessary, the project had a rhythm and felicity undisturbed by whatever might be picking at him more privately. The job-groove here was so powerful, he hadn't even noticed there was an argument going on.

An argument, now he heard it. Outside the basement window. He tuned in only when there was a clatter outside the window.

Deliberately, he shook his head. For a moment there he'd imagined some supernatural hand snatching up the counterfeit materials, whisking them out of the building, then throwing them back at window-well. Madonna mia, shake it off. After that, as he found the dangling switch for the overhead bulb, it occurred to him that some ill-advised jerk might be trying to break in. Some clandestino who didn't know the rules. If that were the case, and if Fabbrizio helped prevent the break-in, that should make his time here easier. That should prove he was loyal. He reached across the workbench, over the girl's skull, to kill the low work-lamp.

But the cellar went darker than he'd expected, practically pitch-black. It took him half a tiptoe minute or more to feel his way across the room. Not till he drew near did he discover that the window now had a curtain, a black rag, hooked on a pair of nails above the corners of the setting. One of the crooks must have hung it before leaving. Still, if Fabbro undid one corner now no one outside would be able to see in, especially when you considered how long it had been since anyone had taken a sponge to the glass. He himself couldn't see much at first, only the porch-style lamp on its tilted pole, giving the alley the same bone-white glow as the moon had given the half-undug cemetery not quite ten days earlier.

But soon enough he recognized Nerone and Treno, squared off against the Paestum night watchman. The guard he'd bribed to get into the dig.

Only one way in or out of the alley, and the mobsters were blocking it. The rest was all padlocked doors, businesses closed now for hours, and pitted back steps without railings. From where Fabbrizio stood Nerone and Treno were closer, their visitor farther off, and for a few moments it looked like the three of them were simply having a conversation. The cammoristi still wore their summer jackets and the guard his uniform. No one was paying any attention to the window, a shadow to them, at the bottom of a garbage-strewn well. Fabbrizio nonetheless suffered a bad flinch, the length of his spine, when Nerone glanced his way. He had to steady himself, putting a hand to the wall. But the gangster out back was only eyeballing the thing that had alerted Fabbrizio to their presence in the first place: a loosely packed duffel bag, one end of which now hung several inches into the well.

A carryall, cheap synthetics, the kind of thing the Africans sold in the streets. One of the seams had given way already and it appeared mostly empty. When Treno had thrown the bag against the wall (Treno, who else?), it had landed with a clatter…

Fabbrizio shuffled closer, his nerves going through adjustments. He heard Nerone speak the word "skeleton," with a put-on affability a bit louder than usual, and with that his suspicions were confirmed. The guard was the one who'd stolen the skull and bones and then—the truly brainless part—tried to sell them himself, in this same neighborhood. A stupid move, truly. The onlooker in the basement couldn't help but think once more of the American, the she-monster. Whatever the rage was in her, whatever she needed to work out, she'd feel a lot closer to satisfaction if she knew what she'd accomplished here. She'd left two grown men staked to the desert floor beside a teeming colony of fire ants, and throughout the entire sickening process she'd had the nerve to call herself Shanti.

Fabbrizio had double-checked the word on the web. The family's internet connection was slow, a dial-up, but Fabbro had had nothing better to do during the sleepless night that followed his screaming and carrying on in front of his half-dead mother. He'd found her, *shanti* or *shantih*, "peace." Talk about a *falso*. The woman's graveyard assurances that she and Fabbrizio could steal and deal any way they chose, that they operated beyond the reach of good guys or bad—she should try telling it to the three out in the alley. She should see what her promise of peace sounded like to the security guard. The man kept jerking his head around, chicken-like, seeing another exit and then discovering it was a mirage. When he answered Nerone, it was in a squeak.

… what do I know? …never done…

Treno barked an obscenity in response, too sudden and flat for Fabbrizio to catch. The guard scowled and even—what could he be thinking?—raised a shaky fist.

"But why do you call me that?" A screech. "I have the goods." He nodded at the bag in the window-well. "I am ready to make an arrangement."

Nerone tossed his long hair off one ear. "Eh, you're late." Easy-going as he sounded, the smaller cammorista had made a fist too, inside a pocket. The knuckles showed through the cloth, though at an angle invisible to the guard.

When Nerone's voice dropped, Treno got loud: "Soon as that dick asked to get inside, that's when a man of *honor* would've come to us."

Again Fabbrizio lost his footing, and in the process missed several seconds of the conversation. He didn't hear how much the cammoristi knew. How could he, when his spiked pants pocket fired off discharges that undid his leg muscles, and he almost tore the rag-curtain off its farther nail? For the second time in less than ten days he suffered a graveyard nightmare, movements too dark to know.

The next words he caught from outside were only the security guard repeating himself. *But I've never done anything like this.*

Made a difference when the danger was on the far side of the glass, didn't it? Like a highway accident in the rear-view mirror, some other rider hitting the pavement without a helmet. And Fabbbrizio noticed, finally, that the night watchman could've in fact used something for his head. The alley lamp revealed the man's bruises, now that he'd given up looking for a way out. There was a bloody spot along one cheekbone, and a sleeve of his uniform hung torn at the shoulder. Fabbrizio, chilled, flatmouth, constructed the argument that if Nerone and Treno had already figured out who'd snuck into the site and made off with the necklace, they wouldn't still be working the guy over. By now they'd have taken his bony goods and—and then sent him home, surely.

"They're businessmen," he heard himself murmur at one corner of the ceiling. "Businessmen."

The watchman hadn't stopped speaking. *...showed me the cash right there in the coffeeshop...* He sounded now as if he were crying. *...a father of children needs to carry plates to...*

Fabbrizio kept his own mouth clamped shut, but he couldn't stop his teeth grinding, his tongue fluttering. When the smaller crook suddenly closed in on the guard, muttering with his face just under his hostage's, the lightless café basement echoed with a long-withheld gasp. At least Nerone kept his fist in his pocket, but it jumped around as if he had one of the local lizards in there. Meantime the watchman (had Fabbrizio ever learned his name?) kept shrugging and shaking his head. He had nothing to give them, even when Treno joined the party, spitting out obscenities and hoisting their prisoner up by his shirt's untorn shoulder. The man in his grip briefly suggested a marionette, a Wooden Soldier marching in place, his trousers trimmed with piping. Then once more the guard's frustration surged; he yanked himself free.

"But what do you need from *me*?"

For the moment the rent-a-cop had abandoned anything like good sense. With both hands he made the you're-an-idiot gesture. "You two, you know everything that goes on from here to Calabria, isn't it true? You have the *world* under your boot!"

The way his gathered fingernails caught the lamplight, he was holding up twinned bubbles of glow.

"A man like me, I might as well be the Iraqis. The Iraqis against the Americans. *Shock and awe.*"

The English had no effect on his persecutors. Treno's dangling hands cast claw-shadows, the sort of effect that Fabbrizio would've sneered at if he'd seen it in a cartoon.

"A man like me, but what can I tell *you?*" Again the guard sounded near tears.

Nerone remained the diplomat, out there amid the scraps of paper and plastic, the discards of the coffee shop and another two or three family places. He showed his big partner an almost goofy smile. Really now, he declared, they could do without these "wild scenes." He got his hand out of his pocket, putting thumb and fingers together to give the insult back to the guard.

"But who's got the world under his boot?" he asked. "My friend here and I, we're just a couple of types with a business. And we need to protect that business."

The cammorista laughed again, and Treno too, but it wasn't till Nerone went on to mention money that the dig's watchman relaxed. For the first time the lanky thirty-something seemed to notice his wounds. With a visible sigh he touched them, and meanwhile rocked his injured head back, getting a long look at the sky. You would've thought he was taking in the stars. Nerone meanwhile wondered aloud how much they might get for the skeleton and the skull together, and though he did drop one hand back into his pocket, he was only checking; in another moment he used the same hand to point towards the window-well. On Fabbrizio's end of things, the action of his knees and lungs had come back within normal limits, and he could make sure he kept the black curtain extended across most of the glass. He allowed himself only a corner to peek through and kept his face back in the dark.

Still he had a clear view when Treno kicked the guard in the ass. Soon as the man from Paestum bent to retrieve his bag, the big hoodlum swung on him.

"*There's* my boot!" Treno hooted. "Right up your shithole!"

The night watchman must've gone headfirst into the near wall, judging from the whack that resonated on Fabbrizio's end, a blow as solid as a shovel hitting a buried box. A few blanched flakes of stucco paint were knocked loose and fluttered across the window-well, while the bag almost toppled in. In another moment the guard too wound up with his face hanging over the well, as he tried to squirrel out of harm's way, and Fabbrizio found himself looking into the man's eyes. Or some freak counterfeit for eyes, glimmering with the fragile unreality of an eclipse. Round with pain, they looked, and yet square with anger; narrow with desperate thinking and yet wide with unalloyed terror. A moment only the onlooker spent with those eyes, all over the map.

Then Treno came down on the man again. "*There's* my boot, shit for brains!"

His victim flailed and rolled, his face going out of sight. After that came a flurry Fabbrizio couldn't entirely follow, not with those eyes still before him, unreal too in how they lingered on the glue-and-metal air. The watchman flung himself onto his skinny knees and got hold of the duffel bag, he erupted with a cry as if his throat were full of raised hackles, and he heaved the bony bundle back at his attacker. There was the clatter of the bag shifting position, the crash of it hitting home.

Except it hit the wrong man, the smaller man. A flying bag of sticks and stones, it caught Nerone flush against head and shoulders and bowled him over. His turn to be the marionette, and someone had cut the strings. The camorrista's limbs and coat-tail splayed in every direction against the concrete, so that you could see how skinny his arms were, how they flounced up limp-wristed after they hit the grease-streaked pavement. Even Treno laughed to see it, another canine hack of a laugh, nobody's idea of fun. And this so-called partner launched into a fresh string of obscenities, or maybe what Fabbrizio heard was the newly-hired part-time security officer from Paestum. He'd kept up his animal howl, still on his knees and with a hand to his unthinking head, until Nerone flung the bag off him and sprang up with a knife.

A knife, a hook of white under the lamp. Fabbro had thought the crook lacked muscle a moment before, but with the weapon out of his pocket Nerone gave the opposite impression, all speed and wallop as he flattened the man who'd laid him out. The guard never got off his knees. His sudden scream was cut short as the mobster drove him back into the Café Sempre wall, catching him in the throat with one stiff arm while carrying the blade down low with the other. The watchman's head and shoulders disappeared, out of Fabbrizio's line of sight, and though he must've continued to kick and flail, for a long moment the blade was the only thing visible. The phantom-white wing of a bird otherwise the color of night.

Then the knife too whipped up out of sight.

All Fabbrizio could see was the legwork, a clutter of man-on-man. Treno joined in, jawing some vicious encouragement. Perhaps he grabbed the guard again, helping to keep him pinned. Fabbrizio wasn't about to try for a better look and get himself…

But, *santissima Madonna mia*, nobody was going to get themselves killed. Calm yourself, Brizio. An unlucky beginner like this poor guy from the next town south, all he needed was a serious scare, a lesson he'd never forget. All Nerone had done was get his lesson-plan out of his pocket. Nobody was going to cut anybody's throat. Off by the wall, off where a person in the cellar couldn't see, the mobster was only holding the blade to some handy artery, raising up the nightmare. Calling up those dark strangers among the long-time dead. But after that Nerone would do no more than tattoo the man's gullet with a shallow slice, perhaps two, perhaps three: a necklace that made a troublesome story for the wife and kids. Nobody was going to murder anybody, nobody needed that kind of headache. Maybe you leave the guy with nine fingers instead of ten. At the worst, you cut an Achilles tendon, so he'll never scamper around another man's cemetery. If you leave him crippled, you also send a message to anyone who sees him and hears his story, any other bright boys out there. But to finish the man off—think about it—it's not the smart move. Nobody was going to get himself killed.

The legwork had stilled, on the far side of the window. At the top of the well wall, over that way, a puddle had started to gather. A puddle that brimmed now over the lip, dark stuff, black in this light, and dripping so slowly down the concrete it recalled the molten metal on the worktable. Except this was too dark for gold.

Nerone gave some gruff order.

Before Fabbrizio closed the curtain, Treno had already ripped away half the uniform, a stretch of cloth glistening with the same black stain.

Sounds of cleanup continued a while. Small sounds, without anyone raising their voice: Nerone and Treno apparently had concerns about the fuss they'd kicked up earlier. Or so Fabbrizio thought, in one of the few sequences of thought that held together, as he squatted against a ragged wall. The stone and mortar at his back felt neither warm nor cold, and for a long time the cellar appeared nothing but dark. Once or twice he believed the cammoristi had taken their night's work and left the alley, but then he had to listen to them returning. They fetched a sort of cleaning fluid, something that made a splash, and one of the killers might've used a mop. At least they seemed to have gotten their bleach, their windshield-wiper fluid or whatever, out of their car. Fabbrizio didn't think he could stand it if they came into the bar.

Finally he made out the worktable, the skull. With that there emerged a glimmer in the mental basement, the name of the Paestum watchman: Torio.

A kind of name, anyway. Ordinarily this came from Vittorio, but the shorthand was common enough that Fabbrizio had heard it used a number of other ways, for instance on a schoolmate who went by the nickname *Purgatorio*. So Torio, perhaps a king, perhaps a sin-cleansing mountain—my unknown soldier, Torio—peace. Somehow this notion or half a notion sent a surge of current through the *artigiano*'s motor functions, and with that and the gangsters at last leaving the alley for good, Fabbrizio made it back to his feet and fumbled after a light switch. Fumbled, reeling, stuck on the stairs like Mama had said. Then before his eyes had adjusted to what seemed at first like out on the beach in the middle of the afternoon, one of these June afternoons, he'd taken up the largest completed piece of the necklace and begun to calculate the final joinings. Blinking, he found his fire-bowl and confirmed that the embers remained hot enough to work with, given the proper stoking. Now how was the colloid solder doing?

The work, its groove, its felicity. Fabbrizio was drawn back in as if without thought, even while the finishing itself required constant thought. Was he retreating into the iPod he'd been born with? Sticking his head into an alternative sand-track?

Yet Fabbrizio understood that these gold and stones before him might be the last he ever looked at, a constellation on the verge of disappearing over the galaxy horizon. Deeply as he withdrew into the odors and patterns, he remained prey to tremors, cold spots, death again so near. Hadn't Torio, back when he was still on his feet, also tried to lose himself in the stars? Hadn't he raised his banged-up face to the scummy port sky? And by that time Nerone and Treno might've heard all they needed to. After they buried the one, now, they might come back for the other. One bad assignment, like Mama had said. The cammoristi had their man in place upstairs, pulling his all-night cover story, a man much too big and strong for the faggot in the basement. Besides, if Fabbrizo did manage to slip out somehow—the window?— then he was guaranteed to wind up a corpse. His employers weren't the type to fuss over mixed motives. If this Fabbro ran out with the contract incomplete, then he might as well have painted the Sistine Chapel after all. Might as well have put God up there pointing the finger directly at him.

Yet these smidgens of clarity, icy touches, bobbed for no more than a moment on the surface tension between the *falso* under his hands and the *terribilità* he'd just witnessed. The memory he couldn't shake was of Torio's face at the window, that jampacked and yet unseeing stare. The better thinking had to do with those places where a man might get free of the *malavita*.

Up north, in the frosty zones above Chianti country, the bastards might leave Fabbrizio alone. But the north was the last place a proud Secondigliano wanted to hide. The barbarians up in Turin or Milan would have the gall to sneer at him, his accent, his choice of salad or pasta. Better to take his chances as one of the boat-people in reverse, packing a toolbox up and down the Somali coast: *Dellaruba il Africano.* The most appealing option, however, remained those rare sinecures right here in town. There were a couple of Southern Italian career tracks on which you could travel without interference from criminals. Mama was right about Art Conservation for instance, or mostly right, and there were the havens protected by NATO, or by the city's UN presence. Shanti, for instance, had found herself some hiding place under the American eagle. She hadn't told him where, exactly, as she'd perched with her kneecaps up, on the frills and roses of her rented bed. But she had said she intended to "go back to Iowa for a while," *Ai-o-*

uaa, and after the last week-plus Fabbrizio believed he knew where she'd meant.

Then the joinings were done and the necklace lay cooling on a pair of jerryrigged props. Only the finials remained, the embellishments dangling off the lower rung, and he'd send up no red flags if he diverged a bit from the picture in the paper. Any buyer with half a brain knew better than to trust such a "rendering." Fabbrizio returned to what he remembered, improving on the paper's Benz-y designs; at the end of each golden tail he wired in a piece of amber or carnelian. He chose those shades of saffron or deep lime that created the strongest alternation. All as he remembered, and when he stood back to get a museumgoer's perspective, he again saw the American lying nearly naked before him. He saw Shanti first and then—the fatigue catching up with him, the fatigue and the dizzy-making odors—another woman in skimpy clothes, more frail, more brown.

"Mama," he said aloud.

Mama, he thought, look at it, look at how I finished it in spite of everything. Now, tell me. Doesn't your Brizio love you?

A small kindness: Fabbrizio got advance warning of Nerone's and Treno's return. He couldn't mistake those matched footsteps overhead, or the tone of their requests for a pre-dawn eye-opener, and he had a chance to pull himself together. Since finishing his assignment, God knows how long he'd been huddled against the stairway wall, crying on and off and hugging his crossed legs to his chest. One foot had fallen asleep. Even after he managed to stand, he needed to keep swabbing his eye sockets, still leaking quiet tears. The colloid paste had lost its smell, the embers in his bowl had gone dark, and the necklace's final connections had cooled and toughened. Taking up the work again, giving it a close once-over, he at last put an end to the crying. He noticed too that before his collapse he'd returned to the tasks of his childhood, putting the space back in order, sweeping the scrap into separate heaps.

As the hatchway opened overhead, he brushed the dust off his butt and pulled his shirtfront straight.

"Eh, how's the poor shepherd, here below? Your angels have returned."

Nerone descended into shadow, corona'd with bar-light. It wasn't till the mobster reached the bottom of the stepladder that Fabbrizio could see he'd changed his clothes. If you didn't count the hair, Nerone looked like a cubicle-jockey. Fabbrizio's father had worn the same sort of outfit in his last years: sportcoat and dress shirt and slacks with a permanent press, the colors never straying outside the range from blue-black to sky-blue. But in Little Caesar's case the ensemble must've come out of the wardrobe some time in the last hour. The one exception appeared to be Nerone's shoes. Those might've been the ones he'd had on earlier, loafers with a gold-plated buckle. One shoe revealed, over the big toe, a half-moon stain.

"But, what?" Nerone asked. "Standing here staring at the floor, what?"

"Isn't the faggot done yet?"

Treno was on the steps now, his own feet in glowing new sneakers. Straight out of a shipment for NATO, no doubt: the Nike swoosh suggested a scoop of coconut gelato. Fabbrizio couldn't raise his eyes, if he did he'd start crying again, but he faked a yawn and brought his arm up in a wave at the worktable.

"Treno, my friend," Nerone said, or purred, "nobody needs that kind of thing. Nobody needs that kind of talk. Look how well our Fabbro has done."

The larger cammorista gave a grumbling approval, moving past the other two towards the table. Only then did Fabbrizio spot, with a flinch that at last brought his head up, the duffel bag with the girl's skeleton. Treno carried it bunched under one arm.

"*Si, bello,*" Nerone murmured, "shake it off. How tired you must be."

Fabbrizio let his lips settle into what he hoped was a feminine pout. Nerone was explaining that he and his partner had been busy too, meeting with "that type" who'd tried to steal from them. "We came to an arrangement," he said, nodding towards the duffel. Treno, studying the necklace, grunted and flourished the bag with a shake. The rattle within set off a tangible echo in Fabbrizio's pants pocket, the first in a while. For the last couple-three hours, apparently, his craftsman's focus and his frightened blubbering had quieted the little bronze poker. Fabbrizio, the better to keep his nerves in their corral, worked up a cynical thought. These two, he told himself, would need another contractor just to put the girl back together.

Now Nerone stood over by the table too, offering further compliments on the work. Carefully Fabbro rearranged his smile and nodded *grazie*.

"But that shit hanging from the bottom," Treno said, "that's not right."

His interior prickling changed. All at once he became the wounded artist, and never mind that it felt absurd, or that lashing out at these two had been what killed the security guard. Thank God Nerone took a hand again, in his continuing role as Cultural Attaché. He made the necessary explanations to his less sophisticated partner, and before he fingered the dangling stones himself, this mobster with the small hands actually asked permission. Of course Fabbrizio still knew a scam when he heard one. In another corner of his brain, too, he went on desperately rehearsing what he might tell these two about Shanti. But what harm was there in enjoying a little sweet talk? Nor could it hurt anyone if he indulged in another calming appreciation of the complicated piece on the table. The yellows and greens checkered the necklace with far-from-ordinary combinations, no small accomplishment for a single man over a pair of extended nights.

Then again, last time he'd seen these combinations, he'd wound up with the knife in his ear. He'd tuned in a ghost who herself tuned in a heart attack.

This time, could he honestly say it was he alone who'd brought off so pretty a decoration, so ancient at first glance, at second, at third? Could Fabbrizio claim sole credit—or did the finished product owe more to tonight's new ghost? Who lent a greater authenticity than the man who'd gotten his throat cut for it?

～～～

Nerone had begun to speak differently, at some point, and now his look suggested he was waiting for an answer. But the most that Fabbrizio could take in, for a tick or two, was the man's fresh beard. Nerone's chin and neck had blackened with growth, after only…

whatever it had been, six hours and at least the same number of shocks to the system. Once again Fabbrizio had to fake a yawn, one that about halfway along no longer felt fake. His gaze dropped to the mobster's stained loafer. Eventually Treno spoke up, profane as ever, but now that Fabbro had heard the question, he couldn't believe it. What did this have to do with jewelry-for-hire? And what additional risk could there be in looking the bigger hoodlum in the face? Treno didn't have nearly the beard his boss did, no more than a touch of blonde down.

"A sports car?" he asked.

"What, you haven't heard of sports cars? This one's a convertible. To fuck, you put the top up."

"Beh, Treno, you know what I drive." With a single slow blink, he grasped the implications. "I have the motorino."

"You have some *friend* with a car like that? Some sugar daddy who'll let you drive his Jaguar if you let him shove his cock up your ass?"

A Jaguar, not even the correct nationality. Of course poor Torio hadn't paid much attention to the car, that morning; the guard had kept his eye on the money in Monte Zu's hand. Now Fabbrizio affected a wounded softness and pointed out that nobody in his neighborhood could afford a Jaguar. But, nobody… Still his nervous system seemed to have absorbed the caffeine from upstairs, its odor more powerful with the hatchway open.

"O-kay," Nerone said. "But what of a, a disco suit, my friend?"

His Penates might've been one of those whirligig toys, shooting colored sparks as it spun on a line strung between the espresso and these new questions. And now Fabbrizio had to deal with another new scent, one he couldn't yet identify. He knew better than to change his tune—*non capisco, capo*—and after a moment he understood that the new smell was on Nerone somewhere. The boss stood close, though this time he kept his hands to himself. Eh, he went on, a suit like the ones you see in the clubs, my friend. You have one of those? A very bright suit, the color of some fancy bird. Like you see on a, a man of certain type.

"With a vest," Nerone concluded. He put a finger in Fabbro's narrow chest.

"*Non capisco.*"

He understood perfectly, of course. He knew just what these two were fishing for, and with the touch at his breastbone he'd discovered that both these murderers were wearing the new scent. It wasn't the Caprifoglio again; that wouldn't last through a decent shower. What he smelled now was stronger, acrid.

"*Non capisci?*" the man asked.

Fresh lime, it was. Nerone and Treno had been working with lime.

"Fab-bri-zi-o?" he asked.

The muscleman must've done most of the spade work. If he weren't on the far side of the table, Fabbrizio would've recognized the odor earlier. Now Treno had taken up the skull again, setting the duffel by his feet. You saw something familiar, easy-going really, in the way he cradled the skinless head.

"But of course I go to the clubs." Fabbrizio would never have believed that the flick of an eyebrow could take so much effort. "I dance with my friends… "

Treno snorted. Fabbrizio tried his pout again, declaring that the discos were hot and crowded, the kind of places where nobody wore a vest. *Sicuro*; that kind of thing went out in the '70s. The big enforcer gave another of those laughs, and he made a crack about Piazza Municipio. Fabbrizio didn't need to hear it—but then the hood offered something different.

"That dick of movie, *Saturday Night Fever*." The closest thing to quiet yet to come from this man's mouth. "That Travolta, with those clothes of his."

He gave the skull a gentle rub. "Neró, you ever see *Saturday Night Fever*?"

Across the table, closemouthed, the smaller crook took his partner's measure.

"With Angela, I saw it," Treno went on. "You know where they show those movies up on top of that castle?"

Nerone glanced at his shoes, nothing you'd call a nod.

"That Travolta. That dancing that night. All he did was dance, and that alone made him the fucking king of the fucking castle."

Fabbrizio didn't want to miss a word. He felt glad for the room's saturation in down-drifting caffeine.

"Listen, Neró." Now Treno gave the skull a pat. "Tonight, it's been a long dick of a night. And things have gone well enough."

The other ground a knuckle against the underside of his chin. "Eh."

"This piece here—" pat, pat—"and also the bones, and also the necklace. Things have gone well."

Fabbrizio had to wonder if this were a trick. You make the victim relax, you get him to open up. But already Treno was saying straight out that "the guy tonight" couldn't have been talking about their *artigiano*. "A type like this Fabbrizio, impossible."

Plus Nerone was the man for tricks, not this one, an overgrown kid who hardly needed to shave.

"The guy tonight was talking about a stud. A big dick of a car."

Though of course the clever one, here, could also lose his head. This very night, hadn't Fabbrizio seen Nerone ignore the smart move?

"A stud who was staring at all the girls, the guy said. A type like this one here, impossible."

The other was flexing his jawline, clenching. Gritting his teeth, preparing for action? Or stifling a yawn?

"Things have gone our way here, Neró."

Maybe the pottymouth was starting to turn squeamish, figuring one corpse a night was enough. Maybe it wasn't the idea of another homicide that put Treno off so much as the thought of cleaning up again. Whatever might be going on in the cammorista's mind, however, Fabbrizio's inner gallery had once more put up Caravaggio. A martyr's fate hung on tenterhooks, in chiaroscuro, among faces so garish that they might've been masks. Between them lay a surface littered by some interrupted task, quotidian bits and pieces themselves half in shadow but composing a life entirely different: orderly, understated, fair in its arrangements.

Nerone was the first to break out of the frame, turning to the table. He put his bristle down close to the necklace, bending between empty outspread hands. Fabbrizio could swear he noticed a change in the air, a lessening in the stench of lime.

But half an hour later, he couldn't stay on the bike.

Fabbrizio had money in his pocket, actually in both his pants pockets, matching thick folds of Euros that should pay for six months and more in the best coronary-recovery program he could find, even Doctor High and Mighty's. Up in the Café he'd downed a cappuccino and helped himself to a brioche, fresh from the morning delivery. As he motored north, too, the rising sun cast the Vesuvian shadow he loved.

He had seen the effect only once before, and again this time he had to pull over to the shoulder and watch the show. So long as the sun remained out of sight beneath the volcano, inland, it cast a long shadow V or W upwards across the sky: the dual cones in reverse. Of course conditions had to be right, the ceiling of visibility, the angle of sunshine. But it could look as if this double-whammy of a mountain, a monster that had smashed and buried more than a few Neapolitan neighborhoods, lived with a peace-giving angel brother, invisible except on those few mornings when you could glimpse the penumbral edges of his wings. The heavenly guardian hovered with head down, so that he might know more intimately the souls over which he watched. Today Fabbrizio caught the epiphany from beginning to end, a manifestation of ten or a dozen minutes. After that, he couldn't stay on the bike.

How far did he get between stops? Three kilometers, even? At least he was making this trip before rush hour, so that when tears blurred the view in his mirrors, tears and gasping, he didn't need to be concerned with more than a few fruit- and vegetable-vendors. Nevertheless this was no way for a man of Secondigliano to behave. A young *fortunato* on his Suzuki, on his way home with the best score of his life, he shouldn't have to pull over a second time and then a third, jamming the kickstand down into place and then spinning, choking, away from the bike. After a while Fabbrizio searched the pocket under his seat for a paper bag. wasn't that what they used on TV, when a person started to hyperventilate? A paper bag, held balloon-like over nose and mouth?

Mama, Mama, you wouldn't believe how your toughneck boy kept crying. Fabbrizio never found a bag and the pocket pack of Kleenex he turned up wasn't nearly enough for him. At one point he discovered himself wiping his eyes with a pair of Euro bills, a ten and a twenty.

Torio, that sorry *stupidagine*, he was going to wind up getting Fabbrizio killed too. This when, in all fairness, the Paestum watchman could hardly be considered his responsibility. Fabbrizio hadn't told him to pull that stunt with the girl's skeleton. Indeed the blows to conscience that the returning Secondigliano suffered over the security guard—though they landed with such a thud that he'd wobble almost out of his driving lane, once startling a nearby driver into hitting the horn—the guilt over Torio was only one of the woes that sent Fabbrizio repeatedly to the highway shoulder, that morning. His burden felt more complicated than that. In time he actually called aloud for help, praying to the angel that hung upside down, the alter ego to the monster mountain. She was no longer visible (or he, or whatever), but then neither was her boss, the Divine. Fabbrizio could find no trace of That in his recent dealings, no Love That Guides the Stars in having the hots for Shanti or in any of the ramifications since, right through to the master-level effort he'd put out tonight for a pair of deep-in-the-pit souls, creatures beyond redemption.

What, for instance, did God have to do with hearing from the dead Greca? A trickster miracle, that one. The experience belonged with the nuthouse theology Fabbrizio had found on the worldwide web. His cracks at the computer over these past, beh—was it ten days now?—his cyber-tours had turned up more than few sites that promised to explain the mystic, the supernatural. One web presence was local, and recently established. It concerned an American rather than a Neapolitan, a boy not yet in his teens who'd performed a number of faith healings since his family had arrived to work with the U.N. earthquake relief. Such at least was the electronic rumor, though Fabbro believed he'd seen something about the case on TV. Anyway whatever this child had accomplished, it didn't deserve such a hysterical reaction as this website. Among its postings and testimonials, you found everything from a prayer in pig-Latin to an obscure scrap of foreign numerology. Everyone believed they had the correct incantation, the password to the Eternal. But during this sunrise drive, stop and go around the Bay, Fabbrizio came to experience himself as beyond the grasp of the larger Net, too slippery for even its least filament. Lately he'd careened from sin to sin, from lust to greed to... to worse? Murder? What name did the watchman cry in the night?

Mama, you wouldn't believe your irregular boy, the questions he was asking himself. You wouldn't believe how the remorse worked him over. At times Fabbrizio leaned against the *autostrada* railing, the metal pressing his twinned bundles of cash into his hipbone, and the only thought he could bear was: six months in the best program. Start her off with a therapist who came to the home.

The time he wiped his eyes with Euros, the son wound up staring down at the bills and growing angry with himself. Nerone had been right, they could do without these wild scenes. He wasn't going to help Mama or anyone else, and he wasn't getting any nearer to salvation either, if he needed a ten and a twenty just to see straight. But while his soul might've gone astray, his moral compass had remained true. Given the runaround life he led, the least he could expect was to trip up some part within, some immortal element less familiar with the daily bump and swivel. But he could still put that brother back on his feet.

Secondigliano, think: you've gotten the money and you've remained in one piece. And down here on the tectonic plates, your problem hasn't been the absence of God, but the absence of brains. It hasn't been an angel going ass over teakettle.

Think, *think* of a place close to Mama yet out of harm's way.

Not that the night was done with Fabbrizio, as he took the Suzuki downtown. He left the *autostrada*, taking care with the gathering traffic and the quake repair-work, and yet more than once Fabbrizio reached for something that wasn't there. He groped for his helmet, believing he'd put it on, thinking there had to be something wrong with the visor. In this early sunshine, things shouldn't look so dark.

The American Consulate occupied one of the best addresses along the waterfront. A handsome and broad-shouldered edifice such as Fabbrizio imagined would be typical of a bank in mid-Manhattan, it sat at the high rollers' end of the Bay boulevard. Both the building and the drive were brainchildren of an earlier wave of outsiders who'd believed they knew what was best for these poor benighted Southerners, the "Progressives" who'd come swaggering into town after the last of the Borbons had dragged his tail out. About two or three Italian Republics ago, or the same number of bad quakes. Thus the drive and the building made a foursquare statement, something like the gladiators' *Strength & Honor*. But hardly a dozen strides inland from the Consulate's security gates—gates that faced away from the marina and the boulevard—the city began its steep rise up from the Tyrhennian. Here as elsewhere the precipitous tufa headlands scrambled the streets or turned them to stairs. A layout pre-Progressive, from twenty or thirty republics ago.

A man could park his bike close enough to watch the Consular doorway and yet remain hidden himself, up some cobblestone *vicolo*. Such alleyways wormed down off the hillside all along the consular blocks. Or so it looked to Fabbrizio, a young man just emerged from interior byways likewise difficult to map. He recognized as well the bureaucracy just ahead, the offices of a changed life.

If he was right about Shanti, about her slipping back under American protection, then he was going to ask her for a job. This consulate by the Bay—nowhere else offered so smart a move, for the woman. Nowhere else seemed remotely like Iowa, not downtown anyway. He hadn't missed it when she'd mentioned some friend on the waterfront, some connection. Now he had to figure that his most promising possibility was to spring a surprise visit, threaten the witch with exposure, and demand in exchange for his silence his own little corner of Desk World. NATO was always hiring local liaisons. They always needed a citizen to circulate one of their questionnaires, and to file the responses in triplicate. If Shanti could work in cubicles, so could he.

A better thought, after tonight. A place close to Mama yet out of harm's way. Fabbrizio sat straddling his bike, near the center of the pedestrian vicolo, keeping watch.

He knew the alley, the garage-sized mall just over one shoulder, occupying a commercial zone past the strictly legal. This by itself was hardly uncommon practice for Naples, but the seller closest to Fabbrizio hawked American wares only. The goods must've come from the Consulate's own stock, or from the warehouses for the U.S compound up in Aversa. Shoppers could pick up detergent with baffling Anglo names like *Wisk*, and that Tylenol painkiller pharmacies in Italy weren't allowed to sell, and the sort of puffy-rimmed sneakers Treno had pulled on before his return to the Café Sempre. The wares were contraband, and yet you found them here, alongside the daily commute of the very people who knew best that they were contraband. And the shop had been here for years, and no one had issued a warrant. If you intended to ambush an American, one of the Consular folks, this was the place.

Not that Fabbrizio sat on his banana seat oblivious to what a long shot he was betting. Not when his knuckles ached from two straight nights of close-up work. He'd shaken the darkness of the ride into town—indeed, things had taken on an edge of pale fire—but more than once his chin dropped to his chest and he started to slip off his machine. Each time, after he'd straightened back up, the Secondigliano steadied himself with a stiff dose of realism. Brizio, it's a long, long shot. It's a bet on an offhand remark, a half-educated guess.

Worse, he was losing track of time. He'd left his phone off, in the bike's boot (besides, if a call had come in, he'd have been too frightened to read the number), and as usual when working he'd worn no watch. One less thing to worry about, over the tongs and the fire-bowl. Now Fabbrizio couldn't tell whether the morning traffic on the farther side of the Consulate, the Bay side, had begun to thin out. Likewise inscrutable was the bustle of the nearest bar, the orders shouted between the bursts of high-pitched steaming, the whiff of 8-to-5ers coming out carrying glazed brioche or fresh-baked cornetti. These set his digestive tract wriggling, a motion sickness after the fact, but he couldn't begin to guess if the breakfast rush were over yet.

Beh, he'd give her a bit longer. Even playing it straight, Shanti wasn't the type to keep normal hours.

And those commuters alongside the Bay, what a show. Look how the cars caught the light! You'd think it was noon already, the fires the sun was setting along the chrome and steel, and on the fishing boats that hadn't gone out today. Those boats, their glossy hulls rocking, teasing glimmers out of the traffic-stirred ripples around the pilings. You'd think those boats were sending signals in some fierce color code, between the passing Fiats and Audis. Or was it the fish themselves? Airborne fish just visible in the sun's unstable refractions, fish or more precisely octopi, pinwheels with arms and mouths sea-yellow, sea-green, and the pink of a wound. So much color speckling the air all of a sudden, in metal and wood and flesh, an orchestration in multiple textures for the voice that was now emerging in the back of his brain.

...death against that filthy stucco, death on top of insult... I had my necklace, for my journey... all he had was the knife...

Fabbrizio collapsed over his handlebars, putting his face to the speedometer. The K in his pocket was another fish out of water, with long teeth and a raised spine.

...death so far from the family... only white stucco and black glass... first the insults and then the knife...

He might've been a junkie, the way he was drooping, nodding. He wanted to keep his head up for appearances but he couldn't bear to watch the pyrotechnics, the Greca's soundless fanfare.

...such truth in my father's hands, as he hooked on my necklace... such lying hands that held the knife tonight...

Again the accent suspiciously contemporary, a Balkan refugee. Knowing which death she spoke of, this time, made the voice more familiar still, even with the reverb-distortion that fanned out from his pants pocket.

...such lying... it has me too away from my family, it has me in pieces... with death so near, I cry out...

Fabbrizio was trying to pray, throaty partials of the Hail Mary that must've been audible to passersby. But the Queen of Heaven felt as useless as last time, as did his halting attempts at a rationale, telling himself he'd had no better moment in his life for a stress-induced hallucination. A post-traumatic breakdown. After all, though the watchman had been from the Greca's home town, and she might've felt a certain sentimental attachment, nonetheless over on her side of things, where they could see the future, the man's murder must be old news. Fabbrizio's thinking however never got far, nor his prayers either. He spoke some part of both aloud, but when he managed to recognize a word out of his own mouth, it sounded like nothing so much as another proof that he was in the grip of a visitor unencumbered by psychology, or by the decades of the rosary. Also he'd started crying again. Quite the spectacle for the alley traffic, this mumbling young burnout who couldn't even keep his arms straight. Fabbro shook his head, his dripping and overheated head. He tried to gauge how far along the vision had gotten. He tried to assess the new presence at his shoulder, maybe flesh and blood.

No one had touched him, no person of three dimensions, but there was somebody close enough to make themselves felt. Fabbrizio choked down a sob, working on it. He couldn't turn around yet, not while he was still licking saltwater off his lips, but this seemed like a woman.

He caught a bath-oil scent, perhaps lavender, and out the corner of one eye he could see a few breeze-blown strands of long hair. It helped that the Greca's visit seemed to be ending. The colors above the traffic had calmed, and the electro-shock out of his groin eased a few notches down the dial.

Fabbrizio cleared his throat and let go a long exhale. Yes, the voice had dwindled to a murmur; the spirits were through with him. He coughed again, trying to come up with a line of talk for this Good Samaritan.

"Fabbrizio?" asked Shanti, after the sight of her had stopped him in mid-word. "What is it?"

She wore an office-girl's suit, so sedate that he might've failed to spot her even without interference from the occult. In one hand a big to-go coffee, Starbucks-style. But the least likely thing about the young woman was her purse, ungainly, unstylish.

"Listen, *ragazzo*," Shanti went on quietly. "I can't have you here making a scene. You want to talk, all right, we'll talk. But with calm, understand?"

Ragazzo, what was all this crying? He'd come down to the Consulate wanting a change, but not like this. Not like he'd never get control of himself again.

"Fabbrizio." A whisper as sharp as the spikes of his Penates. "I can't have you here falling to pieces. Here there are people I work with."

Averting his face from the others going by, using the clip-clop of dressy Naples heels to help flatten the Greca's last jolts to his nerves, Fabbrizio looked the woman up and down. Up and down, and then his teardrop-goggled eyes came to rest on the purse. Down in the Portofino hotel, he recalled, the ghost-message had been transmitted via the conjunction of two ancient pieces: his Roman and her Greek.

"What you and I have between us, it stays between us. Understand? Now, what do you say to a nice cappuccino?"

Whatever l'Americana did at the Consulate, it didn't require a bag so bulky as that. She even had a combination on the clasp.

"Are you... ?"

The best she could with the purse in her elbow, Shanti gave the smoker's gesture. She didn't mean tobacco, that was obvious. But the rattle Fabbrizio heard from inside the bag—the shifting of ancient metal and stone—that was more obscure. That might've happened only in his head, still hot from the highway and leaking tears once more. Not that he had any doubts about the stolen necklace. His former accomplice here kept it with her, she carried it even today, and he remained *fortunato* enough to know that, a man of Secondigliano even when he'd come to this alley in hopes of finding a way to go straight. Shanti had the goods whether he'd heard them rattle or not. The truth had come to him with the same incontrovertible wallop that his one-man remote-access server had delivered twice now. The Greca needed her necklace in order to speak.

But to dig that nugget out of the ground and confront Shanti with it, that was much too much for him yet. That was far out of reach, beyond nerves gone to garbage. Likewise any plan of his...

"But, Fabbrizio." She'd been studying his eyes, his bare arms. "What is it?"

"Help me," he asked, brokenly. "Please, help me."

Third Evening

If hearing from the Greca was a trickster miracle, then what kind of miracle was this? The American had answered his bike-seat prayer. Over the past week (no, more—this evening made nine days) Shanti had helped Fabbrizio settle into an appointment jointly managed by NATO and the UN earthquake relief. The straightest job he'd ever had, with procedures that seemed to him out of another civilization, a distant culture in which inhabitants maintained a parking lot with the same neatness and attention to ritual as a Neapolitan would keep the shrine in his kitchen. And all arranged for him by a playgirl. Shanti had handled the interviews and clearances so efficiently that Fabbrizo came to think this New York City con girl possessed a potent strain of the military bean-counter. In Shanti's case both the Consulate downtown and the NATO compound up in Aversa seemed no more than different branches of the same toy store.

And the gadget she currently enjoyed the most was The Fabbro. The way she'd taken the Secondigliano under her wing had him thinking of the old colonials, the Regional Administrators who would select, as one of their first official acts, a pretty native boy or girl for "personal assistant." When the American had looked over his new documentation, when she'd ascertained that Fabbrizio was just 24 years old, she'd announced, "Now that's interesting." On the first morning he'd found her again, outside the Consulate, even as they talked over coffee she'd declared: "It will be a pleasure to see your sweet ass around here." Your pleasure, sahib, is my gladsome duty. The Secondigliano figured that as of yet, a week-plus into the job, it was only politics that had kept her from laying hands on him. Shanti was waiting for the moment, she was perhaps even now making arrangements for the moment, when she could claim that sweet ass without creating complications around the office.

My duty, sahib. Though naturally the other woman in Fabbrizio's life, his mother, thought the world of his new 9-to-6.

Or she claimed to, Mama. Certainly she made a big, prayerful production out of their goodbye kiss, every morning. After she pressed her face to both his cheeks she would continue to sit up in bed, lighting a candle on the night-table, and then while she fell back onto her pillows she would hold him a long moment more with her fixed gaze alone, her eyes maybe murky with tears, or fogged by medication, or simply still sleepy. Against the collar of her nightgown his mother would hold the rosary, beading it through the fingers no longer brown from sun. She thanked God, she thanked Pio, she called her *secondo* "my resurrected child"... till finally Brizio had to wonder. He had to trot down the stairs to his Suzuki, wondering. If Mama could throw herself into a wild scene such as that, what was she doing spending the rest of the day in bed? If she was taking her prescription and working with the visiting therapist (Mondays, Thursdays, Saturdays), then how was it she remained so slack and goo-goo, locked in near-death doldrums?

Now they were nine days into her son's legitimate employment, a dozen days past her return from the hospital. But according to Uldirico it was about all their Mama could manage just to brew a *macchinetta* of espresso before the therapist arrived. Rico couldn't say for certain whether she stayed in the bedroom all day—he and Brizio had hardly been acting like brothers, anyway, lately. But judging from what the mother showed the younger boy, she'd never been so chained to the Hail Mary and the Our Father, either. Never mind the shrine in the kitchen. Ninety-nine out of a hundred homes in Naples had such a shrine, and Mama after all had been the parent more firmly fixed to earth, the one who'd mentioned the Camorra by name and suggested a job at the lottery office. Then what was this fervor every morning, carrying on as if she might go to Jesus before her younger son got home? And once or twice, when Brizio had eaten dinner at home (before things got ugly with Rico), he'd caught the evening show too.

It felt like a show to him, an act; may Mama forgive him for thinking so. It felt like she was putting pressure on her new straight arrow, seeing if indeed it wouldn't bend. She had reason to doubt her boy, certainly. This was a woman who'd spent her life on the city periphery, hardly *fesso* to begin with, and now all of a sudden she found herself enrolled in a private recovery program, top of the line, extending even to group counseling sessions with other survivors. The mother hadn't attended any of those sessions yet. She'd claimed she lacked the strength. But one evening she'd suggested another explanation, fixing her younger son with a look entirely unclouded.

"And what would I tell them?" Mama had said. "What would I share with those people, about my good boy who made it possible for me to join?"

Her boy was left asking himself some questions too. What had God wrought, for His chosen Secondigliano? On the job he faced the American with the notches on her belt, looking to add one more, and at home he faced the Neapolitan who knew just where to poke him and how hard, in her search for proof that his return to righteousness would last longer than it took to pay off the heart specialist. Pressure on the straight arrow. Fabbrizio didn't know much more he could take.

Yet even as these strains gathered, his changed life had him grateful. The accessories alone felt great, the laminated Treaty Organization ID, the three new numbers in his cell-phone memory, two connecting him with NATO and one with an office in UN relief. He even had a mailbox of his own, up here at the Aversa compound, on the city's northern fringes. Indeed, thanks to Shanti (or Daphne, should he say?), this evening made the third time he'd been allowed into Aversa, home to hundreds of soldiers, sailors, and transatlantic bureaucrats. Though tonight again, tonight especially, he had to wonder whether such special favors made him truly a *fortunato*. Tonight, he and l'Americana had come to the compound in order to commit a crime. And if they pulled the caper off—and why shouldn't they, under the protection of a woman like this, a maker of diabolic miracles?—Fabbrizio had something still more devious up his sleeve. He had a trick that should both rid him of the trophy-hunting American and provide his mother with the reassurance she needed.

Though he needed no scams to make the Aversa base seem like another planet entirely. A rogue orbit around the periphery.

Aversa had been a hamlet for dairy farming, water-buffalo dairy, mozzarella. Then after the last bad quake, in 1980, the U.S. Department of Defense had created a *falso* of its own, making over a broad swath of *Mezzogiorno* landscape as a California suburb. The troop housing seemed incongruous in its very materials, all that aluminum. Fabbrizio's greatest astonishment may have come when Shanti or Daphne or whoever brought him up close to one of the low-steepled homes she described as "ranch style." In the wall siding he found imitation wood grains, cut deep enough to cast tiny shadows. He had to put his finger to the hot metal grooves, just to make sure.

What kind of detail-work was this, obscure and without pattern? Nothing so sumptuous as the grapevines you saw carved on marble columns around Naples; nothing so tale-bearing as the godling Fabbrizio carried in his pocket, a piece designed for display beside a family's front door. Plus these colorless, stippled homes sat huddled around blacktop cul-de-sacs, on small, starving lawns. Each family lived isolated, without so much as a laundry line to connect their window to the next. And as he stood with a dumb finger to the siding, Fabbrizio heard his guide explain, with a certain gleeful malice, that the planning for this "subdivision" had in fact bungled the job of recreating Stateside style, for most of the Marines and Navy stationed here. The vast majority, she explained, had never seen the San Fernando Valley. Most came either from the American South (like Texas, Fabbrizio, *capisce?*) or the African-American inner cities.

Fabbrizio supposed his brother might get more out of her lecture, perhaps a paper titled "Delusions of the Imperial Legions." Himself, on this law-breaking evening, he was bowled over again by the sheer *denial* of it all: that wood grain in aluminum. Where there were colors, they were preposterous candy colors, and the base as a whole pretended to spaciousness while in fact cramming circles on top of quadrilaterals.

The deceptiveness of the place got to him again tonight, as Shanti showed her Daphne-passport at the security gate. In the process she slipped off her bike helmet, and seeing this touched Fabbrizio with a moment's chill, a reminder of his own plan for tonight: the end that would at last justify eighteen months of rule-breaking means. For his scheme to work, he needed the bike. So he was glad for his own helmet, the tinted cover it kept over his face, and he looked away from the guardhouse, allowing himself to be baffled all over again by this pseudo L.A. The strangest thing about it was how the compound's design perverted its very reason for existence. The comforts of the mall put a benign, not to say corrupt face on all the firepower. In fact Aversa was about nothing if not guns and the people who knew how to use them; U.S. armed forces had established no fewer than a half-dozen such sites around Naples, some six thousand miles from Washington and nevertheless deemed "essential to security." With that kind of doubletalk going on, it was hardly surprising to see, on top of everything else, denial of the raging hormones in play.

Troops at the base were mostly well under thirty and in terrific shape. They knew it, too, keeping their uniforms snug and creased, and otherwise parading around in the skimpy togs of the gym and the beach. Fabbrizio had seen fewer pretty people, and less aggressive body-play, at the disco. But to look at the strict cul de sacs, or at the dodecaplex movie theater—a faceless larger box amid the squat steel-and-stucco tract of the PX mall—you would think you'd entered a land of robots. The same went for the sweatshop functionality of the printing facility, where he and Shanti were headed now. After closing hours.

He understood culture shock, naturally, and he understood that Italians generally put too much stock in *la bella figura*. Nonetheless, even as he parked in one of the spaces set aside for motorbikes, spaces designated by bleached white lines of rigid consistency, suddenly his hormones got into play. It might've had something to do with the lot's heat, the tarmac roasting under the long day's sun. The real trigger for his dreaming, however, was two women jogging past in scoop-necked tops while, at his side, l'Americana checked her cozy white shorts for a key she wasn't supposed to have. For a moment there, knotted three-way heavings erupted in his mind's eye. For a moment he forgot the trouble he'd suffered at the hands of tonight's accomplice, this woman with who-knows-how-many names. He was glad he'd chosen loose pants for this trip, cargo pants with extra storage pockets.

But the joggers went out of sight, he and his guide reached the locked front doors of Printing & Publications, and once more he had to wonder.

In time he allowed himself to vent a bit. By then Fabbrizio and the woman had moved onto a path that ran along one side of the facility, a byway almost unseen behind a flowering hedge. Underfoot lay crunching gravel, but he kept his voice at a whisper.

"Why are you doing this?"

He had to ask twice before she responded. "But, what? You know the kind of technology they've got in here."

"I mean—" if only he did know what he meant!—"where do I enter in? Surely you could find a friend with NATO, someone more powerful."

"Come on. Aren't you the one with the connection for taking the goods overseas?"

"*Sicuro.*" This was his cover story; he had to agree. "Nevertheless I, I ask myself. We're breaking into American property, no? It's a greater risk even than three weeks ago, the necropolis."

At least his Penates remained tranquil, unelectrified. Still Fabbrizio kept darting looks over both shoulders.

"I have to go inside, Fabbro, really inside. I need you to watch the outer door."

The dense rows of camellia and the windows of the nearest buildings were all remarkably empty. Shanti had said this was dinner hour, though it was hardly past six. Also she'd described this part of the compound as a "campus." Beh, nothing like Fabbrizio's university.

"But," he said, "you could've gotten your girl to do that. The wife of the colonel?"

She broke stride and eyed him, smiling open-mouthed.

"She'd do it," he went on, "wouldn't she?"

During his last visit to Aversa, l'Americana had revealed that she'd enjoyed a torrid weekend with the young wife of one of the compound's highest ranking officers. While she'd told the story Shanti's almost-Arab features had flickered momentarily with the revenge-taking Fabbrizio had noticed before, a glint considerably higher up the hardness scale than the simple pleasure of breaking rules. But by and large the news came out as a self-assertion unimpressed with itself. She'd made a half-handed gesture in the direction of the couple's home, as if Fabbrizio had been there. He wound up feeling he should've known. The woman's recent swinging the other way had something to do with why she hadn't yet jumped his own heterosexual bones, no doubt, and besides, he should've seen this coming. He should've seen the libertine in her that first afternoon in Café Sempre, when she'd taken charge even in a Mafia front. And it felt a little insulting when, after Shanti had finished the story—her first time "stealing someone else's sweet young thing," she'd concluded, with the thoughtful pout of a connoisseur—she assumed she'd hurt his feelings. Her look turning almost motherly, she'd told him: Fabbro, don't look so discouraged. You know I enjoy a man every now and then. It felt to Fabbrizio like a pat on the head, nice doggy; it set him creeping up the hardness scale.

Tonight, behind the camellias, she went on smiling. "I suppose the girl would do it," she said. "She made me the key, didn't she?"

The weekend fling had included at least one session inside Printing & Publications. Shanti had explained that there were cots upstairs, dormers for the occasional round-the-clock runs (recently, for instance, the fleet had needed extra materials on the Persian-Gulf states). But Fabbrizio got the impression that the women hadn't much bothered with the beds. The colonel himself ran the printing operations, and according to Shanti his office featured leather chairs and a vast executive desk.

"But then," he asked, toeing at the gravel between them, "why don't you have her here? She knows the—"

Shanti waved away the thought, showing him close-trimmed nails. "There could be problems, that way. Complications. With her it was one thing and tonight, it's a different thing."

He should've known. For this woman, even a string of illicit orgasms offered a chance to work a couple of angles, and indeed tonight's stop at the compound had been her idea entirely. If she and Fabbrizio had stuck to his plan—both what he'd told her and what he'd kept secret—they would've come nowhere near Printing & Publications. But as soon as he'd given Shanti his line of talk about the necklace, she'd suggested an early-evening stop up at Aversa. She'd thought of plucking a few illegal leaves from this American grafting. Fabbrizio, for his part, figured the trip would keep her off guard. Between the way there and the way back, he'd get the opportunity he needed.

If only this NATO gravel weren't so noisy! Meanwhile Shanti promised him again that what she had in mind would remain untraceable, so long as the two of them got in and out of the facility undetected.

"Anyway," she went on now, "you know how much I enjoy having you accompany me. You're my, you're truly my *Best Boy*."

He managed a sideways smile, tight, reined in. Best Boy, *ah si*, from the credits for an American movie. Back when he'd had time for movies, he and the other Secondigliani had made their share of jokes about such job titles—and yet here he was, Best Boy native boy. Ah, but tonight the natives were restless. Tonight he was going to steal back the necklace.

The Consular assignment that Shanti had arranged for him, after all, amounted to no more than a stopgap. It wasn't so asphyxiating a safety-space as his father had stumbled into. It got Fabbrizio out on the bike, and the learning curve had an intriguing slope. But the young man's NATO position had nothing to do with the skills that made his fingers itch, or that set him rethinking the layout and architecture here in… what *would* you call this place? The Transplant State? A true *artigiano*, anyway, would soon grow weary of a runaround like Fabbrizio's new posting. It was only a paper chase at bottom, and one that had no future to boot. Another pickup job, that's what set Fabbrizio revving his Suzuki nowadays: an assignment that would serve no further purpose as soon as various post-quake headcounts were completed and collated. In another two-three months, the clandestini would no longer be able to use the counterfeit documents now in circulation, the so-called "Earthquake I.D."

Think it over, Fabbrizio. Think it through, now while it's quiet.

Shanti had posted him as a lookout, inside the facility's most discreet side entrance. She believed she knew the schedule for the security rounds, the MP's, but just the same: Stay, boy. The door was tinted, treated. Fabbrizio could see out but others couldn't see in, and anyway bypassers were so rare, out on the well-kept gravel and lawn between this facility and the next, that he spent most of the time studying his own dim reflection. Shanti couldn't say just how long her chores might take, down in the technology. Printing & Publications had the best digital cameras that the Pentagon could afford. With one of those and a pair of surgical gloves—plus the colonel's password, a pet name for his wife—she could burn a CD of necklace photos and e-mail the pick of the set over to New York. The whole process would take place free of any connection back to "Daphne," and New York at last would get a good look at what they were buying.

Or rather what they thought they were buying. New York and their woman in Naples had never had reason to risk exposure on the internet before because Fabbrizio had never lied to her like this before.

Sahib, you think you're a wiseguy? You swallowed this hook, line, and sinker. Thanks to his new job Fabbrizio had learned a thing or two about smuggling, and he'd worked up a passable story about making a connection, a man at one of the shipping companies who could take the jewels across the Atlantic. He'd embellished his gab with a detail or two he'd picked up recently—and just like that, Shanti had taken the bait. Hook, line, and lie, she'd gone for it, with a look almost dazzled at the possibility, a look like a post-it on the wall of Fabbrizio's awareness. To see her this way reminded him that this woman wasn't so much older than he, and she too had little talent for waiting. Shanti, Daphne, whoever, she must've grown impatient with her new burden, its rattle in her oversize purse. She saw herself as something better than a mule.

She'd had the necklace with her, just as he'd suspected, that morning when she and Fabbrizio had hooked up again outside the Consulate. Just as he'd come to believe: he needed the Paestum tomb jewelry, the Roman hearth-protector, and some death or near-death during this American century, all three close to him in some way, in order to create the internal combustion of the Greca's messages. So Shanti had been holding, that morning of their re-meeting and throughout her workday, because that afternoon she had an appointment with a would-be buyer. She'd kept the appointment of course, a meeting in the bar at one of the waterfront hotels, one of the swanks. After the first vodka, as a kind of consolation prize, the man had proposed what Fabbrizio imagined was an excellent price for taking Shanti herself upstairs (wasn't hard to imagine, though he'd sat out of earshot down the bar, the woman's "backup"). L'Americana however hadn't been interested in either offer. That evening like every evening, she'd hiked back home with the same load as when she'd left.

She'd been ready to tumble. Eager, really; by the time Fabbrizio learned enough to make it sound like he'd found a reliable smuggler, she'd had a plan set up for just such an eventuality. She was going to get the photos out on the Net.

Shanti should've remembered what a slick piece of lying he'd done just to get this new job. During the interview, Fabbrizio claimed a lot more experience with the city's refugee population than he'd had. He'd gone so far as to invent, whole cloth, a trio of soccer buddies from Cameroon. The truth was, a week plus into his new appointment, he was still learning the best way to put a newly-arrived African at ease. Thank God his employers couldn't watch him at work. Fabbrizio was authorized to offer amnesty for the use of the counterfeit I.D.—for that single felony alone—should anyone be willing to turn theirs in. Should a clandestino have more useful information, such as how to find one of the underground paper-traders, Fabbrizio had another carrot or two to dangle. The sweetest was an official Statement of Cooperation, co-signed by officials from both the NATO command and the primary UN relief agency. Fabbrizio could deliver such a Statement only if what the informant had told him resulted in an arrest, but such an outcome meant that the document held considerable sway with the bureaucrats in charge of work visas and residence contracts. If an illegal immigrant fingered a worse criminal, and got a good report from Fabbrizio, he might become legal.

So he began to learn his way around the black blocks, the nearest thing he had to a regular workplace. Out on the beltway the exit was designated by a locomotive pulling into a shed, and just as the *stazione* occupied as ugly a piazza as existed in Italy, so the nearby intersections favored by the Liberians or Somalis—from opposite sides of the southern continent, here they amounted to the same thing—fit no one's notion of urban cute. The blocks were defaced more than most by quake reconstruction. Scaffolding and plastic swaddled half the buildings. Rubble lingered in heaps at the dead-ends where the tracks went through, and over the mounds of broken brick and girder shriveled cats poked for garbage. Underfoot, one was forever kicking away plastic scrap.

Or you were stepping on someone's pavement-level clearing house. Most of the selling in these blocks took place off reed mats strewn with goods: slapdash animal figures, purses of near-leather, or necklaces of amber, carnelian, and gold. Other vendors worked out of synthetic duffel bags in sweatshop-green or -blue. You saw backpacks small enough for a Greek preteen and carryalls large enough to hold her skeleton.

Fabbrizio also learned to spot, here and there among the tubes of gray scaffolding and flaps of blue plastic, the actual storefront shops. The most common properties offered booths for internet connections or phone calls overseas. A handful of others served goat meat and vegetables in concoctions the Secondigliano found sloppy, soupy, plus fruit juices and teas he found too sweet. He liked more the wraparound suits from Senegal, with ballooning drawstring pants and a loose-hanging top, the entire flap-happy outfit decorated in the same madcap party print and worn with nothing underneath.

Also these blocks weren't so black as all that. Fabbrizio had some notion of American "ghettos," segregated and grim, though he realized that both the big screen and the TV showed a lot of fairytales (and then again, what could be more of a fairytale than the mini-America he saw on the screen before him tonight—the door to Printing & Publications—these flatlands and rectangles numbed further by tinted glass, a landscape utterly at odds with what he intended, something radical, something to prove himself once and for all pure of heart?). But the *zona Africana* in downtown Naples included a good number of white Neapolitans, and not just cross-cultural adventurers like Monte Zu. There was also the occasional café family, insuring that this neighborhood too had worthwhile pizza and espresso. And Fabbrizio encountered a number of Pakistanis, the color of unrefined olive oil; he saw pale Vietnamese, hefty Koreans, nimble Sri Lankans. These went in for the garment business mostly, though some of the Pakis ran the internet-and-phone centers. He even discovered two or three pro-bono organizations, staffed by white folks with educations and a conscience. There was a Legal Aid office. Another group, its door almost hidden behind the repair sheeting, struggled to arrange steady on-the-books employment. Construction work, paperwork, staff positions with hospitals and outpatient clinics—jobs such as these had made all the difference for *immigrati* in cities like Paris or New York. But in Naples it remained rare to find an African on the state's payroll. Fabbrizio saw no dark faces, even, around the deeply-staffed clinic he'd arranged for his mother.

Yet while the Secondigliano grew accustomed to his new place of business, his new colleagues and clientele, now and again he still had to struggle against spasms of the fear that had rocked him down in the Paestum graveyard. So many shades of black! Every gesture an unknown!

Monte Zu of course laughed at the problem. The one time Fabbrizio had ventured to talk about his fretfulness in plain Italian, the hash dealer had tugged on one of his Italo-dreadlocks and suggested Fabbrizio try the style. Another time, when Fabbro had merely looked uneasy, Zu had offered a blessing in some Muslim tongue (the language of tigers? was that the name?). Occasionally, too, this friend who'd made the arrangements with the murdered night watchman down by the dead Greek agora performed a similar function up here in the living Italian marketplace. Occasionally he cut away the bristling thorn-bushes that guarded Fabbrizio's terrors, and so allowed the *artigiano* to enter and learn just how silly they were. Monte Zu for instance took the Secondigliano into his first all-African apartment building.

Not that the dealer arranged the visit in the name of worldwide brotherhood. Rather, Zu had a new product. "When's the last time," he asked as he and Fabbrizio were buzzed inside the palazzo, "an item out of Africa really cornered the market? Back when they were still selling slaves?"

Upstairs, on a scrap of balcony with a view of the northbound train tracks, he introduced two friends from the region that used to be called "the Horn," one lighter, one darker. Then back inside, after drawing the curtains, Monte Zu set up a hip-high hookah with a pair of smoking hoses as thick as a boat's painter. The gold-plated trim was exceptional work, its detail clever enough to call to mind the Greca's necklace. That plus the scent of the coals had Fabbrizio yearning for his tools, his metals, his fire. Then his guide loaded the smoking bowl from a pouch with a label in fiery Arabic, tobacco from the smell of it, but something else as well. He insisted his "white friend" sample a good deep draw.

Fabbrizio managed not to cough. The stuff did seem tasty, the flavor—apples.

Monte Zu nodded, backhanding an unraveled dreadlock off his sweaty forehead. Proudly he announced he had a supplier with a dozen varieties of the stuff, fruits both sugary and tart, plus rock-bottom shipping arrangements for the hookahs.

"And now you've got that good NATO money," he reminded Fabbrizio.

In three years, the Afro-*falso* predicted, every Italian under twenty-one would take his tobacco this way. Arrayed around the gilded smoker's tube, while the hash dealer kept his hands raised as if in supplication, the group called to mind one of the Naples Nativity setups. A Christmas crèche, a *presepe*, always included the three wise men from afar, the Moors and Arabs with their retinue.

"I can't think," Monte Zu declared, "of a better investment."

Beh, Fabbrizio couldn't tell him any different. These days he himself was the immigrant, repeatedly miscalculating some vendor's hours of operation or stepping off the curb in front of a Vespa. Sometimes the only familiarity seemed the stairways; these palazzi too never had an elevator. But when Monte Zu led him back down out of his first such apartment building, the taste of apple in his mouth, Fabbrizio realized he couldn't recall the names of the Africans with whom he'd shared a smoke. Didn't even know their *names*. He wondered if he should start keeping a notebook, then thought again: this would only make everyone nervous, a white man walking around writing down names and addresses. Only later would he learn to enter any trustworthy piece of news into his cell phone, a saved text message.

Not that there'd been much "later," either, not yet. Not even with the hash dealer showing him how to handle an Ethiopian meal, how to do without knife and fork, Fabbrizio still hadn't developed much taste for the food. That floppy pancake bread they ate, what would go with that? Fresh-cut bell pepper, perhaps?

He seemed *fortunato* indeed, one lucky young man, the first time he'd convinced a clandestino to turn in his fake ID. By tonight there'd been three such cases and the officer to whom he reported appeared impressed. But the documents had been less than pristine copies to begin with. In the same way, though Fabbrizio had gleaned the name of a likely dealer, he couldn't call one of the new numbers in his *telefonino*'s memory before he'd established just who among his two or three snitches could be trusted. The Africans who'd confided in him each had their own agenda, their own angle on better money and improved legal status; it didn't take a degree in sociology to understand that. But this same savvy meant that his sources did see more of the big Neapolitan picture than most of their hardscrabble streetmates. The problem was, Fabbrizio still couldn't tell how much of that picture was the same as he saw. Then came the whole question of his own way of looking at these documents, or at anything else, and whether that had much in common with what NATO saw.

And whose reality was this, tonight, that held so heart-stopping a passerby?

Outside the door to Printing & Publication, the heavy glass that turned everything gray, Fabbrizio caught sight of a big man in civilian clothes. The clothes were the first thing he noticed, not the race—maybe his days in the black blocks had done that much for him. Though in fact tonight's passerby appeared African. His skin and features were free of the whitening touches you saw in American blacks. While he didn't wear a uniform, and while his lined face and scarred hands made clear he was older than most of the types you saw walking around the compound, he was big enough to be a soldier. The muscles of his chest and shoulders might've been a sack of stout Sorrento lemons.

The clothes: a ribbed and glossy shirt of the kind favored by Somalis. One look, even through bulletproof glass, and Fabbrizio couldn't deny he knew the man.

Shanti had kept the key of course. He didn't think about an alarm till his head and shoulders were back out in the evening heat, and then he didn't hear any alarm. There was no one else on this scrap of lawn either, nothing except the rising white noise inside his head to interfere with his throaty whisper, calling the man over.

"But, what?" he added, still hushed, as the big thirty-something approached. "What are you *doing* here?"

"Fab-bri-zi-o." The Somali father barely bothered to lower his voice.

The family rounded up along the Paestum roadside, the clandestini first accused of stealing the necklace, had profited from their moment in the spotlight. Not that the news clips, like the petition that had circulated, were extraordinary responses for cases such as theirs. Going on-camera with a rock star, as for that, had been a lucky accident. But thanks to these developments the father, mother, and daughter not only got out of jail, but also earned a temporary legal status in this country. Temporary—a matter of days, really—but nonetheless the Africans' new standing opened rare doors. They needed the same thing any newcomer in Italy needed, of course, a position with a longterm contract and an employer's guarantee of a roof of their heads. But in this family's case the father was free to seek such employment, so long as he carried the correct papers and allowed himself to be frisked, anywhere he could get to. His Exemption order even meant he could look for work on territory that was technically foreign, like Aversa.

Too bad his name remained the kind of tongue-twister that didn't allow for easy assimilation: N'mbor-làvà. An unsettling hybrid, a word that suggested the compounds from Fabbrizio's jewelry-making. He'd failed to get the name right in either of his two previous meetings with the father. Their first run-in had taken place outside the Legal Aid office down in the black blocks, just the day before the day before yesterday. At that encounter, naturally, the Secondigliano had at first been so startled and scared that he could hardly speak simple Italian, let alone try on foreign names. But he hadn't done much better at the second meeting—the second, at least, of any length and substance— when he'd actually sought out the briefly-legitimate Somalis, on the piazzetta where they set up their vendor's mats and goods. During that more recent get-together he and the father had set up a strategy for tonight's little scam, and yet Fabbrizio had gone on struggling with what to call his accomplice.

Was it NIM-bohr LAH-vah? Lah-VAH? He struggled with the father's first name, too, neither "Nando" nor "Nardo" nor "Nodo."

But however you pronounced it, the family name was now spared immediate entry into the passenger manifest for a Coast Guard ferry back to Africa. Their pass-through status, the rule that limited undocumented newcomers like these to just 14 days in Italy, had been extended. A figure near the top of the Campanian Regional Administration had weighed in, drawing up a document that granted "Nanni N'mbor-lavá," along with his wife and his daughter, short-term exemptions to the tightening Italian laws on immigration. The family had three times the usual period in which to find a secure job sponsor, an accredited university program, or even NATO employment. The Aversa compound, like its model back in Southern California, tended to use someone other than Americans when it came to scrubbing the pots or dumping the garbage.

"But you understand," the father told Fabbrizio now, outside the door to Printing. "Okay I ask work from the Americans."

At least he was whispering, the old griot—though Fabbrizio, struggling to get a grip on his surprise, reminded himself that this balding African had no more than a year or two on Shanti. And come to think of it, where had that playgirl got to? The Secondigliano pulled his head back inside a moment, but still heard nothing on the stairs. The cross-wired windows on the lobby doors revealed nothing either. He motioned "Nanni" to come inside and shut the one-way glass behind him.

"My wife, my daughter, they know I'm here." The African seemed to think this was reassuring. "I have arrangement for after. After, I phone to my wife."

"After? After you break the law—with me, my help—you're going to call them somewhere and tell them you did it?"

"Is okay I come here. I don't break the law. The Americans believe I am here to find work. The Americans don't know I am search for Feh, Fatti, Fabbrizio."

As usual the foreigner's idioms had him cupping one hand loosely, thumb to fingertips. "You came here to find me? You knew I would be in, in this place?"

"But, how not? You say you have business with the Americans, and this is an hour of the evening when the Consulate is closed."

Fabbrizio opened his mouth but couldn't put it to use. This new man in his life, this guest of the nation... How could the African have so much on the ball as to figure out where he'd gone, and at the same time knock around like the worst loose cannon in greater Naples? Flattening his own Marines all over the deck? The Secondigliano cast another glance towards the inside stairwell, the lesser of two evils here. Shanti at least wouldn't throw them both in jail—though come to think of it, New York was pretty quick herself. She wouldn't need more than a single stuttering evasion, out of either man's mouth, to spot the axial lines of a double-cross. And with her Daphne documents, with the numbers in her cell, there was no telling what havoc might follow.

He balled his hand into a fist, extending the thumb. "Outside, my friend. Outside, and keep low."

Leaving the air conditioning, Fabbrizio was dizzied briefly by the thickness of the camellia bushes, screening the facility's side entrance. But he made the move swiftly, and in a squat, well under the redolent topmost flowers. Also the Somali proved spry for his bulk, not much disturbing the gravel on the hidden walkway. In another moment the only problem was the door, how to prop it open. Fabbrizio didn't want to risk losing a shoe, or crumpling the extended prick on his lucky charm, so he wound up using his billfold. Jamming the fine Campanian leather under the door's base, he left a pinkie-width of a gap, invisible unless you were right on top of it.

"O-kay," he muttered, once more facing his visitor "Now, you, if an American comes, suddenly, yes? If an American comes, if she comes to this door or wherever, you work on the bushes. Understand?"

Raising his hands, he mimed pruning and plucking. "The plants."

"Rrn."

"If you are a gardener an American won't see you."

"Feh, Fabbrizio." The African's whisper had a higher pitch, breathless from his squat. "You are here for the business, yes? For my family."

"It's true I've got business here, and this business will be a help to you and your family. It's true, everything, just as we discussed. But think. The—the American with whom I work, here tonight, it is a criminal American. Quasi Mafia. Understand?"

"This business, tonight, it's the..." the father spread one hand between his lapels, necklace-style. His nails, Fabbrizio realized, were as fat and ruddy as the amber he'd used on other piecework.

"Yes, that business, but it's no business for you. You, my friend, you must go and right now."

"But, the jewel?" the African said. "You are here for the jewel from the, from that place with all the dead?"

"My friend, if you stay here, there will be no jewel. Not for you. If you are here, the criminal keeps the necklace, and she gives you to the police. Here you are between the criminals and the police, understand?

The police send you back to Africa and the criminals…" he gestured at his own neck, dragging his thumb across an artery.

"But, the jewel—with that my family becomes legal. Perhaps."

The brief amnesty granted the N'mbor-lavá hardly solved their problem. One could say that, in the end, they'd gained nothing more than an extra month and a half for slipping back off the books. Worse, this time they might turn into true outlaws, for instance attempting to trade up their Certificate of Exemption, exchanging it for one of the very counterfeits Fabbrizio had been hired to recover. Granted, the Earthquake I.D. wouldn't protect them for long, either, as the government record-keeping caught up with the damage done by the quake's electro-magnetic pulse. But even an additional month or so of legitimacy would carry the three non-citizens a lot further than any interest from the public at large. By tonight, hardly two weeks after they'd been released from police custody, this "Nanni" and the women depending on him (their looks interesting, but hardly show business) had disappeared from the news. The story of the moment was another mass drowning between Tunisia and Sicily, the sea-bitten remains of boat people washing ashore again along the southern beaches.

At least the father had been smart enough to see it coming, their fall from the media radar. No sooner was he back on the streets than he'd begun to stop by one of the black blocks' pro bono ventures, the Legal Aid cooperative. Their office was the only door open in a half-block of scaffolding, down a dead-end alleyway. Often the lone desk was manned by an actual lawyer, though this *avvocato* was generally of more use in navigating Italian legislation than in helping a family through its daily hardscrabble. Getting the three Somalis out of jail had been one thing, it had triggered an Amnesty International Urgent Action Alert, but carrying plates to the table was another. These days the N'mbor-lavá made what money they could as street vendors. The strength in the father's upper body was wasted in toting around plastic toys: whistles, water-pistols, and birds with clear plastic wings decorated like henna tattoos. Mother and daughter, working the other end of the same squat piazza, served roasted nuts and slushy lemon ice out of a wooden-wheeled cart.

Thus the man who'd confronted Fabbrizio outside the *Centro di Assistenze Legale*, the night before the night before last night, had looked like someone scraping the bottom of every barrel in reach. Dripping sweat and wrestling his duffel of toys between the scaffolding uprights, Nono or Nano appeared far older than the newly-hired investigator into identification fraud. Indeed, it was over the course of that same first night's conversation that Fabbrizio had first been startled to discover how young he was, this sagging father of two—and talk about startling, the African had killed a man. He was the murderer of his other daughter's murderer.

That evening of their initial re-encounter, they'd settled on the name Nado. A compromise, this was, like every scrap of understanding that Fabbrizio could hammer out regarding his new friend. Gaps in the brawny African's testimony cropped up everywhere, and that included the story of how his younger daughter had died and what he'd done about it. A few more salient facts had made the papers, naturally. The girl had gone overboard towards the end of the family's night sea-journey. But though Fabbrizio now knew more than anyone in Italy about the drowning and its aftermath, during those wild and sorry hours off the coast of Reggio Calabria, he could hardly say he knew it all. He'd figured that if he questioned the father too closely, it would do more harm than good. Besides, what few exchanges he'd had with Nado had generally been limited to a couple of labored and repetitive phrases. The two of them had managed just one more extended conversation, one more meeting of any length, between that evening outside Legal Aid and this one behind the NATO flower bushes.

And that first night, once the Secondigliano had gotten beyond his dumbstruck terror, he'd stood there baffled by the man's restraint. If he'd been in Nado's shoes, he'd have screamed for the police. But the immigrant's pillowy lips had stretched into an indulgent smile, making him look forty if he was a day,

"Is good we are met when we are met." Nado had been barely audible, too, what with the rattle of the street repairs' plastic sheeting.

Fabbrizio attempted to gather himself, figuring his best move was to play the stranger without a clue.

"If we are met before," the father went on, "I scream and scream. Rrn. Your pretty clothes, your pretty face, it falls to die."

Pretty? Die?

"Now, but now. I think you give comfort to my head, and I give to your head. No? Is the justice."

Fabbro craned his neck to peek around the man. Inside the office, the hole in the wall, the lawyer on duty wore a shirt of police blue.

"I give comfort to your head, no? And of you, me."

"Do you—" Fabbrizio couldn't say whether he was playing the stranger or not—"do you want something from me?"

"We give comfort to our heads, both of us. This way I heard, I learned, from the priest at the other."

Hardly three minutes later, Fabbrizio was offering the African a mango juice at the café he'd come to like best, in this ever more familiar 'hood. The Neapolitan suggested table service, rather than ordering from the counter. He could do no less, and never mind that before he spoke every word he had to flake off its lamina of bewilderment and legal questions. He could do no less because shame had hit him now, like a readjustment of the vertebrae. Now he recalled how he'd gone brainless with fear, simply at spotting this same workingman father outside la Greca's tomb. He knew the name of that fear now, all about skin. For shame, Brizio.

After the juice and coffee had arrived at Fabbrizio's table, he'd declared that he knew the priest that Nado was talking about. The on-and-off clandestino meant a knobby old Jesuit, something of a political firebrand, who made twice-weekly visits to a sanctuary at the edge of the historic center. Another St. Peter's, the church claimed an ancient kinship with refugees. It housed the stone on which the original Peter, fresh off the boat, had baptized the first Christians in Naples, and these days the church bordered the piazza in which Nado laid out his toys and his wife and remaining daughter set up their cart. In one of the rectory offices, every Tuesday and Friday afternoon, this priest offered advice for newcomers to Italy. His counsel tended towards liberation theology, not so by-the-book as at the little office in the black blocks; the seventy-something radical had gone so far as to provide the sacraments for a notorious immigrant-rights group who'd staged a hunger strike. Fabbrizio seemed to recall that Americans too had gotten involved in that case. He hadn't realized, before taking on this new job, how much his city offered its most recent arrivals. He would never have guessed that so many people were willing to lend a hand.

And when the father from Somalia had stopped into the rectory, the priest had been full of ideas. He'd suggested that for a family such as his, the best hope for staying on in Italy legally might be some additional special exemption. Their case thus far could be said to have set a precedent. Now if the N'mbor-lavà could perform some new service for the state, if they could for instance solve some crime...

Thus the logic behind Fabbrizio sneaking into to an American military facility: commit a new crime to atone for an older one. Of course he couldn't take the logic far. He couldn't look too hard at that word "atone."

But didn't breaking and entering here on the northern arc of the Bay's semi-circle offer a natural symmetry with breaking and entering down south in Paestum? He could feel the rightness of it, the straight arrow flying free of all doubts and manipulations in a final and spectacular arc that would take the prize for this entire bumpy month's carnival. Here on the American campus, on the gravel outside Printing & Publications, Fabbrizio could see the same mounting excitement in the face of his drop-in. Nado's enthusiasm for the risk he was taking shone clear as a bell. More often, to be sure, the flecks of gold in the man's eyes remained hard to assess, like sparks thrown off by an interior blacksmithing too whanging and brutal for a light-fingered artigiano. But here beneath the G.I. camellia bushes he had no trouble sensing the momentum that had carried the man so far north of town. When he'd spotted the father outside Printing & Publication, the man had been in the middle of a noble gesture, his most noble since he'd arrived in this country.

Though on second thought, the idea had Fabbrizio anxious again, glancing again towards the facility door (blank of course, useless to him). The last thing tonight's job needed was another freelancer.

"Now, listen, my friend." Soothing. "This necklace, listen, it's safe with me."

"Rrn. But truly?"

"Truly, Nado, the thing is safe. But first I must get it in hand. Then I give it to you, my friend, and you go to the police. You give it to the police, and after that the judge, he helps your family. Yes? But now, I say *right now*, you must go—"

"You say."

Nado's whisper had an edge, something more than the struggle for breath. Even in a squat, he loomed so big that Fabbrizio thought for a moment of Treno.

"You say you give me this," Nado continued. "You say, 'to help the family.' But you are here and the, the thing is here. The jewel. And I am not here."

Was Fabbrizio back up against the Black Hand? "Nado," he asked, "don't you trust me?" Again his gesturing toughened. "What is this fear?"

"I am not here, and I know you know how to steal. To steal this very jewel."

"What is this *fear*? Ma-don-na mia." Maybe this was what life was like as a father: trying to comprehend subtleties and then express them in words of one syllable. "Nado, do you truly believe I'm—I'm a monster?"

The man didn't quite shake his head. Rather what the Secondigliano saw was a shiver, involuntary, right through his visitor's chest and shoulders.

"Please, think a minute." Though for all Fabbrizio knew, they didn't have a minute. Shanti was no novice with digital cameras and e-mail attachments. "Think what will do good for your family."

"My family, what do you know? The pain, and the people who gave us the pain. What do you know?"

"Nado, not here, not now. Think, listen, please."

"I am thinking. In the piazza behind the church I am thinking. I think, now another time, I give my faith to a foreigner. And he knows how to steal."

"But, what, are you calling me stupid?" Fabbrizio struggled against the impulse to shout. "Are you saying, when I intend to take the piece for myself, I would go tell someone else?"

"Rrn. Who knows? You need a person to give to the police, maybe. Maybe. You send the police to my piazza."

"Oh, my friend, my frightened friend. Don't you think this business is already complicated enough?"

The African's gaze turned inward, glittering. He'd come to Aversa all revved up, yes, but he'd had more than one engine going.

"Nado, listen. Instead of this, o-kay." And Fabbrizio was frowning himself, seizing a new idea with both eager hands even while it was still barely hatched. "Suppose you go to my home, Nado? You go stay with my brother, my own mother, there in my home. If you stay in my home, think, it's you who can call the police. You can call them right to my home. Understand? While you are staying with my family I could never hurt you."

When the clandestino once more lifted a hand to his face, to his unsmiling parted lips, you couldn't help but notice those humped amber nails. Like small stones flung against a dark window, to wake a sleeping friend. Fabbrizio meantime fished his cell from one of his knee-level carpenter pockets.

"I'll call him, all right?" When he switched on the phone, he was relieved to find no fresh messages, nothing to distract him. "I'll call my brother, you talk to him yourself. And then, my friend, you *go.*"

Uldirico was the one to pick up, naturally. Before dinner Mama tended to lie down, again, and anyway why should she be bothered with the phone? More surprising was how Rico cut him off. Before Fabbrizio could begin to explain, while he was still clearing his throat, his brother jumped in with repeated exclamations about how glad he was that Brizo had called. They needed to talk!

"You know we've been in a crisis," Uldirico went on, "all of us in this house, in a terrible crisis."

He sounded livelier than he had in months, in fact, the stay-at-home sociologist. Fabbrizio, adjusting his behind-the-bushes squat, believed he knew what this was about. Rico was working up to an apology. Yesterday morning, after Fabbrizio's coffee and brioche but before his Mama's unsettling goodbye kisses, his older brother had, without so much as sitting up in bed, lashed out extraordinarily. Insults, accusations, vicious stuff. Brizio had only gone back into their bedroom to collect his Penates and billfold, before stopping in on their mother, and Uldirico—him with the Bohemian curls unwinding across the pillow—had laid into the second-born like never before. He packed a shocking punch, Rico, erupting with a blackheartedness he must've been mulling over for days. The zingers he came up with, he must've been searching the internet. Fabbrizio was left so burned and confused that since then he'd stayed away from the house. Last night, he'd crashed downtown at Monte Zu's. Why should he stay where, after he'd rolled his eyes and stalked out of the bedroom, his attacker had leapt up and followed him, still hissing and spitting? Could've been the earliest Rico had thrown off his covers since Mama got out of the hospital. The younger brother headed straight out, never mind his kiss, while grumbles of vituperation, the more intense for remaining barely above a whisper, echoed down the graffiti'd stairwell after him.

And Fabbrizio had recalled his own explosion, over his mother's sickbed, a couple of crowded weeks ago. At least he was past that kind of thing, himself. Tonight, who could say, he might even have anticipated Rico's urge to apologize.

"My brother, my brother, o-kay." He kept his voice low, his lips brushing the cell phone. "It's a good thing, truly, and we'll talk. But, for now, listen."

Eyeing the half-inch-open door behind him, keeping his voice low, he plunged into explanations. When at first he heard no response, Fabbrizio rushed on, suggesting his brother pick up the father at the Metro station ("the local busses can be confusing, no?"). He argued that to spend a few hours with this former clandestino, former and perhaps future too, would be useful for Rico. Put a human face on his studies.

"Ask him," he said in rapid half-dialect, so Nado wouldn't understand, "about what happened that last morning on the boat. What happened with his other child."

"Brizio," came the voice on other end of the line, "calm yourself."

As if selecting garlic rather than mushrooms, the brother asked to speak with the African. Rico figured he should introduce himself, if he was going to keep the man out of harm's way for two or three hours.

"You will…" The younger brother actually lowered the phone a moment, checking the screen, a brighter glow now as the evening deepened. Then: "You will keep him with you? *Sicuro*?"

"Well, yes. That's the word, isn't it? *Sicuro* is precisely the word, my brother. Tonight you call me because I alone, out of all the clever ones and the lucky ones in your life—I alone can promise to keep him *sicuro*."

"Ahh, you, alone..." Fabbrizio had to wonder if this was another insult. On the street people might think of the younger Dellaruba boy as the smart one, but when it came to wordplay, to talk rather than business, Uldirico was the sharper. Yesterday morning had hardly been the first example. Brizio had suffered similar bruisings—similar if lighter—during those political squabbles over *scopa*.

"Beh. Solidarity, comrade." The older of the two must've been asking himself the same, because at last he delivered a direct apology for his outburst. "We need to talk," he repeated, "so you can understand what's been going on with your Rico.

"But I'm sorry, Brizio. Truly. I didn't mean a word of it."

There: in plain Italian. Fabbrizio discovered his mouth had fallen open, slack, so that he was looking like a baby-brother tenderfoot at something like the worst possible moment. The only thing that could make it worse would be Shanti. Easy to imagine her at the door behind him, her own look more or less the opposite of his, flashing that playgirl anger. But the younger brother remained the *fortunato*, as the older leveled his voice again, briskly returning to the case before them. The clandestino.

"Put him on the phone, Brizio. If I need to make the man trust me when he can't even see my face, I'd better get to work."

Establishing trust was indeed the first order of business, based on what Fabbrizio heard. Nado needed the address, phone numbers, the name of the Metro stop. He turned out to be carrying a pen and notepad, a precaution they'd recommended at Legal Aide perhaps. Brizio pitched in at one point, suggesting a time limit of three hours. If in three hours he hadn't touched base one way or another, Nado should call the police. Sounded workable, and the way the father nodded over his watch looked encouraging. But when the *secondo* saw his home address jotted down, in the African's hacking scrawl, he was carried back into the sketchy family feeling around the apartment, over the last eight or nine days. With the clarity of digital photography, the trouble revealed itself as beginning far earlier. The way his mother was testing him now, every morning testing his beatification by NATO and the UN, was only the latest and steepest wave of the same difficulty as had kept him bobbing and pitching for a month now. Likewise the older brother hadn't gotten so tangled in his abstruse vocabulary as to lose all touch with the "fractals" and "valences" building throughout the rest of the apartment.

Like Mama, Rico had merely kept a game face, a family face. Yesterday morning he'd thrown his tantrum without a word of it reaching her. Or so he must've thought, knowing how the medication made her groggy.

But who could say how much their mother might be aware of, twelve days after she'd come home from the hospital (more than once, Fabbrizio had counted the squares x'd off on the calendar)? She didn't appear to stay on her feet longer than it took to make coffee, or to get from the bed to the table after one of the boys or a neighbor had made dinner. Certainly she hadn't gone to any of the sessions with the others in recovery, the group who gathered one evening a week in a nearby church. Yet she always arranged, somehow, for dinner to get made. Behind her closed bedroom door, whenever the physical therapist came to visit, Mama apparently gave that woman all she could handle. This according to the p.t. herself, the single time the younger son had managed to stop her and ask a few questions. A battleaxe with a vowel-grinding Polish accent, a woman who'd made a point of working her official worker's visa into her conversation, the therapist declared that his mother put in such a dedicated half-hour of exercise, the two of them barely had breath left to say the rosary afterwards.

Who could say just what Mama needed from him now? Who could handle the mounting waves and valences? When the time came for the mother's first trip out of the house, her first checkup at the office of the heart specialist, the younger brother had used his new job as an excuse to keep from going along. Caught up as he was between so many tugs and provocations, another face-to-face with that Mussolini in a smock seemed like a recipe for a blowup.

He needed to keep such shadows behind him, and just now especially. When Nado agreed to leave, to wait out the results of this break-in at Fabbrizio's home, the younger Secondigliano needed to come across a bit like Il Duce himself, nodding and frowning as if this were merely the smart move. As if his innards remained quiet, rather than leaping all over their bony cages for joy. To be sure, the big man's decision was great news, it meant he and Fabbrizio both would stay out of jail a few more hours at least—but only so long as the African hurried up and got *out of there*. Thus while Brizio listened to Nado arrange a meeting place within the Metro stop, he kept his interior bouncy-bounce out of sight, only straightening in his squat and reaching out to stroke the nearest camellia. His look remained neutral until, after the arrangements had been completed, Uldirico apparently brought up the recent treaty agreements in Somalia. Out of nowhere, Nado began talking about the warlords making peace.

"Is possible," the clandestino said, almost at conversational volume. "Now we see the future."

Fabbrizio allowed himself a show of irritation. Catching his visitor's eye, he put one index finger to his lips while, with the other, he pointed in what he believed was the direction of the gates.

"Is possible," Nado repeated more quietly. "We see a future, finally. Of this I speak more later."

And was there no end to tonight's unlikely impulses? No sooner were these last words out of the African's mouth than Fabbrizio found himself wishing he could hear more. For a moment he almost asked the family's tribe (if that were still the word for it, "tribe"), and whether the father had carried a gun in the recent civil wars. The man's face, its premature rumpling and creases, offered a fresh set of mysteries, all the more intriguing for the clues he'd dropped earlier, the glimpses of the fears that lay behind the jowls and worry lines. Not that Brizio wasted time with his brother, once Nado returned the phone. Also he kept things quick with his visitor, his barely familiar partner in crime; Fabbrizio opened his mouth to speak but instead, frowning again, lifted one wrist and pointed to his watch. He circled the Roman numerals of the face, once, twice, three times, then waggled that finger back and forth between the two of them, eyes wide. In response the African clamped a big hand over his shoulder. The way he squeezed Brizio, for a tick or three, it might've been a warning and might've been a gesture of support.

Then the stranger scuttled away—but not so fast that Fabbrizio could make it back inside, with the door shut behind him, before Shanti showed up.

"How do I know what he was doing here?" Fabbrizio didn't have to pretend he was on edge. "He must've been some type of gardener."

L'Americana was the one to shut the door. Afterwards she continued to lean against the one-way glass, angling for the best view. Nado, a law-abiding semi-citizen after all, had no reason to continue hiding behind the flowered hedge. Now he stood out on the lawn between facilities, looking left-right, getting his bearings.

"He's not one of soldiers," she said, "not with that gut. The haircut—"

"So, as I said, a gardener. They hire Africans here too."

When she faced him, he was relieved to see a smile developing, the lips apart. "But Fabbro, you, you found a need to open the door?"

Talking with the clandestino had left him more aware of the rare missteps in this woman's Italian. "Shanti, but think, suppose he had a key? Suppose he discovered me in here? What then, *bellissima?*"

The word had been a risk, but it worked. The New Yorker turned fully away from the door, and he noticed she seemed to be showing more skin.

"A man like myself"—he tugged at a shirt-button, showing her something—"prefers to take action. If the black's going to come in the door, it's better I step out and confront him, show him my white face. Understand?"

Had she undone an additional button, herself? He didn't recall the woman's Capris hanging so low either, revealing a finger-wide strip of designer underwear, *oro sommerso* again. And in her open purse he could see the necklace.

"Fab-bri-zio," she said. "But what a *cavaliere.*"

"I prefer to take action."

Was this more of the Greca's magic? Was it she who enabled her Neapolitan medium to slip so fast from spirit to spirit? A moment ago Fabbrizio had been hiding his face in terror at Shanti's arrival, and now he'd kindled up an old-fashioned machismo, he'd turned her head. "In fact the black never saw me. And anyway, my dear—I was growing bored."

What gave him the nerve? "Listen, is it Daphne, tonight? Daphne, my colleague, this might be my only visit to this—to an edifice such as this, so American. Must I really spend all my time in one little room?"

"O-kay, Fab-bro." He liked how her eyebrows cocked. "I suppose you and I could go upstairs for a few minutes."

Beh. Whatever might be up there, it wouldn't be the African.

"I myself," she went on, "was thinking of something you might find diverting, up in those offices."

Also Nado might run into delays at the security gates, another frisk, interrogation. The last thing Fabbrizio needed was to run into the father outside a Military Police kiosk. On the way up to the second floor of Printing & Publications, however, he had to wonder again about the company he was keeping here inside.

No matter how sweet a kick Shanti got out of black-market seduction (for wasn't that the way the numbers added up, now? the numbers they'd been playing down in the lobby?)—whatever the thrill she got from such smoky stuff, tonight the whiff of it had led her astray awfully quick. The Secondigliano had needed hardly half a minute to distract her, to change the subject, and this via the oldest trick in the book. Also he couldn't honestly believe that he'd gotten help from the oldest thing in her bag. When this woman had burst back in on him, out of the stairwell and into the little lobby for the side entrance, she'd looked excited already. "Fuckable," perhaps? Whatever; he hadn't much noticed at the time, with his foot still in the door and his wallet not yet back in his pocket. Now that Fabbrizio thought about it, however, l'Americana might well have nailed some sucker out in cyberspace and then hopped up from the keyboard looking to hammer that angry pleasure home in the flesh. She might well have, and so much for Sex Secrets of the Ancients. The magic wasn't the winking old craftwork in her purse, that bulky and unfashionable purse, but the glint of more recent and roughcut structures in her guts. A flicker he'd caught sight of a few times now, quartzlike, all about revenge.

She had her mysteries, this white girl as much as the black man earlier, more subtlety than Fabbrizio would've believed you found in people from the States. For the moment he had to leave off trying to understand her, his eyes dropping from the strip of off-gold underwear at her hipline to the real gold folded in her bag. Even at this distance, Fabbrizio could spot a detail or two he'd failed to get right in the imitation. Though his remained the best, among the dozens of copies out there by now.

Down in the black blocks, Fabbrizio had spotted more of the knockoffs every day. Generally the triple-decker bauble hung around the necks of African women, but some of the darker Balkans or Middle Easterners had taken to wearing it too. Full of sun, the ornament made a fine contrast to a dark and underfed neck. The other counterfeits however lacked Fabbrizio's talent—or his desperate concentration. Below the bottom rung of these imitations dangled all manner of inappropriate geegaws, from silver stars to slugs of onyx. The soldering would be quick and dirty, borax mostly, whatever these amateurs had on hand. Look closely at any half-dozen women wearing the copies, and you'd pick out the same number of variations on the original *falso*.

Yet careless as the workmanship might be, often the piece had him sending his respects back across the centuries, one *artigiano* to another. Of course the sight of it also set off waves of anxiety-static. The scrap of bronze in his pants grew agitated, and once or twice he thought he saw the necklace dripping blood. Nevertheless he had to give the old Greek journeyman credit. The man must've known that this was tomb jewelry, and that the single time anyone saw it, they'd be looking through tears. Still he'd put in his best effort, his most powerful geometry. You could pick out the harmony even in fakes of fakes. And you saw it out along a few of the commuter roads, where the women trying to drum up a bit of highway trade had been the first to start wearing the necklace. It had become part of the come-on.

Design issues, after all, hadn't meant much to Nerone and Treno. Rather, their intended buyer had made a disappointing offer—not that he saw through Fabbrizio's ruses, Hail Mary full of grace. If the fake hadn't been good enough to fool a dilettante, the Secondigliano would've heard about it. To put it mildly, he would've heard, and this when he hadn't wasted any time spending what the cammoristi had paid him. The heart specialist had no problem taking cash in advance.

Nerone and Treno however never came back to Fabbrizio about his technique. Not that he hadn't suffered two or three days of spine-scraping apprehension, in the black blocks and the tent cities, days of bad static and bleeding metal. But in time, Hail Mary, he'd come to understand the mistake his previous employers had made. They'd neglected basic market research. The high costs of production, in this sector, affected profitability, and so to make a decent Euro in counterfeits, you couldn't deal in single items; you needed volume. Fabbrizio even recalled hearing something to that effect during his days at the university. His favorite professor, the live wire with the Post-It notes, had spoken of a royal burial chamber stocked entirely with forgeries. Fakes by the dozen, that was the only way to make real money. So the thugs from Salerno had declined the initial offer, anticipating a better opportunity via another subsidiary. They found a shop willing to turn out knockoffs, people who weren't so finicky as their original contractor, and they asked a percentage on, eh, the first thirty items sold. Also they had a readymade market, buyers who couldn't refuse: the girls who worked the roadsides. Then somebody along the line, maybe one of the prostitutes themselves, noticed how good the necklace looked on the Africans. Some girlfriend had smiled, some John had paid a few extra Euros, and with that the fad was underway. Too fertile even for the Cammora's scattered poisons. Nerone and Treno couldn't complain, anyway, not with their initial kickback. Business picked up out on the roadways, too, with no need to buy new tents or mattresses.

The Secondigliano, just doing his job, had questioned a few of the women who wore the necklace. Prostitutes of course worked a different end of the market from the people in contraband antiquities, but nonetheless he'd learned a thing or two about smuggling. He'd come up with a line of talk good enough to mislead the wheeler-dealer who'd brought him here, the lovely delinquent leading him up the stairs of Printing & Publication.

Thus, the overwrought tapestry of his last week-plus: playing this stranger while she was playing him, in a struggle to convince his battered loved ones that he wouldn't ever play again. Now—what was this further madness?

She'd climbed a step or so above him, her butt falling into something of a sashay, two balls of mozzarella in snug Capri-sacks. Fabbrizio tried again to understand. A type like Shanti was use-and-discard, at this moment in her life at least, and so nothing might seem more fascinating to her than a young man like himself, in one way or another the product of a local history that went back three thousand years. History after all had been the source for her original scam, the ritual to raise the Goddess. But to think of the woman this way felt like a flimsy insight, a fragment, not much use considering what he was getting into. Meanwhile they reached the second floor, and from this angle the sun bulged so fatly over the horizon it appeared to be stuck. Shanti led him to the end of a corridor speckled by that immobilized light, its windows shaded by high-tech roll-down screens. Was this glass too one-way? And did this woman really believe no one would bother with them, no one would notice, as she used her lover's husband's key-card on the broad office door at the end of the hall?

"A little something," she said. "I thought you'd find it diverting."

That last line came across with a hint of melody. Fabbrizio understood where she'd brought him, the facility headquarters. A space fit for a colonel with a trophy wife, its own broad windows filling both corner walls.

Shanti lingered back by the door, punching a code into the buttons above the latch. The Neapolitan found himself drawn to the view. The gilded Tyrhennian and the sun above it could be taken in directly from this height, behind the faintly green effect of the tinting and screening, and another notion came to him, less anxious, the idea that so long as he was here he might as well enjoy it. Along the way to the windows he gave a stroke to one of the recliner-chairs, taking pleasure in the give of the leather, its chuckling squeak. Across from those sat a desk as fat and ostentatious as the Mafia yachts you saw off Ischia or Amalfi. On the only wall without a door or a window, there hung a baroque crucifix, all design and no Christ, gussied up further by twinned silky scarves of purple and white. Fabbrizio had no idea what the scarves were about. Yet after a sighing stop by the window, he realized he knew these interiors. Swank yet hardly out of this world, they were only more set design, the cushy and antiseptic stuff of high-end catalogues. And while the Secondigliano might have struck a pose or two earlier, down by the side entrance, the show now belonged to the Americans. To one in particular. Up here was a good scene for the bad girl, set on a trespassers' stage.

Fabbrizio could watch her movie starting up, in reflection. L'Americana had finished with the lock-box, which no doubt meant that, even if the MP's checked the building, they wouldn't come in the office. And now through the thread-thin screen played the shadow-

and-white of Shanti changing costumes. Perhaps instead he heard it, the rustle of summer silk, the rattle of gold and stone.

How often had he told himself, concerning this woman, that he should've known? This time he'd known. He still couldn't say exactly what good he might do her, among the desk and chairs; he couldn't say whether this was payback or party or exploration, maybe all three in a single wrapping. But he'd known for some time that she'd intended to wrangle it out of him, whatever betterment fucking might bring. Uneasy, Fabbrizio shifted his focus away from her fluttering shape on the window. He wondered a moment about security cameras—about, say, infra-red long-range spy-scopes—and yet soon wound up meditating again, almost happily, on the view. When you saw the compound from helicopter height, like this, the very symmetry that had earlier seemed so loony and dispiriting now delivered stroke after stroke of visual satisfaction. He might've been looking over the necklace. The community's design seemed to carry a comparable promise of eternity, an assurance that the gods and alliances which ruled these quadrilaterals would sit in power forever. A false assurance to be sure, but he fell for it a moment. Meanwhile out over the sea, there remained the intractable Naples sun, and under it nothing glared so harshly as the security checkpoint. The gate and kiosk made a white steel hot-spot.

Still Fabbrizio couldn't say he'd been forced to put off his getaway. He couldn't claim he was a victim, a Best Boy in someone else's movie, now when he took such pride in the considerable compliment of holding the woman's interest. She'd been spooning him sweet talk longer than she'd had her latest name, and in the process she'd fed his own fantasy, no denying. He'd never stopped wanting this, a roll in ripe American hay. He'd never found the transatlantic shape-shifter behind him less than spellbinding. Inside his pants now, his loose-fit business with the extra pockets, the twitching and stirring had nothing to do with any pockmarked bronze stick-figure. He was only 24, after all. He was too young to toss away one promising night after another in fretting over mothers and brothers and making things right.

"Fab-bri-zi-o."

A wrinkle of anger at that—it seemed like no one could say his name at full speed any more. And did it always have to sound, even at this breathless low volume, like something so venal?

"Don't worry, *ragazzo*." Her smile revealed her tongue. "New York is never going to call us here."

Talk about venal, here was the Bad Girl, doing her level best to live up to the title. Shanti presented herself propped on dark-tanned elbows against the bone-white heavyweight paper of the desk blotter. With her butt on the desk's mahogany edge and her parted legs dangling, her pussy sat front and center, bulging up beneath the *oro sommerso* in a way that made it obvious she trimmed her hair. Also she'd slipped back on her jungle-colored sandals. Over the soft swell of her breasts lay the green-gold gravel-texture of the necklace.

"Last time," she told him, "that was a shame. But New York doesn't even have this number."

He could've predicted this, a page from a skin magazine, in an opulent room itself practically airbrushed. But so what? One good eyeful and Shanti or whoever she was overwhelmed every picture in his head. The necklace no longer looked a thing like the NATO compound. The spies' infra-red, as for that, burned in her narrowed gaze, her tongue between her teeth, her greedy thrust-up centerpiece. She didn't need to say anything about the lock on the door, either, or about her interior tubes and eggs. Fabbrizio understood all that in his groin, in its pleasure and undertow, alive in a way nothing like his Penates—and yet these same skin-full moments took him once more, strangely, towards the supernatural. While he was fucking he seemed also to bristle with awareness, he picked up a dozen impressions at a time as he went at the woman, herself gulping and shuddering through an array of tender complications. Certainly their flailing around the room was a matter beneath the brain, all nerve-endings and bodywork. His cock seemed to come out of his briefs and bob as if the muscle itself needed to see this woman yank off the final pale covering for her crotch, and then later, inside her, he jerked and trembled and yet stayed erect right through the end of his first climax, just to see the new shape of her smile, a sideways bite while she sprawled back against the white desk-blotter. One brown arm flicked convulsively at the changing pressure on her clit, and she knocked away a small globe. Yet at the same time his thinking remained engaged and, what's more, expanding. Fabbrizio knew that this globe was an award of some kind, a recognition of good management, and to topple it off the desk excited this woman. To her it was another case of getting even: take that! Likewise the lippy orgasmic bite she took out of the air: tearing a chunk from a defeated enemy. Then some unknown minutes later, after he'd carried her on his reconstructing cock over to one of the recliner chairs, after she was jamming and wriggling on top of him so the clatter of the necklace matched the shrieking of the leather, the insight came round to Fabbrizio himself. He felt suddenly like the world's original grave-robber. What was he if not a grave-robber, when each time he heaved himself up to suck at Shanti's nipples, the Greca's beads and gold-work slapped against the bone behind his eyebrows, and each time he fell back the bottom row of ornaments bounced off the American's slickened flesh? Between the two, indeed, he was the first *tombarolo* ever, taking from skeletons to reinvigorate skin. He was the man who invented desecration and yet, in the same act, invested his day-to-day grind with a kind of ecstasy, the wallop of the original and the inescapable, both.

And, bristling, Fabbrizio also hit on an idea for getting back the necklace. Shanti quivered and went for another peak, and he fell back into the recliner reaching his own, and in there somewhere he figured out how to get it away from her. The play had to start right here in this room.

They finished in the chair, with her on top. Recovering herself, murmuring some satisfied English he didn't recognize, she bent to kiss him. She scooped a last taste into her jar of a mouth. Finally Shanti propped herself at arm's length above him, one of the necklace's caged chunks of amber dangling to tickle his nose. She braced her hands around his throat.

<hr />

"Down in my pants," he said. "We'll keep it down there till we're outside the gate again."

Pausing over a shirt-button, Shanti gave him the smile he'd come to understand better. "*Bello*, I don't see how it would fit."

No point hiding his own smile. This made the third time the woman had mentioned his size, something he'd never heard before, dilatory as he'd been about pursuing a sex life. Not that he believed her, entirely. Under the sugar he could taste the vinegar, the story she was going to make of him one day, a jab to unsettle some future lover.

This young Italian stud horse, you have no idea. Then too, weren't such compliments a way of keeping him in line? A reminder, friendly and chilly at once, that Fabbrizio shouldn't imagine anything more than skin-deep had gone on here. Still he smiled, better a good review than some other kind of static, when what needed to remain uppermost in mind was the plan for the necklace. Now he showed her how low his pants could hang, given the narrowness of his hips.

"Like a rap star," he tried to joke. "And these Americans, at the kiosk they'd never…"

"Fabbro, don't forget I'm American." She didn't merely point to herself, she pressed her fingers against one breast. "I might put my own hands down in there. I might even do it while the guard is watching."

In another moment she'd let go her shirt, stepped close, and jammed one hand into his open fly.

"Wouldn't you like that, Fabbro? Wouldn't you like it if I kept hold of your big cock while the soldiers are watching?"

Which left him standing like a dummy, holding his pants open for her. This pseudo-Shanti, a woman you couldn't begin to understand until you'd seen her in full warrior-princess nakedness. If you wanted further comprehension you needed to hang in through further outlawry, and so he did his best to play along. He tossed off a throaty laugh. Then as Shanti cuddled his meat, crooking her pinkie to stroke it, his mind's eye filled first with flashes of another round, sweaty and bucking, and then unexpectedly with a look into her future. Fabbrizio could see how in years to come, this playgirl was going to tickle her husband this way—her husband, yes, a man who would know her actual name. Didn't a razor-dance like hers always end with a soft backwards tumble into the lap of bourgeois comfort? If you plucked your most glittery gems of self via a risky and close-up betrayal of the square life, didn't you eventually begin to appreciate the stolid framing that made those bright things seem so valuable? And so over time tuck yourself into the box? Shanti's wild past would become by itself all the excitement she needed, precisely because she would live surrounded by well-kept appliances in a foursquare home. She'd remember a night like tonight with a tingle below the hipline, and get still more out of that tingle because she could nurse it in happy secret, out at a dining-room table full of folks she would describe as "perfectly nice."

Fabbrizio had once believed that his on-and-off accomplice was past thirty, a woman of the world. Tonight, in a down-to-earth byproduct of their outer-planets intensity, he'd learned she was young yet.

"*Bello*, think of the, the jealous, you'll give them. Think of the jealous those soldiers will feel."

She was just another girl on the periphery.

"Listen," Fabbrizio said. "I'm anxious, understand? This is a strange place for me, and we've been here a long time."

"Ahh, not that long, judging by what I feel."

True enough. He was unwrinkling down there, moved again by her unwashed closeness and the new familiarity of her grasp.

"Let's not go crazy," he told her. "Look how it's getting late. If you can tear your eyes from me, signorina, you'll see it's sundown."

"But you said midnight, didn't you?"

True again; it had seemed a nice round time for a bogus appointment. Now it wouldn't have been hard to dream up a new kink or two in his story, but with the girls he knew, what worked best was flattery. "Listen, you know I'm your puppy, you beautiful creature. You know you hold me like a puppy on a leash."

There was the smile again.

"But truly, Shanti, I'm a frightened puppy."

"Fabbrizio. Didn't I tell you I know, I know when the police come around?"

"Yes, you know. You know so much more than me, I understand well. But, please. Give me the necklace."

"*Per carita*. Don't you realize, if anyone were going to search my bag, they would do it when I came in?"

"Give me the necklace. I'll put it in my pants."

"When a person's coming in, Fabbro. Coming into the compound. That's when they have reason to worry."

"But, just give it to me. Please, Shanti, the necklace. Let me have it…"

Her hand came out of his fly and the words died on his tongue. His cock shrank and his gestures collapsed. The way the woman's look narrowed, in the grated shreds of late sunshine, suggested Nerone in the basement.

He worked on his own smile. "You beautiful creature…"

But already she'd backed off, pulling her shirt together. She'd started the interrogation, and the look that preceded each question was like the point of a spade. Fabbrizio, why would you insist on holding it? You know whoever's holding it—you know how it would look if the police should discover it—so why would you insist?

The Secondigliano found himself stuck in place again, shirtless and unzipped. Over one of the woman's shoulders hung the crucifix, with its out-of-place scarves. And behind her narrowed eyes there might remain those qualities he'd figured out earlier, here in her bad-girl's retreat, but he'd forgotten a more fundamental issue, namely, how smart she was. Already Shanti had turned their intimacy around. *Tesoro mio*, she was asking, how can you tell me you're frightened about one thing and not about the other, especially when this other carries the more serious danger? Doesn't that sound strange? And besides, *amore*, isn't the one who's holding a piece like this, isn't that person usually the one to sell it?

"In English," she told him, "they say 'possession is nine-tenths of the law.'"

She dropped her eyes, her cutting edge, in order to tug her Capris into place. Fabbrizio noticed she was doing without underpants, then recalled those had gotten ripped away somewhere between the desktop and the floor. Whatever he'd just accomplished with this woman—insight, desecration, thrills—it'd been ferocious, taken to the quick. He worked up a hollow laugh and replied that the two of them could hardly be concerned about the *law*.

She was staring again. "All right Fabbro, let's talk about our business. In our business, possession is everything." She undid the necklace and then cradled the piece in both hands before her, making an ancient, brilliant drapery. She went back to the original question. Why did Fabbrizio want to hold it?

"Because, because I'm frightened." Madonn', he sounded pathetic.

"But, really? This man of Secondigliano, him with the *cazzo grande*, is he really such a helpless puppy?"

He got his pants zipped, he reached for his own shirt. Putting the anger in elbows and wrists.

"My own helpless little puppy on a leash?"

But with his pants done up, wasn't he one step further from getting the necklace? What about... "But," he almost shouted, "how can you talk to me this way?"

"You don't have a smuggler." Gently she looped the necklace back into her purse. "You have a *buyer.*"

"A—*buyer.*" In English the sarcasm took more effort. "You, New York, you think you're so smart."

"Smart." Flatmouthed, she shook her head. "Fabbro, I'll tell you the truth, I blame myself. I was so eager, when you told me. A dick of an eager little girl."

"You, you think you know a man like me. Silly American. *Fesso.*"

Shanti nudged the purse behind her and, propped against the still-disorderly desk, crossed her arms and ankles. "Shit," she said, in English, and then something he couldn't understand. After that, with a sour renewal of her smile, she switched back to Italian, or mostly Italian: "I thought I was all through with that Iowa girl, so eager to please."

He gave the air a disgusted chop. "But what are you talking about? What are you thinking? You think this is about *you?*"

She stiffened in her lean, her elbows coming up. Fabbrizio recognized the pose, and yet this only left him more unsettled. When his mother and Babbo had argued, she used to angle back against the kitchen table the same way.

More unsettled: "Are you saying this is *therapy?* This is all about Shanti, or whoever you are, the girl from I-o-wa? Oh sure, it's therapy, all of it. You need to get in touch with your pain, so you work with the Secondigliano, and—"

"Keep your hands down, Fabbrizio."

"But of course, I understand, you were the girl from the farm! And you went to San Francisco, a big city, a place with drugs and gays. And ever since, even here six thousand miles away, you must take revenge for some ugly moment—"

"*Bello,* to call the Military Police, it's one button on the phone."

"Then I'm right." He jerked his chin. "If you're talking about the police, I must have you right, a little girl who was betrayed. The Americans, when anyone gets too close, they call in the Marines."

Fabbrizio surprised himself with that one, a zinger more in Uldirico's line. He was full of surprises; he had to shut his mouth. The woman took in the silence for a long moment, then allowed herself a slow blink, so he noticed how her eye shadow had smeared. Eventually she undid her smile with a sigh. "All right, Fabbrizio. I never denied that you were smart."

She still had her elbows up, though. The way she checked the desktop behind her looked like military business, a reconnaissance.

"Tonight, imagine—*I fucked Freud*." The English could've been a battlefield order. "But doctor, esteemed doctor, listen. A truly smart man, at this moment he'd be thinking about the police and how this will look."

Why'd she have to squint like that? As if the insights that in him had taken up acres and acres of brain space to her were a cluster of gnats to be brushed aside?

"Yes, and what a fairy tale you'd have for them! What a lie!" Now both his hands were in the air. His voice rang in the sundown-speckled screens.

"Fabbrizio, calm yourself."

"A lie, *another goddamn lie*! Whenever you Americans leave your own country, you talk nothing but lies."

"But, what is this? You sound like a relic. A ghost from the 1960s."

He smacked the knuckles of one hand into the palm of another. "You talk to Italians, you lie." Smack again, louder. "And the worst is when you talk to *Africans*."

At least Shanti no longer resembled his mother. Fabbrizio might've carried on in front of Mama the same way, with the same kind of bellowing, but back at the Camaldoli hospital his mother could never have leapt from her bed and zipped around like a gymnast. Here the con-girl pulled off a kind of half-flip, swinging up and over the colonel's desk with no more than a squeak and a rustle, hardly budging the blotter out of place. For a moment she might've been a skin-and-bone modern dancer. Of course she'd shown him similar acrobatics back when he'd had his cock (large, medium, small?) inside her; of course he suffered the muscle memory now, a prickling in his lower back. And after Shanti had gotten the hefty piece of furniture between the two of them, she lay one hand over the phone's keypad while with the other she dug in her purse. When she came up with a switchblade, when she snapped the thing open, Fabbrizio stopped thinking of his mother. The fitting recollection was Nerone, rather: his showy American-Fifties weapon, pearl-handed.

"One button, *ragazzo*."

Her voice was matter-of-fact, though she pulled a movie-stunt with the blade, turning the thing and making it glint. "And if you come near me, I'll go straight for that precious business down in your pants."

Fabbrizio, over the last two or three days, had managed to hold off recollections of the night watchman's murder. He'd occupied his thinking with the new job, the N'mbor-lavà, the argument with his older brother. Now however he stood watching a knife about the same size throw wedges of light around another square space with a single exit. The air conditioning in here kept the room as cool as a basement. Again Torio's last few minutes alive and their encouragement to get out of this runaround once and for all came down full weight on Fabbrizio, even seeming to hamper his deliberate inhale and exhale. When he spoke, he heard himself echoing the slaughtered rent-a-cop.

"But what do you need of me?" A murmur. "You have the world under your finger, there."

The American kept her hands where they were, but her gaze might've softened.

"What, what did you ever need of me?"

"Fabbrizio. Don't try to play the innocent."

"People have died, you know. To you this is just another touch of the button, it's a game. But people have been killed."

"Oh, the poor innocent. Oh, with his tales of the murdering Siren, 'people have been killed.' Fabbro, what are these lies you're trying to tell me?"

"Shanti, what I want is *no more* lies. No more of this sickness."

"*Per carita.*" Her knife-hand had relaxed enough for him to see that it had a handle of mere hardshell plastic, nothing so fancy as the gangster's. "What is it, Padre?"

He bowed his head and touched his Penates, gathering his strength. If he was going to tell the truth about the Somali family, he owed it to them not to cry.

Shanti didn't seem to be getting it. Fabbrizio had been trying to sell her on his conversion for a few minutes now: the beauty of these N'mbor-lavà, the irresistible good of giving them the necklace. He'd come clean even about his innocence, if you could call it innocence, if such a state of being had ever existed for the likes of him. In any case he'd admitted that the Paestum break-in was the worst crime he'd ever committed, a felony far more serious than whipping up a counterfeit antique or two (especially when, in the latest case, the work wasn't sold as antique). The American had listened respectfully enough. She'd settled into the executive chair, another technophile piece, its woven-mesh design in a shape that suggested a butterfly. But she twiddled her dangling knife-hand so the blade batted against the soft plastic of the armrest. The other hand remained just a twitch away from the phone, and her smile had lost its variable depths. Fabbrizio still suffered the occasional glancing strike of anger—wasn't the whole situation an embarrassment?—but he was through with histrionics. He couldn't sit, yet, but he reined in his gesturing and kept his voice at café level.

The sun meantime slipped below the humpbacked crest of the PX moviehouse. Fabbrizio was actually going to turn on a lamp until Shanti raised the knife and waved him off. He tappped his forehead with a fingertip, *che stupido*, and decided to get into the high drama.

"This father," he said, "what a man he is. You know when they left Africa, they had two daughters."

The family had caught a ride to Italy on one of those boats you read about, its pilot a Moroccan with veiny eyes and a snubnosed shotgun. The former fishing craft, badly overloaded, had slogged through the springtime chop for two or three days—Fabbrizio still wasn't certain of the details, given Nado's slapdash Italian. It sounded as if fresh water had been limited to a single morning cupful for each passenger, and as if, on the first night, a man had died. A man not much older than Nado himself, it sounded like, and the father had been the one to try CPR on the poor guy, or as much CPR as he'd picked up second- or third-hand. But the crew had come prepared for this eventuality; they'd packed an extra length of heavy chain. The smugglers also had something ready in case the Coast Guard caught up with them.

The captain might've been a hashish freak, but he'd known enough to avoid the usual Italian drop-spots, the bootheel and the instep. Nonetheless, on what should've been the last morning at sea, indeed with the hills of the Cilento in sight, the boat was spotted by a *Guardia* coastal sweeper. The captain first took up his cell phone, right there in front of everyone, asking his contacts ashore if they couldn't buy his pursuers off. But then the Guard's hydrofoil went up on its risers. They switched on their forward speaker and started bellowing orders. With that the captain went for his shotgun and told the crew to grab the nearest children.

"Think of this father," Fabbrizio said. "Think of how far he brought his family. Then he had to see his daughter thrown overboard."

Throwing the kids in the water had become standard practice, when a smuggler found himself under pursuit. The Guardia had to play the good guys. They had to downshift and go for the life preservers, while the crooks got a chance to run off. Fabbrizio had seen something on the news about it, stories that made him wince and shout at the TV. In fact he'd needed to recall those stories, when Nado's recollection of that morning off the coast had broken down into tears. The man had cried with the gut-wrenching lack of control you saw in older Italians, like something out of those brutal black-and-white movies from after the last war. It sounded as if the girl had hit the water in the middle of a scream, without getting a breath.

Likewise the father's growls of murderous satisfaction came across as more animal than human, as he tried to describe his attack on the captain. If the Secondigliano hadn't had the stories from the news to fall back on, he would hardly have gotten the picture at all. As it was he knew only that the Somali mother had followed her first daughter overboard, while the father had taken advantage of a mass abandon-ship. Perhaps the crooks had ordered everyone off, or perhaps the crowd on board had panicked at seeing the shoreline so close. Meantime Nado somehow made weapons of his shoes; Fabbrizio couldn't help but think of Torio and his duffel bag.

"Think of this father," Fabbrizio repeated. "Think of the tragedy and the nightmares he—"

"Enough," Shanti said. "I understand."

Eyeing her, he thought: I was just getting to the *point*.

"I've heard enough, Fabbrizio. But, truly. So this man got the shotgun, killed the captain, and then escaped the police by swimming ashore."

"He didn't even need the shotgun, I don't think. It was a tremendous thing. He took the other man down with his own…"

This time she didn't need to say anything. L'Americana only gave a long exhale, long and weary, and with that Fabbrizio bit his tongue. At some point he'd fished out his Penates, and now he let that hand drop, closing it around the figure.

"Look at it my way," she went on finally. "A month ago I met a young *settebello* who would do anything for a fuck."

He tried to find the most comfortable setting for the poky statuette.

"But now that man's turned into some kind of, of idealist. Fabbro, you think you can speak for this clandestino?"

"He's not a clandestino. He has a chance, tonight, a better opportunity."

"Tonight the man isn't even here, Fabbrizio. Oh, this father, you keep saying. Oh, what a man! But look around, he's not here. He's a ghost in this room and a ghost in this country."

"I believe I know him, or let's say, I know enough. I found a connection." Fabbrizio touched the god-hand to his chest.

Shanti, allowing herself a fraction of a smirk, heaved another chesty sigh. As recently as half an hour ago, just to see her cleavage rise and fall like that would've cleared every other thought from his head.

Outside the streetlamps were coming on. American brightness, blue-tinged halogens on gray steel stalks.

"Fabbro, think what you intend with this African. Truly, think, how well do you know him? Have you spent even, even half an hour talking with him, by now?"

Unable to answer, once more he was drawn to the window, the possibility of some clarifying reflection. But the woman behind the desk stopped him after the first step; she warned him against throwing a shadow across the glass. Then Shanti was looking matter of fact, folding her knife shut and slipping it back into her fat purse, while her tone of voice shifted to a schoolteacher's. "You've known him so little, and even so you've told him enough to spoil everything."

A schoolteacher giving a lecture. But Fabbrizio noticed again how young she was, this desk-jumper, swinging the chair sideways in order to stretch her legs.

"You've told him," she said, "way too much."

This he didn't need to hear. Granted, the woman had knocked him back a bit with what she'd said about Nado, reminding him how much the man remained in shadow. But these latest complaints were old business. Of course Fabbrizio had ruined the last frail possibility of a New York deal. He'd pulled the plug on her arrangements as soon as he'd told the father about the missing graveyard goods, day before yesterday, back in the shadow of the church beside which the African sold his toys. The Secondigliano had known what he was doing, too, wrecking a plan that had stretched back who knows how long before she'd turned up in that sketchy Salerno coffee bar. Yet the day before yesterday, over the African's whistles and dancing birds, Fabbrizio had perched a restless foot on a milk-crate and gone into as much detail as he could.

By tonight, the witch was dead. Dead, even if she returned the favor somehow, if she transformed herself magically into Nerone, cut Fabbrizio's throat, and buried him under high-potency NATO lime (just a thought…). Too late, the damage was done, a wild hair set loose among the tight cornrows of her transatlantic setup. And now that she'd gotten the picture too, now that they each understood the other better, he'd give her a break for the rest of the evening. Fabbrizio backed away from the office windows and sank without a word onto the extended foot of a recliner. The leather still carried the odors of sex, but never mind; it was time to fold his sleeve back up over the heart he'd wearing on it. There'd been enough of that, just as Shanti had said.

She was returning to her purse, tugging out the necklace. As she extended it towards Fabbrizio, over the crisp white blotter, he tucked away his spiky figurine.

"But look," she said. "Look how the American Empire is fallen."

He shifted on the leather, its moist squeak making him wonder if he was picking up anything on his pants. He couldn't take the jewelry, not yet. To see it hanging from her hand, its bottom semi-circle of caged amber splayed against the blotter's heavyweight bond, you would think the piece was already in a museum where it belonged. Nonetheless

Fabbrizio was made uneasy by her continuing claim that he'd "won," somehow. In the old painting and sculpture he'd studied, whenever some vainglorious mortal believed he'd won, it was only a matter of moments before the gods whopped him back down into the worst slum in the afterlife.

"I always thought you were pretty as the David," she told him. "Now look how you brought down Goliath."

The American declared she didn't need this trouble, a calming thought, one that set him nodding. Never mind the gods—around Naples there were plenty of mortals who packed a mean lightning bolt. The last thing she wanted, no matter what passport might be in her purse, was to have the wrong people catch her holding the goods. The black-market yellow and green.

He did see one problem, though. "Also, your friends, over in New York?" Fabbrizio asked. "After what you told them in the e-mail?"

"Fabbro, and now you are a detective? You don't know what I told them."

Couldn't he follow her logic even when it came to this kind of thing? "You were down there so long…"

"I will—" she broke into one of those multi-level smiles—"I will confirm that I took pictures. I am in possession of a zip drive."

Fabbrizio had the necklace by now, spread carefully across his lap between both hands. But he was frowning again.

"You know, *raggazo*, I could write to New York from up here." Playfully she swept her fingers across the narrow screen of the desktop computer, a gesture that recalled their earlier desktop groaning and flailing, all the more outlandish when you looked again at the expensive machinery sharing the same space.

"You understand," she went on. "But surely you understand, my dear doctor Fabbrizio Freud. I was thinking, first Secondigliano, then New York."

He managed another airless laugh. "Still, there had to be something else, down there. Why go through all this just to take some photos?"

"Beh, enough. Even lovers have their secrets."

Lovers? To hear her say the word triggered a more genuine laugh, and after that Fabbrizio took a quiet moment to assess the gold and amber in his lap. The piece hadn't been made for folding, not with such delicate joints. When he'd said he could pack it into his pants, he'd been trying to sell the woman a line of talk.

"Listen, Shanti…"

"Oh, don't call me that any more. You might as well know, my name is Nuncia. From Annunciata."

His head came up. Her eyes were the color of an espresso after the first few sips, the foam drunk off. "You're… Italian?"

"*Sicuro.*"

Now the fear. Strange: his evening had already put him at risk a dozen ways, out squatting under the camellias and up splayed across the colonel's desk. But only now did his nerve-ends start banging their alarm bells. As Fabbrizio first got out of this extravagant headquarters for Printing & Publications and later smiled his way past the security kiosk at the base exit, then next as he made a quick stop at the Secondigliano Metro station for… was it Nuncia, really?… through all that, he was at last racked by a dread which, come to think of it, should've have been cramping his style from the time he and l'Americana had first climbed onto his Suzuki. He should've been far too frightened, number one, to put up back-to-back erections.

How could he have failed to keep his pants on? His plan for tonight had been a hellacious ropewalk, and he'd almost had the African up and teetering beside him. Yet it was only now that fear began to burden him, to shrink him.

He and l'Americana took more time than he would've believed necessary just working out a way to put the necklace in his pants. Tonight in fact—and getting his brain around this idea also took improbably long—he made his first close-up assessment of the piece. Back when Shanti Annunciata had made away with the jewels, a month ago or nearly, he'd never gotten to weigh it like this. He'd never had the chance to feel out the hookups within its balance of glint and polish, to test their barbed or scratchy spots. Finally, after long minutes drawing the necklace over first one spread hand and then the other, Fabbrizio wondered aloud if he couldn't wrap it somehow. At that the woman had pointed out the purple and white drapery hung round the crucifix. In fact these proved perfect for the job, two wide head-scarves or bandannas, the material a durable synthetic. As soon as he pulled the soft package together, he lost any misgivings about using cloth that was more or less sanctified.

By then he'd grown aware of his rising chills. Nonetheless this shrine he'd disturbed was nothing to worry about, only some screwball American hoodoo. The colonel had gotten the colors wrong, hanging the purple and white of Easter when tonight was almost July. Though Fabbrizio liked the effect once he got the interacting pale and dark wrapped around the necklace. The overlap put some six or seven different colors in play, as he turned the package over, trying to guess which way might fit best. Nuncia meantime had come up with duct tape, and there was nothing sexy about the way she eyeballed his crotch and thighs.

But then she cocked an ear and raised a stiff finger. Visitors. Bootsteps.

In another minute she was hugging him tight, again with nothing sexy about it, no matter how her curves swelled against him. Rather this was about keeping his shivers under control, the spastic fit that had him all but dropping the wrapped-up necklace, as the Military Police paused outside the door and ran a few numbers through the lock-box. There the cops found whatever they were looking for, naturally. Fabbrizio's partner in crime had known what she was doing when she'd punched her own code into the keypad on this side of the door. The soldiers (there seemed to be two) exchanged some sort of significant grunt, and in another moment the clomp of their unsummery footwear dwindled away down the corridor.

The embrace lingered with Fabbrizio, a benchmark in his gathering dread, the woman's spread hands across his goosebumps providing a carpenter's measure. It let him know what he had to deal with—for instance when, fifteen minutes later, he got a grip on the bike's accelerator. Flex the fingers, Brizio; loosen up. Likewise, after that embrace, keeping a close an eye on himself mattered more than anything he sensed in the woman who hugged him. Naturally, while the men with guns stood outside the office door, this Nuncia-for-now took a renewed thrill in veering so close to disaster. A familiar buzz: *Right under your noses, assholes.* With that Fabbrizio might even have achieved a larger perspective on her point-scoring, a glimpse of its place along the continuum of a growing girl's spirit. But tonight was no longer about New York. From now on he had to conserve his moth-eaten good judgment, as he took matters towards a final stop that didn't lie along the *Tangenziale*, a workshop where he could both sweep the scrap from his conscience and resolder his family.

He and Annunciata made their goodbyes outside the farther Secondigliano station. The closest stop, as you came south from Aversa. While he geared the Suzuki down, on the city streets, he spotted a pair of his friends from the block. Their eyes followed him past, him and the hot number with her hands linked over his belt-buckle.

Look at that *fortunato*.

During the ride, however, he'd paid more attention to how the necklace hugged him. Before he and the American left P&P headquarters they'd found a remarkable fit, and out at the security kiosk, once she took off her helmet and flashed a smile the guards allowed them to sign out without so much as single followup question. You had to admire a person for that. On the highway, more good news, the duct tape held snugly. One corner of the bundle pressed against his cell, down in one of his lower pockets; good thing he'd left the gadget switched off since he'd made the arrangements with Uldirico. Then with the arrival at the Metro stop came another trial—he needed to step off the bike. He braced himself for a pinch or two. But it turned out he had more trouble with rider's cramp than with the package at the top of his thigh. Rico was the brother with the hair, after all, and hadn't this woman said he looked like the beardless David?

Shaking out her own cramps, Nuncia hoisted her dowdy bag, searching it again. No doubt she'd be glad to switch to something more stylish.

"So," she said, "can I give you money for gas?"

For a moment the dread cleared off and Fabbrizio had to laugh. He propped himself against his bike as, under the parking-lot lights, she showed him yet another grade of smile.

"Why not?" he said, and highballed the figure: thirty Euros.

"Fabbro." Opening her wallet. "You would think you drove me all the way back down to graveyard."

"I think," he found himself saying, "tonight, it's as if I did. I think, with those pictures out on the web, it's as if you got yourself another necklace."

Now there was a smile he knew. For once in fact the woman appeared easy to read, even as she kept both hands largely hidden by her billfold.

"That's all you need," he went on, "the pictures, the zip drive. Don't forget, this is my business too, the fakes. Also the Earthquake I.D."

The seed of this must've stirred inside the helmet, then flowered under the halogen sunshine. "My dear friend, with this *buyer* in New York, you'll make a sack of money as soon as you put the pictures on his computer."

The woman gave a sort of hum, a sort of groan, not unlike the sounds she'd made up on the desktop or the recliner, in the grip of climax. "It's all in the Defense Budget," she said. "The best digital technology on earth."

"With those pictures, you can sell the necklace in New York, then sell it again over in San Francisco."

"Beh." She remained as quick on the uptake as ever, returning to business, pulling bills from her wallet. "Such a smart boy, you've become. I ask myself, how did you get so smart, in just a month?

"Listen," she went on, holding a twenty and a ten against her chest. "In days to come you'll thank me."

To get hold of the money, his fingers had to brush against a half-erect nipple, a backhand caress.

"In days to come," she said, "you'll thank me for a lot more than this."

This traveler, still young—she certainly looked Italian. Her hair for instance, its swing and bob as she turned and walked. Plus her parting shot left him wobbly, as if this moment at the Metro contained more of past and future than he could hold in balance. The continuum of a woman's developing spirit, that seemed like the sort of thing only an Italian could make manifest, somehow present in Annuciata's kinetic outline before she disappeared, her hips and shoulders against the ticket booths. She waved goodbye without turning to look, her fingers waggling over one shoulder.

As he motored away past his friends, Fabbrizio used the same smug salute.

But the fear had him again a few minutes later, when he walked into in an empty home. The Secondigliano wasn't concerned when no one answered the buzzer—that had been broken more often than not lately, and he only rang it as a heads-up. But he didn't like the way the crone on the streetcorner was eyeing him. The old woman looked as if she might actually get up from her chair, revealing the stash of Lucky Strikes beneath her. Before she could move Brizio rolled his bike into the lobby and strapped the chain around the wheels. As he went up the three flights of stairs that had nearly killed his mother, the taped and folded bundle against his upper thigh took more of a toll than it had when he'd been getting on and off the Suzuki. Or maybe he only noticed it more, given how his skin started to creep again as he trotted around his home's empty spaces. At least someone had thought to blow out the candle in front of Padre Pio. And the older brother had made his bed, Brizio hadn't seen that for a while.

He came across no broken furniture. Blinking, frowning, he suffered a recollection of that black drip down the basement window-well out back of Café Sempre. But there was nothing like that here, the walls clean, the floor too. Nevertheless the absence of the hour's usual kitchen odors, of whoever the mother had arranged to make dinner calling to her from the stovetop, plunged Fabbrizio into such a frightened moil he couldn't take time for other sorts of clues. He seemed to recall that Mama had some kind of therapy available outside the home, a standing invitation perhaps. But he lacked the patience to go rummaging for a scribbled prescription, especially one from that doctor. And Uldirico was the kind to leave a note, these days usually on the computer. But how could the younger brother settle down enough to enter passwords and poke at an icon or two, those soulless sticks and boxes? He'd spent all afternoon and evening right in someone else's face, in their lap, and he couldn't so easily switch to the two-dimensional, voices on a screen or a scrap of paper. Fabbrizio might've lasted as little as three minutes up in the apartment before he rushed back down to the sidewalk. He needed the old technology, the gossip on the corner.

Then with the first words out of his neighbor's mouth, he regretted his choice.

"That ape," said the cigarette lady, "that big black ape. What's your family doing with a thing like that?"

Fabbrizio touched a finger to the lump in his lower pocket, the cell phone. Another better possibility. After a moment he came up with three words that would fit the atrophied coils of the old hag's brain: *A little arrangement.*

Slowly she nodded, the folds of her wattles like those in her long skirts, now as she readjusted them over her chairlegs. "Might as well help a dog scratch its own fleas. Eh. In any case it looks like you ran into some trouble now."

He hid his face, getting a look uphill. Of course that way was residential; if there were trouble, it tended to come from the other end, the principal Corso for this part of the periphery. Roughly he brought up the cops.

"Come on, *ragazzo*. Would I be sitting here if there'd been cops?"

That brought him back around, glaring.

"Eh," the woman said. "The black, he had some trouble in the city. Downtown. Your brother, he had to go with him. But how should I know why? You work with apes, soon only the apes understand you."

Fabbrizio raised one hand, flapping it by his ear, letting that do for thanks. As he wheeled his Suzuki back out between the parked Fiats, he paused only to make certain of what the old woman had to add about his mother. Mama seemed to be doing better, said the cigarette-crone. "She went out tonight too, you know. Some chit-chat with others who have the heart sickness."

The group therapy, yes: it came back to him through his fright and his overload. Sessions were held in the church a couple of blocks down the Corso, and the walk home would be safe for hours yet. More reassuring still was the way his mother had left the kitchen, taking care to snuff the shrine-candle. And what good could he do her—this was the question—what further good could he do for Mama out here in Secondigliano, when plainly she'd seen the proof of his changed nature that she required? Nado's arrival at her home might've constituted the evidence she needed, by itself, and then on top of that was whatever the frightened Somali, himself heartsick, had to tell. The ape had got rid of the monster, in the mother's thoughts. Now for the first time in nearly two weeks she was up and out of the house on her own. She was reaching out to someone other than Brizio and Rico to help absorb the blows she'd taken, and trying to gain some traction for whatever years (could be good years) she had left.

Then how could he waste any time getting down to the black blocks? The current of his difficult night had at last been disconnected from one of its sources, all well and good, but that meant also that now its electricity ran all the more powerfully through the conductor that remained, the purple-and-white strapping round his thigh.

Fabbrizio was so fired up, so confirmed in what he'd intended for this evening, that he didn't think to switch on his cell phone till he reached the first traffic circle. Then, sure enough, the lone incoming call was from the home number. The message, Uldirico's, explained that Nado's wife and daughter hadn't been where they'd said they'd be. The N'mbor-lavà had set an appointment to check in via someone else's phone, a business phone, in one of the clandestini-friendly bars. The father, Fabbrizio recalled, had mentioned the arrangement while they'd squatted under the camellias. But the women had never showed up. Now, according to Rico's message, he and the Somalis would be waiting by the church where St. Peter had baptized his first converts.

That last might've been the one truly surprising piece of news. Since when did Rico know about that piazzetta—about a church that didn't object to street vendors right outside the door? You couldn't find that on the internet.

No sooner had Fabbrizzio planted his feet to either side of the ticking Suzuki, in the oddly shaped square on the edge of the black blocks, than he could see there'd been trouble. This even before he spotted his brother. One good look around was all the Secondigliano required, by this time, in order to assess the intensity level in the multicolor coming and going. He'd picked up the semiotics, for instance the sticks the Africans had going in their mouths, every stick still bobbing with some aggravation that wasn't long over. News of anything out of line traveled from here to the far side of the train station in no time—just as it had when he'd first hit the neighborhood, a NATO man from Secondigliano, and after that when he'd started keeping unusual company. Tonight too, he could see the word-of-mouth beginning as soon as a passerby caught sight of him. Their sticks settled briefly between their lips, a pause for the chewer to gather himself, or herself, before they passed along the latest chapter. Meanwhile Fabbrizio, his internal alarms clanging louder at each fruitless glance, couldn't find the Somalis anywhere. It took him two-three minutes just to spot Uldirico. The brother wasn't hiding, but he'd found a quiet spot before one of the church doors. His head was down too, in conference with some priest or friar in Franciscan browns.

The cleric appeared too old to be out so late, in such a *zona*, and he was little more than skin and bones in his sacklike habit. But the man proved spry, ducking back inside the sanctuary before Fabbrizio got a decent look at his face. It seemed, too, that the priest rushed away at a suggestion from Uldirico. Brizio couldn't be sure, it'd been so long since he'd seen his brother calling the shots. Rico hadn't changed much otherwise, still the sloppy bell-pepper shape. He wore a Disney World T-shirt (a top with an agenda? a political commentary?), on which the Florida yellows had long since faded, and this was slashed crossways by the olive-green strap of a fraying ammo bag.

His opener was likewise soft: "Brizio, listen, yesterday, yesterday morning. The things I said, I'm sorry."

The bag's pocket flaps were open, and from one Uldirico removed a lemon soda. There was the brother Brizio knew, couldn't go anywhere without books and sugar. The piazza seemed to shrink for a moment to the size of their bedroom.

"You know better than anyone," Uldirico went on. "For months now, maybe ever since our Babbo… I've been in a crisis, you understand…"

"Rico." He didn't bother to gesture. "The clandestini, that Nado, his wife and daughter. What happened?"

Uldirico got a long drink, noisy, the way he raised one arm and cocked back his head calling attention to his size. He must've been hot, big as he was, with all that hair. "I've been demoralized, truly."

"The police," Fabbrizio said. "If I'm not mistaken, the police have been here, and they've taken someone away."

"Yes, yes. It's with the police now, Brizio. You let them handle it."

With that the younger brother got hot himself. Never mind the illogic of it, the insignificance of the old quarrel, there among Africans pointing and whispering. "Demoralized, you say, Uldirico? That's all you have to tell me after the other morning? That trick with my name, that 'Fabbro' trick, that was a terrible thing."

"Okay." English, mournful. "I'm sorry, Brizio, truly."

"And I'm no better than the cammorista who puts a gun to someone's head?"

Rico had worked a couple fingers of his free hand into his beard. "Maybe I shouldn't have mentioned the black work. Your Nado, as I say, he's with the police now. With the law. And Mama, after that man came by our house, she put a stone over your past."

Fabbrizio gave the air an upwards chop, flat-handed.

"But have you forgotten," Uldirico went on abruptly, "you did some shouting of your own? Up in the hospital?"

The younger brother left his hand in the air, but the way he dropped his head he might've been warding off a blow.

"Brizio, calm yourself."

Good advice. What was this sudden trembling in his fingers, this clotting in his lungs? "I'm sorry. I was scared."

"Scared, yes." At least Rico's voice had dropped too. "*Sicuro.*"

Fabbrizio backed off, for the first time in a while noticing the bundle around one thigh. Dropping his hand, steadying himself against his bike's gas tank, he had an impulse to jump back on and get as far away as thirty Euros could take him.

His brother was talking again about feeling demoralized. "I was living under a heavy hand, Brizio. I thought I would never get out."

He drained the rest of his soda and crushed the empty. The way he flexed his fist, you would've thought he was crumpling up the latest figures on some debt that still weighed on them both. And it wasn't till Uldirico disposed of the can that Fabbrizio noticed the piazza had a receptacle for recycling. The thing might've been an alien, a green and humpbacked voyager from a better world. It had a better smell, even, the last sugared drops in the cans and bottles. Someone else might've found the odor sickening, but at that moment the sweetness struck Fabbrizio as a relief. The usual downtown stink was diesel and mortar, traffic and construction.

"Rico, Rico, all right." Fabbrizio ticked his open hand at each word, the fingers under control. "We understand each other, we're making progress, all right. But now the Numbra, the N'mbor-lavà, what happened?"

The older one was still crumpling up paper, wiping his hands on a Kleenex.

As the story unfolded, the latest piece of bad luck for these clandestini, Fabbrizio found himself thinking of other visitors to Italy, transients on the opposite end of the legal and economic spectrum. The tourists from the U.S., he thought of, and how he loved to sneer at their romantic folderol. Jet lag, nothing—the real disorientation was the dream of some soap opera, a night with Loren or Casanova. But now who was playing the high drama? Fabbrizio, once he wrapped things up here downtown, would set off on yet another dead-of-night gallop around the periphery. He'd go Musketeering in the shadow of the volcano, with the necklace that could rescue a pair of damsels under the knife. What's more, he'd be sent on this hero's journey by his own brother, the two of them almost reconciled, almost. His elder still required one thing more of him, one last noble deed that—should Fabbrizio survive—would once and for all prove him righteous enough to hold his head up at the family table.

Not that the earlier episode in this piazzetta, the trouble with the clandestini, had been the stuff of Hollywood. It was only another mob kidnapping. Another couple of young women had been smacked and rough-housed into submission, in this case the Somali mother and daughter. They'd wound up in the back seat of Nerone's Audi.

Yet as Fabbrizio got the picture, he thought he'd found something that could match tonight's dread, namely, an onrushing wild finish. The ultimate drama. This critical exposition was provided, after all, by a bearded lecturer with the pack-strap that underlined the word *Disney*. Moreover, that Rico should show up in the black blocks, sooner or later, felt likewise unavoidable. After all he'd made a study of the population's changes and margins, and he remained young and ambitious, so long as he wasn't drowning in grief. Naturally he preferred to get out into the field and work out face-to-face encounters with his subject. Then where but in a place like this would Uldirico show up, sooner or later, with one, two, three pens in his pocket? Then too, didn't the recent changes in both brothers carry the same implacable movement towards this neighborhood? A near-match of a conversion experience, in fact, seemed the least you could expect between *primo* and *secondo*. And Fabbrizio also had a sense of other forces nudging them together, broader powers, stronger and yet more vague. For instance there were the statistics he'd seen in the papers, the figures on unemployment across Campania. The worst numbers were for men under thirty.

While Rico explained—the wife and daughter seized, the father gone to the police—Brizio couldn't think about sitting. He kept pulling his bronze antique from his pocket, juggling it a moment, then jamming it back in. But he could've sworn that he was the toy in larger hands. He was the figure put in just this spot and no other by some god with six or seven additional fingers and a considerably farther reach.

Eventually the older brother spelled out a key connection. "This necklace, Brizio? I mean the one that put that poor African on the wrong side of the Camorra. I imagine it's you who got the bad people involved in the first place."

Fabbrizio shifted his attention to his bike, the trunk beneath the seat. The climax he saw coming would need a gun, there under the seat. He tried to recall a name, a toughie rumored to be in the weapons market, down in Portici.

"You're the *artigiano*," Uldirico went on, "the one who makes the copies. But before a man makes a copy, first he needs a crooked contact."

Rico had to be the only law-abiding citizen who got the whole picture, tonight's trouble and just what it had to do with his brother. Rico alone, unlike either Nerone or Nado, could sit out in public and talk about it in plain Italian.

"Beh," Fabbrizio said, "anyone can see how this must happen."

"Must happen, brother? Listen, I'll tell you what must happen, you've got to go to the police yourself."

What? The police? Fabbrizio went on pacing alongside his machine, juggling his Penates, glad he didn't have to cross the two-three blocks to the protected parking space behind Monte Zu's. Plainly Uldirico had chosen to ignore the inevitable. He didn't have so firm a grasp on matters as his younger brother, suddenly harping, instead, on this secondary business of making a statement to the cops. Time enough for that, Rico—after the gunplay that would at last make your Brizio a hero.

"The father," Uldirico was saying, "Nado, he left here with the police. Do I have to spell it out for you? He's down at the station and he's talking."

Nado had done a lot of talking lately, it turned out. Perhaps the father had been acting on some instinct towards East African brotherhood, or possibly he'd believed that sharing the news would provide him with a safety net, a friend at his back. In any case Nado had let slip his plans for getting the necklace and taking it to the police. He'd confided in a man who'd made the crossing years ago, the one who supplied the N'mbor-lavà with their toys and junk food. This wholesaler however came from Ethiopia. Uldirico, in a transparent ploy to dull things down, explained the danger; Ethiopia, he said, was one of the southern continent's oldest and most sophisticated cultures, the land of Prester John and the Falasha Jews, and therefore its natives tended towards a laissez-faire amorality in their dealings on this side of the Mediterranean. In their homeland, Mussolini had held sway for a mere nine years, a blink of the Black Emperor's eye. Whereas in Somalia the Italians had kept control for decades…

"Rico," Fabbrizio put in, getting his hands back on the bike-handle, "you're not going for an examination here."

The upshot, for the N'mbor-lavà, was that their immigrant brother sold them out. The Ethiopian had swapped favors with a pair of mobsters who, in the quiet of dusk, had pulled their expensive German car right up into the piazzetta. According to Uldirico, the gangsters "sounded like a clown act, one big and one small."

Killer clowns, Fabbrizio thought, more drama. Tarantino.

At first the cammoristi had pretended to be immigration officials. Then once it was clear that they didn't have the whole family—once they'd made sense of the mother's frightened stuttering, enough to understand that the father was off visiting, of all places, a NATO base—Nerone and Treno had simply gotten out the knives. One of them had been careless enough to mention Salerno, as they'd wrestled the women into the car.

"The father knows that much," Uldirico said. "And he's with the police."

Fabbrizio reached into a different pocket, pulling out his keys. He figured Treno had gotten hold of the mother, the bigger of the two, and it wasn't hard to imagine what the thug had said: *Down in Salerno we'll teach your daughter to be a good little cunt.*

"The cops, Brizio," his brother said. "You need to tell them your story."

Didn't Uldirico realize how many years he'd wasted, under the painted thumb of killer clowns? Him and all his family, and now this brown new father in his life as well?

"Brizio, are you listening? That Nado, he listened."

Uldirico and Nado had arrived not quite an hour after the kidnap. Before then, up over fruit juice and reheated pasta at the Dellaruba family table, the Somali father had realized he could trust this family. He sensed no doublecross in Rico, no secret agenda in Mama. And anyway, once the mother and daughter failed to show for their phone appointment, whatever might be going on downtown mattered more to Nado than some gold-and-amber bricabrac out on the periphery. So Uldirico and the African had climbed into the old 600, and they arrived at this piazzetta to find the slush-server's cart still in place and two cops working their way around the crowd, buttonholing the vendors that hadn't fled. Brizio's brother had actually lent the police a hand, with one of these peddlers, having picked up a smattering of Amharic during his years before the computer screen. He'd made the introductions for Nado, too, and he'd helped to ease the father's fears about going off to the station. He'd made the former clandestino understand that, just now, cooperating with the authorities was the best thing he could do.

Also Uldirico hadn't been so buried in his books that he'd forgotten how the *malavita* worked. The older brother didn't need Nado to tell him (rather, to groan miserably up towards the flaps of dangling laundry, useless and damp as his own baggy body) that the two gangsters had been hoping to get their hands on the necklace itself.

Taking the wife and daughter had been an improvisation, Plan B. The crooks had wanted no part of any hostage crisis, always a drawn-out affair, and one that could get messy. Also they'd known better than to cut anyone's throat. Murder in the middle of the street could likewise lead to trouble you didn't need, especially outside your own turf. Besides, where was the profit in it? Rather, once Nerone and Treno had sized up the stuttering mother, the daughter with the fists up under her chin, they'd gone for the better investment. The younger one alone could bring in thousands before the year was out.

But Uldirico understood what the camorristi had been after.

"Brizio, think." He framed the point with raised hands. "You know those women, they'll tell those two everything."

The younger brother wondered if he could get a sawed-off shotgun, a *lupara*.

"Then there's Nado, my brother. You know he's telling the cops about you."

As for Uldirico, the easiest way to handle him would be to lie. Just say he was heading for the police station.

"He's got to be telling them, Brizio. What are you to him?"

Fabbrizio turned and put a finger in the bigger man's chest. "But let me tell you who I am—allow me, my brother! I'm the man who's going to save those women. I'm going to show the whole fat and callous *world*."

Rico raised a shaggy eyebrow. "Oh dear. The artist in the family. I was afraid of this. I was afraid you'd take off into Dreamland."

When Fabbrizio talked about "the whole world," the older son was saying, where did one begin? "For example I must ask," Rico went on," how you can believe that whatever you might do for the N'mbor-lavà will make a difference for any of the others? Think, brother. Their case is an exception."

Brizio had his head down again, looking at his hands and wondering about the feel of his brother's chest when he'd touched it. Uldirico had seemed almost as fleshy as Nuncia, and likewise soaked in sweat. Hardly a reminder to reassure the artist in the family, especially when through his spread fingers he could see the black vinyl of his bike's banana seat, the trunk beneath it utterly wrong for a *lupara*. The older brother however wouldn't allow him to drift off into silent recriminations. Rico stayed so close you could smell the pseudo-citrus on his breath. He admitted he didn't know what Fabbrizio had in mind, but he knew for certain that any gallivanting around intended to help the N'mbor-lavà, even in the unlikely event that it did those three any good ("but, *highly* unlikely, Brizio",) wouldn't mean a thing for the other three hundred thousand or so like them.

"And that's just counting from Rome south," Uldirico said.

Statistics? His brother was giving him statistics, and getting loud about it? Fabbrizio hoisted one leg over his still-warm bike, a last spasm out of a still-warm dream, his notion of playing judge, jury, and executioner. But Uldirico threw his own leg over the Suzuki's front wheel and grabbed hold of the handlebars. The younger one had to slide back on the seat, a move that tugged at the tape around his thigh. Rico's glare brought out how much he'd taken after their father, down to the traces of nicotine in his eyeballs, and the street noise seemed to quiet, the others in the piazza thinking perhaps they were about to see another scuffle. At least there wasn't any static from Brizio's pants pocket.

"There's only one place," Uldirico declared, "where I'll let you go now."

He'd put his lecturing behind him. When Fabbrizio didn't respond, when his struggle to get his head on straight again became obvious, the older one turned an appraising look towards the church alongside them. Wasn't much to look at, its stonework chipped in the quake and gone black from exhaust long before that. Nonetheless Uldirico declared with some warmth that his professor had been right about this St.Peter's. That priest he'd been talking to had mentioned some fascinating case studies, anecdotal evidence at the least, useful for Rico's latest assignment.

"A new project," said the sociology student. "We worked it out this morning."

Fabbrizio dropped his hands from the accelerator and gearshift.

"It's my own arrangement, Brizio, a course of study I designed myself. I met with the professor this morning, and he suggested I talk to this priest here."

"A new project?" This the younger brother could talk about. "Uldirico, you mean, a course for credit? Have you been so busy?"

Rico nodded, giving the brake-handles a squeeze.

"You went to the professor," Fabbrizio said, "right after you—right after yesterday morning. Those terrible things you said"

"Beh, you understand. My investigations had reached the limit of what could be accomplished via research on my own."

Was that a smile, under Rico's dampened mustache? A smirk like Brizio used to see across the *scopa* table? The second-born found himself chuckling, or almost, as much of a surprise as his choking up earlier. Yet again he dropped his gaze, shaking his head at the wide medieval paving stones. Eventually Uldirico added that his professor had agreed to a formal acknowledgment of his student's help. His name would appear on any interview data. "And once we have that material in presentable form, we'll set an examination date."

"But, an examination, truly Rico? A final examination?"

The brother shrugged, perhaps adjusting the hang of his bag. Fabbrizio preferred to think Rico was swallowing some quip that had occurred to him, some one-liner that, however zingy, would cheapen what was taking place.

"An examination, Rico, that's good news. It's a tremendous thing—"

"Yes, Brizio, yes, all right. Thanks. Good. But listen."

His lips all but disappearing in his beard, the brother repeated that Fabbrizio needed to go to the cops. "Think of Nado. He's down at the station saving *himself.*"

Fabbrizio sighed, not quite giving a nod. His dizziness here downtown, he was starting to realize, had more than a little to do with the orgy out in the colonel's office. At the clubs he'd seen couples like that, tottering back onto the floor.

"You want to help the immigrants, the clandestini? Then don't get in this man's way. Help him to speak for himself."

Again Fabbrizio was studying his hands, small but hardly incapable. It came to him that this entire furious month had begun with the notion of summoning up some "ancient power," a resurrection ritual that was nine-tenths nuts. Yet to judge from the crowds at the temples down south, to see what happened to the girls especially, that power might've been alive and kicking the whole time.

"*Sicuro,*" Fabbrizio repeated. "I'll go to the Salerno police and no one else."

By this time Uldirico too had let go of the handlebars. Arms crossed, he'd shuffled backwards, making himself as comfortable as he could while keeping his legs to either side of the front wheel.

"Rico, what are you worried about, really? Listen—bless me, father. I have sinned. I confess it again, ten or fifteen minutes ago I sinned in my heart, I had a truly crazy idea. Tonight for once, father, I was the one with my head in the clouds."

Fabbrizio cricked his neck, making a sifter of his upper spine, shaking out flakes of his earlier bad intensity. "Tonight," he repeated, "for once."

In the nearer intersections, passersby no longer took an interest. Most had their backs to the two whites, so you noticed the loose hang of their djellabas, the winking bits of mirror on the tops of their braided caps.

"Rico, what do you think, I'm lying? When I leave here, I swear, it's straight to the Salerno police."

The other pawed momentarily in his bag, as if he hoped to find another soda. "I believe you, Brizio," he admitted. "But you do realize, the Naples police, the ones Nado is talking to, all they have to do is pick up a phone."

"A good idea, Rico, and I'll make a call too." He pulled his cell from his below-the-bundle pocket. "Considering how long it's been, how long ago those bastards took the women, better not waste any time."

The older one leaned closer, eyeing the phone's small screen, the three digits that appeared there.

"I'll make the call," Fabbrizio repeated, his thumb over the Command button. "The emergency number. But then I have to go down there."

"Brizio, now, you can understand why I'd worry, when it was only ten or fifteen minutes ago—"

"Come on. Now you sound like Mama, the same worries over and over, the same reminders. You sound like you're saying the rosary for Padre Pio."

The brother used a thumbnail to flatten the hair beneath his lips.

"But, Rico, this is still Naples. That's why I have to go visit in person. You don't think that, in one evening alone, we've caused the whole city to be born again?"

Button: call. Fabbrizio dipped his head and cupped a hand behind the phone, he didn't want to shout but he didn't want to go unheard either, and he took care to have the woman taking the call repeat the details for him. Uldirico kept silent throughout, then went on thumb- and finger-combing for a long moment after the phone was back in its pocket. Eventually he acknowledged that he hadn't believed Fabbrizio was lying. Most of the time he could tell when that was the case.

"Yes, and especially tonight, Rico. After the way we talked tonight, if nothing else, you know I'm not lying or crazy. Your brother's a good man, you know that, I know that. But this business now, going down there to make the report in person, there's more to it than just you and me."

His phone call, he pointed out, amounted to nothing more than an anonymous tip about an address the police were already watching. They had to know all about the Café Sempre, the Salerno cops. But here in the South, this usually meant the reverse was true as well, and someone in the precinct house was on the Camorra payroll. Could be, even the woman who'd taken Brizio's call.

"Then there's Nado," the younger brother went on. "You're right, Uldirico, he's telling the cops everything. He's given them my name already, probably—but who is he? Who, Rico, really? Here in the city the same as down in Salerno, a man like that, he doesn't have any friends. He's just another illegal."

Uldirico had dropped his hand, nodding.

"If I go down there, if I show up in person, now that's the smart move."

And Fabbrizio saw no harm in reiterating that, lately, he'd seemed to go looking for trouble. "Some wild scenes, sure." He wasn't bothered that this might've been his third apology in less than ten minutes.

"Solidarity, comrade," his brother cut in. "From each according to his abilities, to each according to his need."

Fabbrizio grinned. "In any case, when I drive down to Salerno, it's not like that."

"It's not another case of trying to prove yourself to, to—who knows? To all the gods of our time."

He couldn't quite laugh. Uldirico tugged at his cartoon of a T-shirt: "So. The citizen will do his duty?"

The give and take came more easily. Uldirico backed off the Suzuki's front wheel and Fabbrizio shifted forward into driving posture, though with that his fears resurged a bit. He needed to get his spiky charm out of his pocket. But he could talk through it, here in the sugar scent out of the recycling bin. Also he had no difficulty getting the brother to agree that he should run over to the city's downtown precinct house, himself. Rico should visit the Naples station that stayed open all night, and add his own in-the-flesh impact to that of his younger brother down the highway. And in so far as Fabbrizio needed one final calming touch before he hit the Tangenziale, Uldirico provided it. The older one returned to the soothing rhythm of academics. *If indeed this location you've mentioned serves as the de facto center for illegal activity in that sector...* It sounded like the gentle farther ripples of something, a good distance by now from the initial splash.

Even if some of the police were on the take, the brothers reminded each other, the crooked ones had reason to be concerned. The cops had to start making arrests, if the local mob threatened to create a mess that reeked all the way to Rome. Tonight, maybe, Fabbrizio would only need mention that the Somali mother and daughter had already made the news. Plus if the women were the stick, he also had a carrot. He had the necklace.

Not that he could tell Uldirico. On the contrary, when it came to the contraband strapped to his thigh, his brother was the last person he wanted to know.

Now as the two of them touched on a couple of final details, as one or the other changed the subject to Mama, Fabbrizio didn't come off the bike. Uldirico announced that even before their mother had headed out to her group therapy, she'd made an actual shopping trip. While Uldirico and the unexpected African visitor were busy with a formal interview—before Nado had failed to reach his wife and child down in the black blocks—Mama had descended to the street and then climbed back home with a sack of fresh produce. Hearing this, the younger son felt briefly like a full sack himself, the happiness for a moment plugging the spaces wrenched open by his fear. Even as he and Rico shared a hug at the news, however, he took pains to keep his brother on one side of the Suziki, away from the necklace. After that he sat on one buttock so he faced out over his unencumbered leg.

Uldirico tugged again at his shirt, its logo almost an insult in this neighborhood.

"Brizio, something else. You should get back to the university."

Taking Rico's measure, readjusting on his seat, Fabbrizio thought of Nuncia or whoever she might be. The incomputable angles in her smile.

"Think about it, *secondo*. At last some work you wouldn't have to hide, a degree from the university. Mama would put it on the wall. Under mine, of course."

Maybe something of l'Americana had rubbed off. From this night on, maybe, the effects of any healthy new thought or feeling could no longer ripple in a single direction only, but rather there'd always develop some countercurrent of subterfuge and playing for advantage. *You will thank me*, the woman had said.

"The sons of Dellaruba," Fabbrizio said, "*primo e secondo*."

He worked up a grin to match his brother's. Was it so venal a deception, anyway, to keep Rico from knowing about so dangerous a piece of contraband? The wondering only dropped out of his head when Uldirico kissed him.

A formal kiss, both cheeks. Again tonight, someone else's hair in his ear.

But this time it must be love, because Uldirico was telling him to get a lawyer. Sensible advice, really. Rico was saying he could understand why Fabbrizio had to show up down there in person, but should the police turn their attention to him—should the younger brother find himself under interrogation—his should demand a lawyer.

"Brizio, understand? You said it yourself, you're a good man."

Both of them kept smiling.

"Nevertheless, my brother, in a certain sense, you still look dubious."

Getting back to the highway was a crawl. Several times Fabbrizio had to extend both legs and walk his idling Suzuki, every move of his legs a reminder of his hidden package, as he nosed by street vendors lounging alongside rolled-up mats, or plastic tables with tinkling clusters of empty Cokes and Fantas. Only as he reached the train station could he get up to running speed, and when he came out onto the *Tangenziale* he couldn't be bothered with the helmet. He left it hooked to his bike's rear bar. At this hour the cops had more important things to worry about.

As did Fabbrizio. Once the gray-on-black outline of Vesuvius loomed above the highway, once he was out of the city proper and gunning past the newer housing, the barely legal apartment clusters, the Secondigliano remembered that in one of those places he could've bought a gun. He could've had a pistol jammed in his pants right now. Now there was something to worry about, his state of mind less than half an hour ago, and never mind how sorted-out and pulled-together he'd felt so long as he'd had Uldirico with him to help. If he'd gotten on top of his darker impulses, after all, why had he needed Rico to remind him that he could use a lawyer? Frowning into the onrush of air, Fabbrizio told himself Salerno was city enough to have legal services round the clock. Plus before he called in an attorney, he needed to figure out what he was going to say to the police; that should keep his head in line. Mental rehearsals, just what the doctor ordered. Should he confine what he had to say to the two women? Should he mention the necklace at all?

Or here was a rehearsal—skip the cops and run. Take his thirty-something Euros, his ten-or twelve-thousand-something necklace, and stay on the bike.

The hub of his thinking remained on task. Maybe his best way to handle the police, he told himself, would be to drop a couple of hints about the Paestum piece but refrain from anything specific till it was morning and he could request a public defender.

But on the periphery of his brains flashed a darker glimmer: down in Reggio di Calabria, hardly three hours farther south, he'd find plenty of boats for Africa…

Fabbrizio tasted tears. Of course his eyes were unprotected, their leakage blown down his face. He was bone-tired and blood-anxious. But it took no extra effort to remember that across the mountains was

Bari and across the Adriatic were cities and towns where his goods could set him up like a king. And who could say how long his rule might last? Who could say what lucrative fiefdoms he might claim? Maybe he'd discover some way to cash in, even, on the photos Annunciata had broadcast across the web. Fifteen thousand, or twice that, no telling.

Just open the throttle, *ragazzo*, and ignore the Salerno exits.

His personal timeline had been reversed, turned inside out. Whatever Fabbrizio was about to do, it had already become some anecdote out of his past, some story he was looking for the most entertaining way to tell. *Listen, that was a tremendous thing, a night that changed my life.* At least he knew where the dislocation had begun, the American again, her witchcraft. Perhaps he muttered the name aloud, *Nuncia.* Her elbows sharpened to endless ambiguity, that woman could nudge any preparations ass over teakettle. She could make him half-crazy even when, Fabbrizio reminded himself angrily, since leaving the university he'd in fact spent dozens of highway hours doing just this, motoring along and talking himself through some ticklish encounter ahead. To turn the timeline inside out could well have been the defining movement of his freelance career. He was thoroughly familiar with the strain, as the present groaned under the scaffolding of both past and future. Yet ever since he'd gazed upon that Iowa Harpy, wherever the *artigiano* had found himself careening, every likely-looking blueprint had turned out to contain some failure, some flaw, some crack just wide enough for a beautiful parasite such as Shanti-Daphne-Annuncita. This evening, for instance, there'd been that stunt Nerone had pulled, up on the border of the black blocks. Nerone, a so-called wiseguy. He and Treno couldn't have called more attention to themselves if they'd tried. They'd hit town like a pair of Navy men after six months at sea; they'd gone out of their way to catch every girl's eye. Now as Fabbrizio reached the first Salerno exits, he felt as if he'd spent the last three-four weeks in a metropolis inhabited entirely by drunken sailors, the kind of folks who took their evening *passagiata* where they were most likely to break a leg. Everyone tottered along the crest of a disintegrating wall, Roman or Greek or older. The structure was riddled by weeds and flagged with warning posters; the risk was as old as perversity itself.

Himself, at least he had a sensible program in mind for the police, as he pulled off the highway. Thanks to his brother and his Suzuki, he'd worked out the best sequence for what he had to say, and what sounded like the right tone of voice as well. He was going to save the women and at the same time lose his excess baggage—a weight that was starting to feel like a lot for a grownup's thigh, let alone a teenager's neck (it'd been made, after all, for someone who no longer had to worry about stress on the spinal column). And Fabbrizio himself had been reforged. In the stink and fire of his running around, he'd become whatever sort of person it was who wouldn't take off with the Greca's goods.

Naturally he still had his fear to deal with. He would've thought his shoulder blades had grown roughage. But he'd gotten his performance ready for the cops—and he'd hammered out an interior peace over the extent to which it was a performance, a flow-chart tacked up over a half-dozen kinds of chaos, dangerous or selfish. Some of what he had to say was worked out word for word, and some he could improvise, given the peace and quiet of the hour. Even the docks had shut down.

Though Salerno appeared to have a lot of sparkle, tonight. The passing streetlamps—was this some trick of his helmet's visor?—were erupting in colored pinwheels, rainbow refractions.

But he wasn't wearing the helmet. He squeezed the brakes, a spasm.

The spasm went into his head, setting it sagging. His mouth opened and closed as if in some children's party game, as if his hands were behind his back and he was trying to bite an apple that hung on a string. He set his feet down to either side of the bike only after it started to lose its balance. Around him the silent pyrotechnics gathered, sparking up and trickling down across the strip of sky overhead, its balcony railings and TV antennas. Fabbrizio may have reached back for his helmet, as if it could protect him somehow. Perhaps instead he was waving that hand around to try and disperse the rising static out of his crotch.

The two times previous, the godling and necklace hadn't sat so close together. Now however the bronze and gold each amped the other, the charges firing through the duct tape and the plastic bag, the vibrations mounting by occult geometry. Fabbrizio had to shift on his banana seat. When the vinyl squeaked beneath him, audible in the empty street, the sound triggered an unnerving flashback to his and Nuncia's madness up in Printing & Publications. While the colonel's recliner had complained beneath him, while his erection had felt electrified again and again, the office windows had presented another shoebox full of colored sky (the sundown, the lamps on the base).

Here in the Salerno street, he couldn't say how long he sat blinking, gulping, flapping whichever hand wasn't holding the bike. He couldn't move till the Greca's voice began to emerge from the static. Her first whisper at once out-shouted all his rehearsals on the trip down here: *...th'again s'near....* And no sooner had he deciphered her next phrase, *...this alley again...*, than he'd cranked the accelerator and, at the first intersection, put his back to the waterfront and the police station.

He couldn't wait—the women couldn't wait—not when the ghost warnings swiftly grew louder than his barely-muffled engine. *...death 'gain so near...* Fabbrizio wondered at how he could drive, with all the moaning and fireworks. But keeping control of his bike wasn't any stranger, finally, than the kind of thing he'd seen outside the dance clubs, the drivers who poured themselves back behind the steering wheel after two or three hits of X. So he kept on the accelerator as much as the road allowed, imagining that Nerone already had his knife against the mother's throat. That was the way they did these things, wasn't it? They gave the daughter an incentive to cooperate. Though after Treno had put the girl through her job training, made a better investment of her, there was no telling how they'd handle the mother.

Fabbrizio didn't like the woman's chances, no. Not with these warnings in his ear, their accent still unnerving, an up-to-date Serb or Kosavar. Worse, however, Nado's wife didn't seem like the kind to hold her temper. Her stutter, her grim excuse for a smile, gave the impression she might lose her cool worse than poor Torio, heaving his bag of bones in the hoodlum's face.

As he reached the Café Sempre, thinking a bit more clearly, Fabbrizio realized he didn't know the woman. He doubted he'd exchanged three words with her, the mother, the wife, and he could've read her looks all wrong. The entire family remained obscure to him, stick figures, in which each stick stood for some variety of desperation: a lost homeland, a drowned child, a crying need for a paycheck. You could even say the Somali woman was like a funhouse mirror held up to the American.

Nuncia of course wanted for nothing—yet she too was a sketchlike trick of the light, leading "Fabbro" on towards God knows what.

He was thinking more clearly; he parked the bike a long block away. He hooked it to a burnt-out street lamp, in a dark spot where the popping colors of his visitation gleamed on the coffee-flavored air.

Also he took a moment, in that same blackness, to undo his pants and rip the necklace out of its pouch. The piece was his best defense, and the women's too. It was a bargaining chip, a way he might buy some time, or at the least a distraction. Then as soon as Fabbrizio got his hand on the linked stones and gold, they buzzed so fiercely that he hardly felt anything else, even the duct tape peeling away from his thigh. ...*bones*, the Greca seemed to be saying, *he makes me lie on bones...* After that, once the Secondigliano got himself zipped up again, he could for the first time distinguish between the necklace and the Penates, their different levels of shudder and hum. Tonight's episode had come on more intensely than the previous two, and it was running longer as well. Even with both the elements of the mystery on him, even learning something about their symbiosis, Fabbrizio couldn't help but worry whether anything more ordinary had contributed to their extra zap. Was he exhausted, merely? Or hellbent on getting even, like the former farmgirl? Meanwhile keeping to the dark, his back against the plaster-shedding walls, he moved to the alley that led behind the café.

...*that light in my eyes*, the Greca seemed to be saying, *that awful naked bulb...*

With each snaking stride Fabbrizio felt both out of his young mind and hyper-alert, all his senses spiked for any possible advantage, and in any case it didn't seem to be his own legs carrying him along. Instead (he could only hope this wasn't another variety of the gun-toting fantasy he'd suffered not long ago) what drew him up the alleyway was the tidal pull of affairs far more vast, as murky as the theories in Uldirico's texts and as solid as the man who'd blocked the door to the jeweler's shop in which Brizio had worked so happily beside his father.

By now he could hear the crying, too. A woman with a working tongue, no ghost, crying and trying to talk. She wasn't speaking Italian.

The mother, calling to her daughter across the scabby paving of the lot. The older woman was closer to the alley, and closer to upright, even with Nerone on her. The younger was out of her pants and lying on her back in a sloping far corner, while Treno stood at her feet, pulling off his silly summer jacket.

Fabbrizio discovered he was leaking tears himself, it was everything and the kitchen sink tonight, and he could only squat against a corner at the entry to this backyard killing ground, at an angle where the light of the jerryrigged lamp-post couldn't reach him. He had a notion that the mother might be his best chance, that she might pitch in somehow. The older woman didn't look too tightly bound, insofar as Fabbrizio could tell, through his weeping and lightshow. Nerone hadn't taken much care in strapping the mother's bony wrists to one of the shop-stoop railings over her head, winding the duct tape (what else?) no more than two or three times around both her arms and a single narrow horizontal. It appeared that the mother had already sawed partway through the tape; the bar was that twisted, that rusted. Of course Nerone also had his knife on her. He had her just as Fabbrizio had imagined he would, and beneath the unshaded bulb, the blade gleamed each time the woman spoke. It bobbed with the muscles of her neck. Nerone held her around the shoulders too, those uplifted skin-and-bone shoulders, their lines likewise harsh in this light. And what did Fabbrizio have in his own hand, meanwhile? What kind of a weapon was this, finely crafted, intricate? For a moment he glimpsed the woman and the man holding her as a kind of artwork, another detail off a museum krater.

He blinked, he frowned, and with his free hand swabbed away the last of his tears. The mother, he reminded himself, was his best chance for help. The daughter was hardly more than a baby, a scared kid.

He checked Treno. The larger crook stood undoing his pants, emitting some noise you couldn't define, a whoop and a growl.

"...that cunt... I'll *teach* you..."

Fabbrizio, half around a corner, couldn't be sure of the words. But he knew when a man was trying too hard. This "soldier" always had to ratchet up his viciousness, one obscenity per notch, even when the scene was already some half-lit pocket of hell. The African girl—wasn't this obscenity enough?—had a bag of bones as a pillow. The crooks had laid the teenager out on a collapsed box of corrugated cardboard, and then for better leverage or something they'd tossed behind her head the clattering duffel bag that they'd taken from the Paestum watchman, not even a dozen midnights ago.

Hadn't the Greca mentioned the bones, earlier? One of the first warnings Fabbrizio had heard?

You had to wonder why the camorristi hadn't taken the women inside the café. And then you had to admit that out here on the concrete, on the skeleton, made for a more thorough degradation. Out in the alley, the lesson was more likely to take hold. You could see the impact in the way the African teenager eyed the big potty-mouth above her. The girl looked as if she'd heard the same death-dealing bulletins as Fabbrizio had, in her case picking up the signal from the leftover bits of the sister behind her head.

The mother cut in, wailing something for her child. Behind her straining shoulders Nerone grinned, unbothered. Or was it the ghost Fabbrizio heard, that often-torn thread of murmurs between his pants pocket and his open hand?

Now Treno had exposed his underwear, a silky bikini, pimp stuff. They were green and gold and Brizio didn't want to think about that. He didn't want to watch, either, once the camorrista slipped his thumbs under the briefs' back waistband, and so the Secondigliano was looking at the mother again when she broke free of her tape-straps. The rusted bar above her head had been a ready-made saw-blade, damaged long before the quake. In fact down in the café basement, mother and daughter would've had a lot more trouble like that on which they could lay their hands, wouldn't they? In Fabbro's former workshop, under the bar, the Africans would've had potential weapons lying around everywhere. This must've been part of the gangster logic, preferring the back lot for breaking the women down. Out here, even with her hands free, the mother got nowhere. So frail that even a smaller-model thug could keep her pinned, she managed only to free her arms from the elbow down. Nerone seemed to enjoy the action, the rocking and squirming that budged his knife down from neck to collarbone. He coughed up a doglike laugh.

A laugh, then abruptly a howl. Eyes wide, mouth working, Nerone's head snapped back.

Fabbrizio was watching the knife; he peeked an inch or two out from his shadow. The bad guys weren't going to pay him any attention when, with her free half of an arm, the mother had got hold of her captor's hair. She'd got a fistful of that proud black mane and yanked. The woman had such a vicious hold that, while the jewelry in Fabbrizio's hand shuddered again, she could put her face against Nerone's face and take a bite. She tore out a graffiti-style slash, the kiss-mark of a nasty party. She came away with glossy fresh slather over her lips.

Then there was what Nerone came away with. A murderous vanity—*Nobody does that to me.*

The mother had bit the man high on the cheekbone, up where you got a lot of blood. Now she wanted more, another piece of him (Fabbrizio had a nuthouse thought about the crook's cologne), and with jaws spread wide she wriggled almost out of her shirt (Fabbrizio glimpsed scarring across the upper chest, marks intentional and significant, a world apart from what she'd left on the gangster's face). At last Nerone got his blade moving, whipping the thing up wildly across his attacker's nose and brow. He seemed to've just missed the eye.

Nobody does that to me. The mobster broke into a screech: "Cutting her throat's too *good* for this bitch."

But the mother was hard to get a bead on. Nerone needed a moment to find an angle of attack, when he got her next he wanted it to hurt, and by then Fabbrizio was up out of the alley. The absence of cycle or wall, that alone shocked him; he stood in emptiness. When he flicked his arm it felt like he was shaking off the chill. But this was the arm that held the necklace, and though it seemed to move in a spasm he knew what he was doing—flinging the heavy piece of work, like a handful of stones, into Nerone's bleeding face. Expertly he placed this latest effort, blinding the camorrista and making him howl again. What good was the work if it couldn't serve as a weapon? What use were its linked and tripled adornments, when everyone had gone back to cave days? Its clink and rattle might've been a bead curtain in the breeze, and all around it strangers and newcomers had ripped away their curtains and gone ravaging.

Beyond that, Fabbrizio had no idea. He couldn't even lower his throwing arm.

The emptiness in which he found himself, as if the tape at his thigh were the only thing holding him up, that alone kept him in shock. His gaze was fixed, wooden. He could hardly tell the difference between

Nerone before him, swearing and wrestling the mother off him, and the commotion between Treno and the daughter in the farther corner of the lot. Over that way there might've been a groan, a man's groan, decidedly out of character for mob muscle. But then Fabbrizio might've groaned himself, as Nerone flung the older woman into the stoop behind them, stilling her with a knuckle-slap, a knuckle- and necklace-slap. No down time for the bad guy. Put the mother down, rather, stun her and leave her on the tarmac beside the three-thousand-year-old jewelry. Nerone dumped the necklace, yes, as he leapt to his feet with a glinting upsweep of his knife. Fireworks, it was, the way the blade caught the light. Fireworks again, a fresh burst and sizzle before Brizio's eyes, and then in another moment the man of Secondigliano was left breathless and crumpling onto one knee, unable even to utter the sort of groan he'd heard a moment before from Treno's end of this madness. His face felt seared from jawline to eye-socket. It seemed to take forever just to raise a hand to the wound.

"Fucking queer," Nerone grunted. "You too, wherever you came from. Sick of your pretty face too."

Whatever Fabbrizio could see appeared warped, splotched. The flashes going off around him might've been the pain and might've been the ghost. First he thought that all he'd done was save his killers the trouble of hunting him down; then he thought of the bashed-up Torio, his eyes hanging over the window-well. And what was Brizio looking at, just now? What wreckage, what futility?

"We'll cut everyone's face tonight," Nerone said.

Half blind, mostly blind, Fabbrizio cast around for better. He found Treno looking—out of character. The big cammorista had also collapsed, in his case going down on both knees. He sagged with hands crossed over his crotch.

But when the nearer gangster was hit by the duffel bag, the poor watchman's bone-bag, it wasn't anything Fabbrizio had thought of. It came like yet another visitation from Beyond. An angel, this time, a guardian angel in the form of a flying black blob with corded green handles. It appeared less divine still when, for the second time in ten days, it caught Nerone when he wasn't looking. Only the clatter seemed supernatural, an enormous noise. Fabbrizio flinched; he may have heard a bone break.

Yet for the moment he might as well have been cringing on the other side of a basement wall. Nerone was attacked from both sides and Treno woozed around on his knees, all while Fabbrizio sat watching. The women were free to tear into the smaller of the two crooks because the daughter, he at last understood, had kicked the larger one in the nuts. She'd got him more than once, it looked like. Treno had been distracted, what with this faggot thief coming out of nowhere and this jungle mama biting his partner. His hands had been occupied with wrestling his briefs down over his butt.

The daughter, the older sibling. She leapt on Nerone while he was off-balance, and before he could get the duffel bag off his face the half-naked girl had sunk her own teeth into him, into his knife-hand. The mother remained shaky, meanwhile. When she sat up you could see that her face had gone puffy, under its spatters of blood. But the woman kept her wits about her enough to see that—yes, Brizio—the necklace was no good unless you could use it as a weapon. With a scream she once more seized Nerone by the hair and, her other hand wrapped in the heavy jewelry, she slapped him back and forth. Either that or the teeth in his hand set the kidnapper screaming too, though his noise turned blurry when the mother went for the weak spot. Showing a furious pleasure, her markings suddenly war-paint, the woman jammed the thorny folds of gold and beadwork down into her kidnapper's open mouth.

The uproar seemed to shake down dust. Even a Neapolitan might've called the police. Fabbrizio too found his voice, a grunt louder than necessary as some mechanism in him at last caught gear. He went for the fallen bag of bones, stood and shook the carryall's weight down into one fraying end, then took a long step towards Treno. Nerone's enforcer remained in a low squat, digging in the clothes that bound his lower legs, shaking his cauliflower head. Fabbrizio broke into a cry and swung what was left of the Greca into the man's ear.

The bedlam cranked up worse. Now you could catch an actual word or two. ...*fuck... asshole...*

Brizio, the one who always had an idea. He checked the mother and daughter, at Nerone's hand and mouth; they'd wrangled the undersized bossman onto the ground, onto his back, the crumpled gold and amber blooming out of his mouth like he was coughing up mosaic. Fabbrizio figured that if he got Treno one more good whack then he and the women should have the head start they needed. Three on a bike was nothing new for a Secondigliano. He cocked the bag again and swung hard—and wound up yanked off his feet, thrown onto the buckled paving.

The larger camorrista had regained his balance, one foot at last free of his pants. He'd had no trouble getting hold of the duffel and using it to yank Fabbrizio off his feet.

Now when the mobster tossed the bag aside, the reinjured *artigiano* noticed a couple of bone-ends poking out through a seam. They were lovely, really, bones of that age, the shape of script and the color of olive oil; a good thing the Bureau of Antiquities had experts who could put all the broken bits back together. But Treno wasn't wasting time with schoolboy thoughts, nor with any make-do weapon. Instead he brought out what he'd been searching for in his puddled trousers, a knife of course. Another glint of edge, under the lot's naked bulb. Treno carried a woodsman's model, a bulky toolkit item, and that made three tonight, counting the one that the American had waved at Fabbrizio earlier. You'd almost think there'd been some oversight, with all these knives in play and still no one dead on the floor. Or so Fabbrizio was thinking, in so far as he could think at all, down on the floor. Hauling himself into a defensive crouch, glancing behind him, he winced at the fresh dirt burning in his cut. The two underfed Somali women had all they could handle, each at one of Nerone's arms while the mobster bucked and kicked. Through the knotty stuffing in the man's mouth rose a barking splutter, a noise more vomit than speech. Meanwhile Treno lumbered to his feet, his blade hardly a foot from Fabbrizio's eyes. The thug was keeping his hands low, protecting himself, a fist to either side of the swag between his legs—the skin there, Fabbrizio couldn't help but notice, as dark as sub-Saharan Nado's.

At the first shot, the warning shot, the lot became a vacuum. Noiseless, airless, and packed in concrete.

A shot, a vacant tick or two, and then everyone started screaming again. Even the cops in the alley were screaming. But Treno came on the loudest, nearly naked and entirely crazy, lurching forward with his weapon raised.

No doubt the police didn't mean to hit the man in the face. They'd only wanted to stop him, *sicuro*. Later Fabbrizio could see that a couple of the half-dozen or so shots he'd heard had in fact struck the camorrista in his trunklike legs. But the cops were as susceptible to the jangle of hysteria as anyone else, and Fabbrizio's call alone must've sounded to them like serious trouble. Then there must've been the followup from the Naples office. One jurisdiction had contacted the other, the greater metropolitan system for public safety functioning the way it was intended to.

Salerno had sent a response in force. The squad must've gotten their guns out when they pulled up before the café, and they must've flipped their safeties off as they snuck along the alley. First they'd had the howling and banging, and then they'd had this crewcut gorilla in full roar, a knife in his hand and his balls hanging out. No doubt the police had only wanted to stop the man. Nonetheless they cracked Treno's head open, above a mouth twisted to spit out obscenities. They gave him a jeweled headpiece, or was it still more pyrotechnics, a splatter of unreal color?

Fabbrizio got only a glimpse. After that he buried his own face in the pavement, spineless and racked by sobs. Racked by horror, by relief, even by a recollection, in there somewhere, of the Military Police up in Aversa, the two outside the office door. They'd been the first tonight to come close to putting a bullet in him. Cowering now, snuffling, Brizio drank in his own heavy odor. A lot of odor, after near non-stop jerking around. He couldn't lift his head till he heard the police settle into a more businesslike give and take around him, and when he did he needed first to wipe his eyes.

He slipped his shirt-tail over his hands. A glittery clubgoer's shirt, over finicky jeweler's hands.

The new quiet needed corroboration. He looked for the women. They'd had it worse, those two, manhandled into this stone box. The cement dust that covered them might as well have been lime, and the Africans had better reason than Fabbrizio to doubt that they'd made it safely beyond that kind of thing, rape and murder. Better reason than he to worry about what might lie in store, when for all they knew their tumbling between doom and rescue wasn't yet over. In fact he found mother and daughter whimpering together, in an embrace that had him thinking of all the duct tape earlier.

But the way they met his look, now that he could live with.

Maybe Fabbrizio was at last learning to read these damaged newcomers. Or maybe the hard gratitude in their eyes, a wary acknowledgement of his help that, at the same time, warned him not to expect much in return—maybe this was one of those communicating devices that, for all its intricacy, lost nothing when crossing the Mediterranean. Anyway the wear and tear and bloodstains didn't interfere with the signal. He even believed he could read the younger woman's lips, despite their smearing, as she mouthed a word of thanks. He could see the Neapolitan in those lips, just now, the fleshy play that would last till her heart was as worn and weak as his mother's.

Not that the women could say anything to the police, just yet. Fabbrizio himself couldn't tell how many had come up the alleyway. He did manage to raise a hand and shush the nearest cop, a man who at some point had squatted down beside him and started asking questions. But he had no sense of what the guy looked like, other than the bulky police vest, which seemed to Fabbrizio the same blue-gray as Treno's upflung brain matter. Only after a long shared look with mother and child did he regain the power of speech. He confessed, first, that he was the one who'd called 911. And he got across his need, his and the women's, for a bit more time to recover.

Too much… too much all at once… Words to that effect.

He might also have admitted that he was glad that the cops had made it. Whatever he said, however, the police could never understand the ritual that had taken place here. A mystery of reversal, more than a little supernatural, had turned the tables on the powerful and left the avenged striped with their victims' blood. Between them lay their sacrifice, a man who'd swallowed stones.

In death, the face of the long-haired capo was at first as hard to take as Treno's. The blood vessels in his eyes had burst. More mottling showed on the neck, the nose, and he had a few simple bruises too. As he'd choked on the necklace, Nerone had been made over into a blotched alcoholic and aged a good sixty years. Indeed Fabbrizio, as he grew more comfortable with this corpse in its starfish spread, could see that perhaps there hadn't been anything mythic about its passing. The man had got a chunk of material lodged in the windpipe, the sort of mistake a tourist might make. Every summer you heard of such cases, accidental asphyxiation, some German or Russian too eager over his *cozze*. Tonight might not be anything more than that: another stupid move.

The creep had never let go of his switchblade, his hand tightly clenched. Where the daughter's teeth had broken the skin, blood continued to dribble.

Each detail sent fewer shivers through him than the last, yet the Secondigliano hadn't gone numb either. Rather he'd risen to a new interior plateau, from which he could both take stock of himself, sometime-student, sometime-jewelsmith, a decent son and brother, and consider as well the other fallen bastard. Treno's naked and hefty legs, with their ugly new holes, left Fabbrizio in a calm that was almost churchlike, a space of contemplation. So much of his night had set high sensations pumping through him, like a second circulatory system, but now he was free of twitches and goosebumps, even on his slashed and aching face (and when it crossed his mind that he might've lost his status as a *settebello*, that didn't bother him either). He was getting no static out of the afterlife. His Penates lay so still, he wondered if the piece had gotten flattened in the struggle. He saw too that the Somali mother might not have realized what she was doing, shoving the necklace down the throat of her would-be pimp, but the camorrista had known even less. He'd had no idea about these N'mbor-lavà, Nerone, or what they were capable of. Such a power-haunted little man, he hadn't even taken time to notice the real power around Naples and its periphery: the way so much unstable living could be jammed into the cavities of a single long moment, past and present and future all bursting through the seams of the same moment, so that a single mistaken step would leave you out of time, down some clotted and inescapable hole. One bad move could make you history. Here any person who sought to remain on top of some game or other needed to recognize that essential of citified play, the unstable tectonic pressure on the rules, the shakeups without end. The metropolis could delude you with its sempiternal figures made of skin or stone or society, pretty figures, intriguing, which seemed to cycle round endlessly, inevitable as sinning itself. But anyone who subscribed to a closed system like that needed to meet

Nuncia. Daphne, Shanti, whoever—by any name, the woman was one of those who proclaimed, too vividly to allow argument, that only invention was inevitable. And the reality a person needed to grasp was that none of these city shapes, whether pleasing or hurtful, would hold together long if they remained mere reiteration, mere imitation. Even the temples to the Original Mother over in Paestum, and the timeless numen within, required a fresh workup in the hearts of each new child-bearing generation. Otherwise they soured into the same dreary business as the sun-bleached postcards across the access road, another gimmick for turning a buck. Bribe the guard and get a geegaw or two, bribe the mayor and put a hotel over the necropolis. In Fabbrizio's own case, what did his recent overwound nights amount to if not a series of walloping reminders that the past might still send living green shoots through the pus-yellow crust of the present, through the harsh economics and hurt feelings? That the past had the power yet to carry you into a future otherwise too harsh for even the strongest and best-exercised heart?

All too easy for a traveler to fall into the avoidance behavior encouraged by the elongated ovals of the Naples map, to keep to the soul's periphery, refusing to notice the sulfurs and poisons cooking for centuries. All too easy, and soon enough those grooves became tombs. No home base, no home crowd, could remain endurable unless you embraced the notion that even the meanest artifact onsite, a chunk without a face and caked by parasites, could be cleaned and rebuilt. Any item could be made serviceable once more, and claim a worthy place along the roadway. Anything was possible.

Oh, Brizio. Calm yourself. Save it for the professors, after you get back to class.

Here in the back lot, on a flooring dotted with bloodstains, he had the police. He counted six. Among them was a female officer, a woman now down on hands and knees over the dead boss. Small world: the woman might've been Annunciata's sister. If Fabbrizio had seen the two of them together, he'd have realized right away that the con-girl was Italian. As he watched, the policewoman slipped on thin rubber gloves and lightly separated a linked strand of the jeweled tangles poking up from Nerone's darkening mouth. Outside that mouth, at least, the fastenings still held. Could the piece have remained intact, after all? Anyway that reminded Fabbrizio, something else he needed to deal with tonight. The necklace.

The African father, up in Naples, by now had more than likely given the cops all the information they needed. This Nuncia-clone with the gloves, for all Fabbrizio knew, could be some detective who specialized in antiquities, called in for tonight's action. Likewise the Secondigliano had no idea of his own legal status, once this business got sorted out. He'd both stolen the piece and brought it in—what did that amount to, in the end? Since the night began he'd been going on the belief, like a wish upon a falling star, that he could make a decent case for himself. He could come out looking like a great man. And now even someone with the Legal Aid office, some part-timer who hadn't yet finished his exams, could strengthen Fabbrizio's case based on what had just happened here behind the Café Sempre. Never mind that so far as Fabbrizio himself was concerned, this tooth-and-claw episode had been the worst five or six minutes of his life. The last thing he felt like was a hero.

Still as he looked over the necklace, crumpled into a wedge and shoved in where it wouldn't go, and as he also took in the woman who might arrest him, Fabbrizio began to smile. He had to smile, and widely, enough so he could feel it in his cuts. He hadn't lost the sense of coming to an overlook, seeing things from a distance that put them in place and rendered them shapely, and all at once he was overwhelmed by a breeze-fresh awareness of how lucky he was. A naturalborn *fortunato*, he was, sitting here in one piece and free of the hoodlums who'd been breathing down his neck. Then why should it end here? Why couldn't the police make a mistake too, and fail to realize what they had?

Up in Naples, Nado might be talking, but Fabbrizio knew better than anyone how difficult it could be to figure out what the man was saying. Or maybe there'd be some other breakdown, some police memo mislaid.

He couldn't help thinking, enjoying a new energy. Guts had been spilled tonight, and hadn't his ancestors divined the future in that kind of thing? Checking the entrails? The future that played in his mind's eye now had a terrific beauty, its parts as catchy and balanced as in some extended deejay jam that thronged the club floor. The police would assume the necklace was another of the recent copies. Once they no longer needed it as evidence, they'd return it to the African teenager. The father would see no harm in that, figuring the piece might come in handy some time. A family never knew when they might need extra cash, or leverage with the courts.

And the ghost would be at peace now, too. The Greca's bones no longer had to wander in search of a home. At the same time, her long-ago fatherly gift would've found its way to a righteous new purpose, garnering status and attention for another young woman in another life-to-come. Years from tonight, the necklace would glitter beneath the Somali's beaming face on the day she married an Italian and became a citizen. She would pass it on to her own daughter, too: the first in this new Neapolitan configuration of a family to go to college.

Only then, somewhere in halls of learning, long after Fabbrizio himself had earned an advanced degree and moved on to a conservator's position, would he spot the original masterpiece in all its glitter and clatter. He'd know it at first glance, and with that the ornament would begin again to assert its undying power: to connect far-flung lives and reinvigorate their corrupt and suffocating world.

Books Available from Gival Press
Fiction and Nonfiction

Boy, Lost & Found: Stories by Charles Casillo
ISBN 13: 978-1-92-8589-33-4, $20.00
Finalist for the 2007 ForeWord Magazine's Book Award for
Gay/Lesbian Fiction
Runner up for the 2006 DIY Book Festival Award for
Compilations/Anthologies
"...fascinating, often funny...a safari through the perils and
joys of gay life."—Edward Field

A Change of Heart by David Garrett Izzo
ISBN 13: 978-1-928589-18-1, $20.00
A historical novel about Aldous Huxley and his circle
"astonishingly alive and accurate."
—Roger Lathbury, George Mason University

Dead Time / Tiempo muerto by Carlos Rubio
ISBN 13: 979-1-928589-17-4, $21.00
Winner of the 2003 Silver Award for Translation, ForeWord
Magazine's Book of the Year ~ A bilingual (English/
Spanish) novel that captures a tale of love and hate, passion
and revenge.

Dreams and Other Ailments / Sueños y otros achaques
by Teresa Bevin
ISBN 13: 978-1-092-8589-13-6, $21.00
Winner of the 2001 Bronze Award for Translation,
ForeWord Magazine's Book of the Year ~ A bilingual
(English/Spanish) account of the Latino experience in the
USA, filled with humor and hope.

The Gay Herman Melville Reader edited by Ken Schellenberg
ISBN 13: 978-1-928589-19-8, $16.00
A superb selection of Melville's homoerotic work, with short
commentary

An Interdisciplinary Introduction to Women's Studies
edited by Brianne Friel & Robert L. Giron
ISBN 13: 978-1-928589-29-7, $25.00
Winner of the 2005 DIY Book Festival Award for
Compilations/Anthologies
A succinct collection of articles for the college student on a
variety of topics.

The Last Day of Paradise by Kiki Denis
ISBN 13: 978-1-928589-32-7, $20.00
Winner of the 2005 Gival Press Novel Award / Honorary
Mention at the 2007 Hollywood Book Festival — This
debut novel "...is a slippery in-your-face accelerated rush
of sex, hokum, and Greek family life."—Richard Peabody,
editor of *Mondo Barbie*

Literatures of the African Diaspora by Yemi D. Ogunyemi
ISBN 13: 978-1-928589-22-8, $20.00
An important study of the influences in literatures of the
world.

Lockjaw: Collected Appalachian Stories by Holly Farris
ISBN 13: 978-1-928589-38-9, $20.00
"*Lockjaw* sings with all the power of Appalachian
storytelling—inventive language, unforgettable voices,
narratives that take surprise hairpin turns—without
ever romanticizing the region or leaning on stereotypes.
Refreshing and passionate, these are stories of unexpected
gestures, some brutal, some full of grace, and almost all acts
of secret love. A strong and moving collection!"
—Ann Pancake, author of *Given Ground*

Maximus in Catland by David Garrett Izzo
ISBN 13: 978-1-92-8589-34-1, $20.00
"...*Maximus in Catland* has all the necessary ingredients for
a successful fairy tale: good and evil, unrequited love and
loving loyalty, heroism and ancient wisdom...."
—Jenny Ivor, author of *Rambles*

Middlebrow Annoyances: American Drama in the 21st Century
by Myles Weber
　　ISBN 13: 978-1-928589-20-4, $20.00
　　Current essays on the American theatre scene.

Secret Memories / Recuerdos secretos by Carlos Rubio
　　ISBN 13: 978-1-928589-27-3, $21.00
　　Finalist for the 2005 ForeWord Magazine's Book of the Year
　　Award for Translations
　　This bilingual (English/Spanish) novel adeptly pulls the
　　reader into the world of the narrator who is vulnerable.

The Smoke Week: Sept. 11-21, 2001 by Ellis Avery
　　ISBN 13: 978-1-928589-24-2, $15.00
　　2004 Writer's Notes Magazine Book Award—Notable for
　　Culture / Winner of the Ohionana Library Walter Rumsey
　　Marvin Award
　　"Here is Witness. Here is Testimony." –Maxine Hong
　　Kingston, author of *The Fifth Book of Peace*

The Spanish Teacher by Barbara de la Cuesta
　　ISBN 13: 978-1-92858937-2, $20.00
　　Winner of the 2006 Gival Press Novel Award
　　"...De la Cuesta's novel maintains an accumulating power
　　which holds onto a reader's attention not only through the
　　forceful figure of Ordóñez, but by demonstrating acutely
　　how ordinary lives are impacted by the underlying social
　　and political landscape. Compelling reading."—Tom Tolnay,
　　publisher, Birch Brook Press and author of *Selling America*
　　and *This is the Forest Primeval*

Tina Springs into Summer / Tina se lanza al verano
by Teresa Bevin
　　ISBN 13: 978-1-928589-28-0, $21.00
　　2006 Writer's Notes Magazine Book Award—Notable for
　　Young Adult Literature
　　A bilingual (English/Spanish) compelling story of a
　　youngster from a multi-cultural urban setting and her
　　urgency to fit in.

A Tomb on the Periphery by John Domini
ISBN 13: 978-1-928589-40-2, $20.00
This novel a mix of crime, ghost story and portrait of the
protagonist continues Domini's tales in contemporary
Southern Italy, in the manner of his last novel *Earthquake
I.D.*

Twelve Rivers of the Body by Elizabeth Oness
ISBN 13: 978-1-928589-44-0, $20.00
Winner of the 2007 Gival Press Novel Award
"*Twelve Rivers of the Body* lyrically evokes downtown
Washington, DC in the 1980s, before the real estate
boom, before gentrification, as the city limped from one
crisis to another—crack addiction, AIDS, a crumbling
infrastructure. This beautifully evoked novel traces Elena's
imperfect struggle, like her adopted city's, to find wholeness
and healing."—Kim Roberts, author of *The Kimnama*

For a list of titles published by Gival Press, please visit: *www.givalpress.com.*

Books available via Ingram, the Internet, and other outlets.

Or Write:
Gival Press, LLC
PO Box 3812
Arlington, VA 22203
703.351.0079